Maggie,

I Have Your Baby

The Haunting Of Maggie's Bridge

By Kelly Lidji

For Kaiden

You are my inspiration.

I can call spirits from the vasty deep.

Why, so can I,

or so can any man.

But will they come when you do call for them?

William Shakespeare

Chapter 1

Maggie

At the beginning, and for a long time thereafter, I did not understand I had died. At first, everything was darkness. No bright white light welcomed me, as my church has always led me to believe. No Almighty God there with the singing of a heavenly choir to welcome me to the hereafter. No warm and loving embrace of my long-deceased relations reaching out for me when I awoke in the darkness.

May 31ˢᵗ, 1880

Midnight

I am face up in mud. Cold water is hitting me hard. I open my eyes and immediately blink as they fill with water. My lips are trembling, and my body is shivering all over. I can feel my heart pounding in my ears.

I lie here, soaked with water from the storm, so confused and full of fear my arms and legs are limp. I cannot will them to move. My fingers remain sunk down into the muck at my sides. Lightning flashes across the sky directly above me and I lift my head, squinting my eyes against the flashing light. I pull my arms under me and push myself up to my elbows. Peering through the darkness, I see I am surrounded by tall trees, laying in mud and rocks. Half in and half out of shallow water. Woods are dimly lit on the brightest night. Even when the sky is full of stars the tall trees filter out the light. When traveling in darkness, you rely on the desire of your horse for home and warmth and his knowledge of the way. There is no horse, no road, no light. Nothing around me but trees, sharp rocks, cold mud, and pounding rain.

Another bolt of lightning crashes through the sky with a grand clap of thunder. It illuminates the woods, making the trees glow silver in the dark. I have the brief opportunity to see more clearly around me. The scene is reassuringly familiar. I am on the bank of an offshoot of the Nanticoke River. A tiny tributary that reaches out like a snake from the river, just down the road from my family's farm.

For some reason I am alone, in this terrible storm, next to the wooden bridge. I must try and get my breathing to slow. Closing my eyes and covering my face with my hands. At least I know where I am. I am not far from home.

If only the moon were visible! But even the brightest moon could not shine through the storm overhead. I shakily turn over onto my knees and try to stand up. There is mud caked to my face and hands and I wipe away what I can. I remain still until the lightning flashes again so I may fix in my mind where the road is. When it comes, I begin to work my way, feeling blindly between the sharp rocks and making my way up the bank to the road. It is steep and slippery, so I grab at the thick marshy grass to pull myself up fist by fist. I know that this road is often travelled on a sunny day. Folks taking the ferry the short stretch across the river. However, it is further down the road, near our church. There are few families living out this far. In the dark of night, during such a wicked downpour of rain, no one will be passing. I am alone.

I stand on the road in the dark. What now? I rub my forehead with the heel of my hand, feeling the grittiness of the smeared mud sticking to it. I look around, hoping the scene will somehow explain itself to me. What has happened? How did I end up here? Why am I by the road in the middle of the night? I am afraid of the dark. Not one to venture out when the light is gone. How did I get to this empty spot of the river?

Suddenly a clear thought comes to me, and I stand up straight, my fingers tingling. I am *not* alone. I feel determination fill me. My baby. The precious child that sleeps in my womb. I recall the tight swelling of my belly, gently rounded, early enough that I've yet to face the wrath of my family. The child is still a secret held by only Elias and me. A most precious gift, made from love. Our future. Quietly slumbering in me still. I reach to feel the hard curve of him. To reassure myself that everything is the way it should be.

There is nothing there. No firm, hard tightness. No gentle roundness to my stomach. Just the soft, level flesh covered with filthy wet skirts. As if it has never been there at all.

That is when I finally begin to scream.

Chapter 2

Claire

June 9th, 2017

Well, obviously I have to take him there. What else is there to do around here? Mom has that stupid tracking app on my phone. The minute I got within 5 miles of Rehoboth beach or anywhere remotely interesting I'd be grounded till I was married. That little dot named "Claire" has to be within the city limits, or damn close to it.

He is hot, from New York City, and he loves horror movies. What more could a girl want? Of course, the fact that he is twenty years old to my seventeen might not be cool with my mother. Not that I want her to find out. That won't be happening. Don't get me wrong, as Moms go, I have a great one. I have more than my share of freedom. No curfew. Unlimited screen time. If my grades stay up and I act like a decent human being I am free to be myself and do what I want. The one rule is she must always, *always* know where I am, and I have to stay local. She says my Gram was the same way with her, and she turned out just fine. Although in the 80's, it meant she had to call home...a lot.

We meet at Curtis's party. Curtis is year ahead of me and his graduation was this afternoon. Normally I wouldn't go to the party of someone I didn't really hang out with, but my best friend Toby has a crush on him. For reasons I have not yet figured out. I'm there for moral support. And possibly beer, if we are lucky.

Not so much, turns out Curtis's parents are the stalking type of adult. Creeping on every conversation by standing silent in the corners of the room and basically daring us to misbehave with their eyes. I can practically see the rod up their butts. So we are basically a bunch of teenagers standing or sitting in small groups looking uncomfortable. Even Curtis is not being particularly cute. Sitting with his best friend, obnoxiously rating the various body parts of Tinder matches on his phone. Wild times, indeed. It feels like study hall with more comfortable seating. I may as well be home with a good book. At least there I can wear my old pajamas. Toby and I sit in the living room on their alarmingly matching 70's furniture and give each other quietly desperate looks, texting about how to escape the "forced merriment."

Toby: We MUST FLEE! Curtis is obviously a straight pig. Any minute his parents are going to pull out board games. Kill me now.

Claire: Are you saying you aren't having fun?? It could be worse. You could be at the dentist.

I see him laugh.

Toby: Watching paint dry is better than this.

Claire: Hey, drying paint can be an extraordinary thing to witness if you just open your mind to it. It allows you to meditate on the endless passage of time.

Toby: You are my guru. Wait. Crisis averted. DO YOU SEE the guy in blue? The tall one in the kitchen with the dark hair and those amazing eyes. Talking to Noah?

I look. At first I just see the random teenagers I spend every day with. Then a few people walk back into the living room, and I see him over near the corner. My breath catches in my throat, and I think I forget everything I've learned so far in High School. I don't breathe. A warmth radiates through every part of me.

Claire: OMG, who is THAT? I've never seen him before. I would remember that.

Toby: He must be a friend of the family. Or came with somebody from school. Well? Are you going or am I? You won't meet him just sitting here.

Claire: I can't. He looks older. And way out of my league.

Toby: You better do something. Don't make me go over and tell him about how you sometimes do the jitterbug with your mother in your living room.

Claire: OK! You ass. I have a plan. All of a sudden, I'm hungry. Watch this...

I get up in a way I hope looks casual and make my way to the snack table sandwiched in between the refrigerator and the back door. I nonchalantly fill a plate with chips and cookies shaped like a graduation caps while eavesdropping on their conversation. Noah, who I know from homeroom, and Hot Guy are having a heated conversation about which is better, modern or classic horror movies. Hot guy is firmly on the side of the Classics. Excellent. This…I know. I take a few quick breaths, clearing my throat. My mouth is so dry I can hardly start to speak.

'Noah" I start, "How can you compare the lazy torture porn remake sequel horror crap we get today to a classic like the original Halloween? Carpenter manages to convey dread and terror with almost NO blood. Practically nothing but setting, tension, and mind-blowing music. And what about The Omen? Rosemary's Baby?"

I think it's a good opening line. Noah's mouth falls open as he stares at me. I'm not sure he's ever heard me say so much at once. Hot Guy's eyebrows slowly rise, and a smile seeps onto his face.

He steps quickly to my side. "Exactly! That's what I'm trying to get through to him. Look at The Shining! *That* is what scary really is. Creepiness, dread, absolute master levels of symbolism. Plus, more great music." He winks at me and smiles, revealing a dimple in his left cheek.

"Speaking of Halloween, did you know they made the Michael mask off a William Shatner Star Trek mask?" he challenges.

I'm ready, "Did *you* know the mask looks different in part two not just because Dick Warlock had a bigger head but also because Nick Castle had carried it around in his back pocket during the filming of the original? It even changed color because Debra Hill kept it under her bed where it eventually turned yellow from her heavy smoking."

11

The smile grows wider across his face. I feel the spark from it all the way to my toes.

"I'm Jesse Mumford." He said, staring down directly into my eyes as he reaches out his hand. I try not to *grab* it. It's soft and very warm. Black hair and piercing green eyes with lots of dark lashes tower above me. He is aggressively tall. I like tall, but this is almost asking too much. 6'4" or 6'5" at least. Towering over my 5'4" self. I'll need a ladder if I ever get to kiss him.

"Hi Jesse Mumford, I'm Claire Ludlow," I start, trying to keep my voice casual. Not succeeding at all. I can hear the slight tremble in it. "How do you know Curtis? I haven't seen you before. And in this town, that's definitely saying something."

"I don't, not really. I'm roommates with his older brother. We go to school together at NYU. I'm studying to be a veterinarian. We're on break right now and he didn't feel like driving down for this big event by himself. But after the ceremony this afternoon the temptation of his ex-girlfriend was too much and he's out somewhere with her. Leaving me abandoned and alone at this thing."

He is slowly eyeing me from the top of my head with my dark, out of control curly hair, past my mom's old college sweatshirt and jeans, down to the beat-up moccasins I can't bear to part with.

His voice is like warm honey poured over an upright bass.

"A vet? I sputter, "That's incredible. I'd love to do that if it weren't for the blood and stuff. What kind of vet do you want to be? My mom has parrots. Macaws. We need an avian vet around here. She has to drive out of state to take them to the doctor."

"Not sure yet. I've got some time to decide. And luckily, I'm used to blood and stuff. Remember, I watch all those horror movies, classic *and* new." He laughed. "Although I'm told it's different in real life. The blood looks a little less fake."

I laugh. At least I wish it were just a laugh. What comes out of my mouth sounds more like the cackle that a witch living in the deep forest makes after capturing a tasty kid sized snack. Crap. I always embarrass myself if I'm even mildly attracted to a guy.

"So what kind of macaws does your mom have? My uncle had a Blue and Gold when I was a kid. He was a riot. He had belonged to a neighbor before my uncle, so the bird was already thirty-five when he got him." He said. "He lived to be almost sixty years old. But by the time I knew him he didn't fly too much anymore. Just liked to sit and curse loudly at football games on the TV. A habit he picked up from my uncle, I guess." Jesse laughs affectionately.

"She has Hahn's macaws, a type of miniature parrot species. So they are small. Like a big conure. A pretty emerald green. Rufus is five. He's a handful." I explain. "Finn is only a year old. We just recently got her. A rehome. Mom was told it was a boy. She got her tested and whoops, it's a girl. So it could eventually get interesting.

"So why a vet? What made you decide to go for that?" I'm genuinely curious but I also want to keep him talking. His lips are beautiful when he talks. I can't stop looking at them.

13

"I've wanted to be a vet since I learned what one was. My mom likes to tell the story of how when I was little, I brought her a dead frog and ask her to fix it for me. I thought she could do anything." He laughed. "She explained that it while it was too late for this guy, someday I could learn to keep other animals alive and help them when they are sick or hurt. There were people who learned how to do that. I was hooked. She made it sound like I could be a wizard."

We keep talking for a few minutes. Moving to the most remote couch in the rapidly emptying living room. Toby is in top best friend form and made himself scarce, going to the kitchen with Noah and a few others to talk comic books, so we have relative privacy.

"I've just finished my 2nd year at school and I'm hoping to get into the University of Pennsylvania after for vet school, he said, "I'm originally from Yonkers. Big family. Four brothers, two sisters, I'm the youngest. Um…let's see. What's interesting…I love bats. Every spring I volunteer counting bats in colonies for the state. We count them as they come out of their roosts at dusk. It's awesome, except for the mosquito bites." I laugh.

He starts firing questions at me. "So how old *are* you? What's the first horror movie you ever saw? What are your plans your life? What do you really want to do? What's your biggest fear?

I laughed. "Is this an interrogation? Don't you need to shine a bright light in my face?"

He looks down at his lap and says quietly, "I just want to know." Oh wow. I feel that all the way to my toes.

"Well," I begin, "I'm seventeen, so I start my senior year this fall. My favorite thing to do is read. I think I actually like books more than people most of the time. The last couple years I've done this challenge where I read 100 new books a year. I'm up to sixty-three since January."

"Sixty-three?" he sputtered. "You've got to be kidding!"

"No, I read really fast," I laugh and go on, "Halloween *is* my favorite movie. The first horror movie that I ever saw. Mom watches it all the time in the fall. It's her favorite too. At my house Halloween is every day."

"All year long?"

"Sort of. She has a huge amount of Halloween decorations and horror movie memorabilia and lots of it just stays out. We have a scary movie night every Thursday." I raised one eyebrow and look sideways at him, "Not like it's influenced me or anything. I'm perfectly normal." I laugh.

"I don't know what I want to do yet. I think I want to write. But everyone who reads enough books starts to imagine they can write. Most often, they can't. What sounds great in your head is crap on the page.

"My biggest fear? Um, authority? Cockroaches? Ventriloquist dummies?" I look down at my lap and frown. "Maybe not having an exciting life. Being stuck in this town forever. Not that it's bad. I just want to experience other places. Never getting to travel or see any of the world is too depressing to think about."

This conversation is the most personal I've ever had with a virtual stranger but somehow it's easy. He's making it easy.

He seems so relaxed. Sitting facing me with his arm draped over the back of the couch. I bet he talks to nervous girls all the time, looking the way he does. I try to mirror his position and look calm.

"So, is there anything fun to do around here? What about down at the beach? We aren't that far." he asks. Obviously choosing to ignore the fact that I am one of the more awkward humans he is ever likely to go out in public with.

I'm not ready to admit that I am bound by an app to stay local. No sense in having him scared off before I even get to know him better. I do really want to get to know him better, older than me or not. There has to be something interesting we can do. Just then, a thought pops into my head.

"Um…do you like scary stuff in real life or just in movies?" I blurt out. "Ever gone to haunted bridge? We have one nearby. Kind of a local legend."

"Oh, for real? Let's go. Right now," his eyes light up, "I'm up for anything. How close are we?"

"Just a few miles. A little outside of town. Although we need to have four people for us to have a good chance to see the ghost." I'm not ready to be alone in the woods with a twenty-year-old guy I'd just met. I may be young, but stupid, I'm not.

"Yes! I like it already. Your friend should come. And we can bring Noah too. He needs a good scare to show him it's not all about the blood." He calls across the living room to Toby and flashes that smile with his hand out. "By the way, hello Claire's friend, I'm Jesse. I usually have better manners in public. It's just your friend here is very charming." I feel a traitorous flush creep across my face. I cover my eyes with my hand and slide a bit down in the seat as every other teenager in the place hears him and looks over to see who it is that is so charming.

Toby laughs out loud and comes from the kitchen; doing a much better job than I did of shaking his hand and speaking like a sane human being. He'll have to teach me how to do that.

"Claire said there's a haunted bridge nearby. Want to come with us?" he said.

Toby grins at him and then at me, " Claire wants to go there? Well that's interesting. I'm ready, let's do it."

Jesse turns back to me. "I'll go grab Noah." He heads to the kitchen, and I feel insistent poking in my side. Toby, trying to control his laughter, leans in and whispers in my ear, "Ok, if you want to head *there*, he must be something."

"He wanted something to do, and it was the first thing I could think up. We can't *go* anywhere."

"Fair enough."

Curtis's parents have gone out the back door and are at the grill. I can hear them through the window, arguing about whether the burgers and hot dogs they already have are enough. Considering the rapidly emptying living room, I'd say there's plenty. It's the perfect moment to sneak out the front door. Night arrived several hours ago, but the stars are bright. The moon is full and glowing in the sky. Perfect.

Toby spoke up, "Want me to drive?" I look at Toby's tiny car and back at Jesse. "It will not exactly comfortably fit all of Jesse unless he hangs his legs out the window."

Noah speaks up, "My car is bigger and has four doors. I'll drive." Jesse will have more leg room in the back seat, so he and I climb in there while Toby jumps in up front with Noah.

We head out in the direction of Woodland Road, and I settle back to tell him the story.

"So in the late 1800's a pregnant young woman named Maggie was going over a bridge near her family's house, driving a horse and buggy. It was late at night, there was a thunderstorm, and she was all alone. As the story goes, her horse got spooked by a loud clap of thunder and she, the buggy, and the horse went off the side of the bridge. When they found her the next day, not only was she and her unborn baby dead, but she had been decapitated.

"I guess her spirit is not at rest because if you go out and park by the bridge between midnight and one, on the night the moon is full, things happen. Your car will stall, or the horn might honk. The car can slip out of gear. Your cell phone won't work. If you are brave enough to get out, you take your friends and stand on the four corners of the bridge and call out to her.

"Maggie! Maggie! I have your baby! And then again…Maggie! Maggie! I have your baby! And one more time…Maggie! Maggie! I have your baby! Then you wait."

"What happens after you call her?" Jesse asks, leaning towards me, clearly into the story.

"You could hear screams. Lights can appear off in the woods. You might hear the wails of a crying baby. You could hear a horse and buggy off in the distance. But if you're lucky...*really* lucky, and you did everything right, Maggie herself will appear to you on the bridge. Covered with mud, blood dripping down from the stump of her neck. Holding her severed head in her hands. Pleading for you to reattach it. So she can live again and find her lost baby. And hopefully... she doesn't take you instead," I ended with a creepy smile.

For the first time Jesse looks a little unsure. He looks around at us, swallowing hard, his Adams apple bobbing up and down, "You all know about this?"

"Sure," said Toby. "You live around here; this is the thing to do if you want to creep out your friends or yourself."

"If you believe that crap," Noah says, "but I don't. I've been out here a few times with my friends, and nothing ever happens except you stand around listening for every little noise and trying to scare yourself. I don't know what you expect to see. But anything was more exciting than that party."

Jesse seems mildly relieved, relaxing back into the seat. Maybe not as brave as he originally thought he was. That just makes him even more human. And a little more adorable. I'm a big fan of scares in movies. Go right for it. Freak me out. This is different.

We are deeper into the woods now. The houses getting further and further apart. The dark is creeping up the sides of the car. With the road becoming narrow and the trees pressing in closer, it's increasingly claustrophobic. All you can see is the headlights shining in front of us through the blackness. Jesse's face next to me has disappeared in the gloom.

"Well, I've been coming out here since I was little," Toby said. "Mom would come out here as a teenager with her friends at night and she loved it. Her mom did it as well. People have been coming out here for decades. Paranormal investigators have YouTube videos of themselves at the bridge getting freaked out. Mom brought me out in the daytime once and showed me that it's really just an ordinary place where a sad thing happened. That Maggie was just lost and lonely and probably needed help."

Toby's acceptance of the supernatural is unmatched among my friends. This is just a natural part of life to him. He's played with a Ouija board, which I can't bring myself to even touch. I envy him that. I still get scared the whole idea of real ghosts. Horror movies and scary books are one thing. A living person sat down and wrote that. Brought that story out of their head. Paranormal things happening to and around my actual human body are not so easily managed. I wouldn't be out here at all if I were not trying to impress Jesse. I'm desperate enough to try any excuse to spend more time with him.

We're getting close. Turning the corner to the right past an old empty house on the corner near the entrance to the Woodland Ferry. The ferry was built to take you slowly across the river to the other side of the Nanticoke. It's pretty, but it's really only a few hundred feet to the other side. Not time enough to consider it a *trip*. And boy is it deserted out here this time of night. Only a few lights and fewer houses. Less than a mile from the corner, my breath speeds up as we approach.

MAGGIE I HAVE YOUR BABY

The whole car has gone quiet. It's 11:56 pm. We are there.

Chapter 3

Claire

To the average driver going past, Maggie's Bridge would not attract attention. You might not even notice you'd been over it. It's less a bridge and more a flat road with guardrails to help people avoid what looks to be swamp and cypress. Half fallen and dead trees dot the narrow expanse of water on either side. Dense underbrush along the edges of the woods is thick enough to discourage anyone from exploring.

The only thing remotely out of the ordinary for the area is the excessive graffiti lining the tops of each low guardrail and over the asphalt of the bridge itself. People have left messages for Maggie, questions and well wishes. These are interspersed with typically untalented anatomical drawings and profanity that get regularly covered over by the city. But Maggie's messages tend to stay. It's a lonely place. Hiding in plain sight. Ignored till you look for it. Totally invisible most of the time. Seemingly deep in the thick woods even though the actual Nanticoke River is just a stone's throw away. It's easy to picture the past. A dirt road. A higher wooden bridge and more danger. The woods around us are just as dense as they have been for 200 years.

Noah pulls the car to a stop on the packed dirt past the bridge to the right side of the narrow road. We are quiet. The darkness in the woods is as thick as black ink. Yet the bridge and the water are visible with the bright moon making the trees along the water's edge cast shadows on the surface.

Nobody moves.

"Well," I say, "who's ready?"

"Fine. Let's do this," Noah started, "I'll turn on my camera light so we can see."

"NO!" I say quickly. "No flashlights, no headlights, no recording with our phones. We go just as we are. In the dark. That's how we need to do it if you want it to work."

"Good grief, Claire," He grumbles, but he puts his phone away. Opening the doors lets the scent of the river hit our faces. Cool for June, with the smell of water and rotting leaves. It is silent. Very silent.

Jesse and I slowly climb out of the back of the car. I crawl across the back seat to his door on the left as mine is facing the slope down into the woods. Tripping over my own feet and rolling headfirst into the darkness would not make a good impression. Toby manages to get out the passenger door and around the front of the car to join the three of us huddled together on the edge of the road.

"So Claire, how do we start this?" Jesse speaks softly down to me.

I press my lips tight together and bite them. My palms are sweating. I find myself answering him in the same hushed voice. "We need to find the edges of the water. Each of us stand on a corner of the bridge right above it. Everyone faces out into the woods, our backs to each other. Then we call to her like I told you."

Nobody moves for a minute. My eyes begin to adjust, and I can see deeper into the trees. It is strangely beautiful. The water is still enough that the trees and even the moon are reflected in it on both sides of the bridge. It is totally quiet. No crickets chirping, no frogs croaking. Nothing but silence. It's ominous and eerie.

We slowly separate into pairs. Toby and Noah staying on the end nearest the car and Jesse and I crossing back over the bridge together. Then I go to the left and he goes to the right.

I find my edge above the water, get in place, and look back at everyone. Noah is still trying to find the right spot; peering down to see the water through the rocks and brush. I'm glad he's at least trying to do it right. Jesse and Toby are in place already. I wrap my arms around myself and try to stay calm.

While I wait, I see through the moonlight that fifteen or so feet across the water a tiny finger of land sticks out into the river. A few tall, thin trees lean out from the very edge. They are close to a large fallen tree rotting in the water. The bit of land looks like a tiny island. An adventurous kid would be desperate to reach it.

I look back again. Noah has found his spot. We are ready.

"Ok," I call out softly, trying hard to keep my voice from trembling, "let's start."

And we all call out,

"Maggie, Maggie, we have your baby!"

"Maggie, Maggie, we have your baby!

"Maggie, Maggie, WE HAVE YOUR BABY!

Nothing.

We wait, each of us silent on our corners, staring out ahead. I am terrified to look out, but I do. All I see is the dark woods.

We wait longer. Still nothing.

"Let's try it again," I call out, "Ready?"

"Maggie, Maggie, we have your baby!"

"Maggie, Maggie, we have your baby!"

"Maggie, Maggie, WE HAVE YOUR BABY!"

We wait again, and I'm holding my breath. Squeezing my elbows to my sides and glancing in every direction. Looking for anything out of the ordinary.

Suddenly, a fluttering swoops past my head. I jump and shriek, flailing my arms wildly, terrified. I drop to a squat and wrap my arms over my head. Noah and Toby are screaming because I did. Noah flings his arms back and forth around him. The bats fly right on by, oblivious to our reaction. They head in Jesse's direction, and I hear his gentle laugh. *He* can laugh. He loves bats. They fly gently past without bothering him at all.

"Bats, Claire," Jesse reassures me, "Relax. Don't move and they won't hit you."

"Uh huh. Got it."

I turn back facing away from the bridge again. The air feels thicker. I didn't know if it's a reaction to the bats or something else. I concentrate on breathing slowly and peer back out across the water.

There's a light. It's faint, deep in the trees to my right. Far away from us. It's not moonlight. It has a soft glow that's not a reflection. Then I see another. Then more. A bit apart from each other and close to the ground. They aren't lightning bugs because they're not flashing, the light is solid. I feel my blood turn to ice. My mouth opens but no sound will come out. The lights start to get bigger and brighter, and I realize they are moving closer. I finally find my voice.

"Um, guys? Do you see those lights?" I back slowly towards the middle of the bridge, never taking my eyes off the glow in the trees behind the water. All the blood is leaving my hands and feet and my heart is thumping hard and fast in my chest.

"What lights?" Noah calls. I hear him walking over just as Toby reaches my side. Jesse is frozen in place on his corner. He doesn't move.

"Out over there," I point, "Beyond the edge of the water, in the trees.

"See? Four lights."

No wait.

"Five…"

"I see six," said Toby, speaking easily. He seems perfectly calm, although the wonder in his voice gives away his excitement.

"Whatever," said Noah dismissively, "I guess it's lightning bugs. Or it's probably just someone in the woods trying to scare us. Anyone could be out there."

"Be serious!" Toby said. "It's after midnight! The woods are full of brush and poison ivy. And what isn't covered by brush is mud. You could hardly stand up in there. Who would even know we were coming out here? We didn't tell *anybody*."

"Jesse?" My voice wavering as I call to him. "Are you ok? Do you see them?"

"Jesse? Come here man." Noah said, "It's nothing."

Jesse seems to get control of his legs again and walks rapidly to the three of us. He reaches out and takes my hand. A quick blast of heat races through me coming directly from the connection and up my arm. It quickly thaws the blood that froze in me when I first spotted the lights.

I grip his hand tightly. He still does not speak.

"They seemed to be moving at us," I offered.

"Just take a deep breath everybody," Toby smiled, "It's just lights. Nothing is going to get us." The three of us who have our voices share nervous laughter.

An unearthly scream pierces the night all around us.

It starts out deep, raising in pitch and volume as it fills the space around us with a shriek. To me, it feels like the scream is as much inside my head as it is in the air.

More voices are suddenly screaming. Those screams are coming from us.

Even Jesse.

The scream falls silent. So do we. We stand there, frozen. Noah claps his hands over his ears and shakes his head wildly back and forth. Toby looks around himself, a wildly excited expression on his face. I want to run, right now. Just take off down the road into the darkness. Be anywhere that is not this bridge. Only Jesse's grip holds me in place. I can feel him trembling through our joined hands, but he is here. Standing right next to me. I'm breathing so hard and fast I feel myself getting dizzy.

"Relax! Everybody just *relax*!" Toby attempts to calm us down, but it's not going to happen.

Noah's face is stark white in the dimly lit night and for once he has no comeback. He turns and heads for the car, fumbling his keys out of his pocket. They slip from his panicked fingers and tumble down past the guardrail towards the muck of the water's edge.

"NO!" he screams. Dropping to the edge of the road he reaches down below the guardrail to try and get them back. His arm disappears in the darkness.

"Ow! Damn it!" He pulls back and I see a dark spot of blood well up on the back of his hand holding the found keys. He must have cut it on a thorn bush or one of the rocks along the edge.

Another horrible scream pierces the air. Even louder this time. Closer than before. Again, ringing through my head as well as into my ears.

"Let's GO!" I yell in a panicked voice. Enough of this. Too much. I'm moments away from a total panic attack.

We run back to the car as Noah pushes the button on his keys and unlocks the doors. Opening the driver's door Toby goes through it and climbs over the gearshift, not willing this time to cross to the other side that faces the woods. I do the same into the back seat with Jesse right behind me.

Noah gets behind the wheel, shoves the key in the ignition, and turns it. Nothing happens. No click, no sound at all from the motor.

"Come on…come on you stupid piece of junk!"

He tries again. Still nothing.

The third try and the engine finally grinds to life. He drops it in gear and peels out, fishtailing wildly and leaving black skid lines along the road.

There is total silence in the car for more than a minute. Everyone breathing hard. Noah speaks up, "I'm, uh… going to take the long way back to town since there's no good place to turn around back here."

I'm sure it's because he doesn't want to drive back over the bridge. I'm fine with that. I don't want to either. I'm busy trying to catch my own breath. My ears are still ringing from the screams.

We are halfway back to town when Jesse notices that his hand is still gripped tightly to mine.

"Sorry," he says, and gently releases it. "That really freaked me out. You sure as hell weren't kidding about that place!" He turns and stare out the window into the woods, "What do you think the screaming was? Maybe a mountain lion? I know females can scream when they are in heat." I didn't speak.

"Outside *Seaford, Delaware?* In Woodland? Not hardly." Toby said, turning around from the front seat, "The last report of a mountain lion I heard of was from before I was born and about as far upstate as you can get. We don't get them down here. No way." He is adamant.

"Well, it has to be some kind of animal. I've never heard a human make a sound like that." Noah said. "Not even in Saw."

I feel Jesse start to relax next to me. He leans over next to my ear and softly says, "I'll do some research on that sound when I get home on Sunday. You should give me your email and I'll send you what I find. I'm sure there is a logical explanation."

I feel the warmth of his breath on my ear. Smiling back at him, I nod. Elated he wants to remain in some kind of contact with me for whatever reason. He is going to get my email, for sure.

I know, however, that whatever he finds will not be the real answer. I already know the truth. When Noah had been trying to start the car that third and final time, I had looked back out the rear window. I couldn't help myself. I had to.

She was there in the middle of the bridge. Maggie. Standing alone in the moonlight as we drove away. Her dress, covered with dirt and blood, went all the way to the ground. Water streaming all over it. Clenched in her left hand was a shock of long, dark, knotted hair growing from her hollow-eyed severed head.

Her mouth was open wide. It was screaming.

Chapter 4

I scream for an age. It feels never-ending. Every breath I take comes out in a screaming wail. I fist my hands in my hair, pulling madly. I cannot control myself. When my voice finally gives out, I drop to my knees, coughing from the hot dryness of my throat. I begin to sob, keening and rocking back and forth. Holding my empty belly, I try to make sense of this. Where is the baby that I dreamed was a son?

I have no memory of the events that brought me to this place. All I know is that I must get myself safe and out of the rain. Somewhere warm and dry. A place to calm myself and clear my head. Which direction should I go? Heading back south on the road will lead me back to the farm. Where my parents are no doubt waiting for me. To the north leads me towards our Church, and the ferry. To Elias, whose family lives but a few dozen yards away from the floating platform that in daylight hours carries people and buggies across the water.

A piece of my memory clicks into place. Elias and I are going to leave, to run away! Is this the night? Where is he now? Was I on my way to him? Why would we choose to leave during such a terrible storm? Will he be coming to find me when I do not arrive?

I struggle to my feet, looking first one way and then the other. Finally I begin to head northward, towards Elias. If he knows I am coming he will be waiting for me. He is no doubt already worried that I have not arrived.

My eyes have become accustomed to the darkness but still I cannot easily see the road ahead through the deluge of rain. The going is slow and difficult. Rain is streaming down and running in rivulets down my face and into my eyes, obscuring my vision. The hard packed dirt of the road has softened to unstable mud. Thick and hard to move across. I have to keep my arms out to maintain my balance. My shoes are sinking with every step.

How far is it to Elias's family house? A mile, perhaps? It does not take long in a horse and buggy. It is just a pleasant ride on a sunny day. A couple lots past our church.

I have not walked this road in years, since I was a child. Now, at the age of seventeen, most of my travel is as a passenger when my parents go to market or visit our neighbors. I usually spend the ride searching the woods for birds, deer, or any other woodland creature. The birds are my favorite. I am responsible for the flock of chickens on our farm. I love going out in the early morning and collecting the warm eggs tucked under hens that fuss when I disturb them. But the birds in the wild are so much more beautiful. And so unreachable. I love the blue jay best, with their bright blue colors, even though they bully the other birds.

If any are around me now they are huddled in safety. Keeping warm and dry. I do not have even the comfort of their singing for company. Only the cacophony of pounding rain.

My legs are tired from the constant pulling to get my shoes out of the muddy ground, and I have to stop and rest. I sink down to my hands and knees. Dropping my head, I close my eyes and breathe slowly. I am used to hard work. I have been helping to run a farm since I was very small, but it did not prepare me for something this hard. A weariness has sunk itself bone deep in me. I do not know how much longer I can continue. I hope the road ahead soon reveals that I am where I want to be.

When I do reach safety, I muse, there will be no cleaning or repairing this dress. It is too far gone. Better to focus on getting there and worry later about the hours of work it will take me to replace it.

I soon push myself to my feet and start again. Walking on slowly for a long time. Every step is a struggle. I stop for rest when only when I must. After what seems like hours, I stand still and try to figure out how far I have come. There is no change in the woods around me. The road itself has been curving sharply both to the right and left, twining like a snake. This is not how I remember it. It is generally a straight line. The only real curve in the road at all is right before and after the bridge itself. With the bridge almost catty cornered to the road. Built when I was a child to accommodate the shortest reach across the water. I should be able to stay walking straight and find myself coming up to the church and then the Hastings land.

As I work my way around another curve, and I can finally see the trees open up ahead of me. As I walk forward, my heart fills with hope. Something is here. I have finally arrived at some other place! I stop dead in my tracks and stare around me in mute shock.

I am at the bridge. Have I somehow turned around? When I stopped to rest, did I mistakenly start back the way I had come? Not realizing in the darkness and rain that I was retracing my steps?

I walk back over the bridge again, confused. Slipping and sliding across the wet and muddy boards. Once over it I look down and find the indentation in the mud where I sat and wept before. It has filled with water while I was walking. I have not retraced my steps. I indeed have come upon the bridge from the other direction. Before me is the very way I had walked.

How have I made a circle? There is no circle on this road. How can that be? The next crossing ahead of me should be the corner on which Elias's family home is sitting.

Where am I?

Chapter 5

Claire

May 8th, 2023

If you had asked me a year ago if I could ever be convinced to move back home to Delaware, even for a short time, I would have said you were crazy. That you were nuttier than a five-pound fruitcake. I made my escape from there. I had gotten away to a place where everyone I knew didn't know everyone else I knew. Granted, Philadelphia is only a few hours away. But to me it's a whole different world. This city is alive and breathing. There are so many amazing ways to spend your time. Cozy cafés to grab coffee, the Zoo, the Italian Market, and oh my god, the cheesecakes. An unbelievable amount of amazing restaurants, filled with unique and different people. And the nightlife! Concerts, great bars, fabulous culture. Always something to do. I will miss it.

And Jesse. I will miss Jesse Mumford.

The things we do for love. I look over from my desk and watch him sleeping. Arms and legs flung wide open. I swear, he sleeps like a starfish most of the time. I have to fit myself in the space around him. I really don't want to leave him. How can I leave?

Not that we haven't worked out. Far from it. He emailed me the 1st time two weeks after we had met and gone out to Maggie's Bridge together. It was just the start of many messages. At first, the emails were just him trying to rationalize what had happened that night, and me agreeing with him. Even though the idea of a mountain lion making those terrible screams had been quickly shot down with a little research.

We started emailing each other friendly messages a few times a month. Mostly about what was going on in our lives. What movies we had seen. How our classes were. I sent him passages from books that I had read. Trying with moderate success to make him a voracious reader like myself. It wasn't as easy for him. His mind was filled with classes and examinations. His final two years of college were a blur of heavy studying. He worked so hard to get into vet school. Hitting the books nights, weekends, even holidays. I was proud to at least be his friend.

His college graduation in 2019 was the first time I saw him in person again. I begged my mother to let me go to New York for the weekend of the ceremony. I was freshly 19 and had never been to the city. She put up a fight. One of the few real ones we ever had. But the fact I was officially a working adult and had never given her trouble as a teen, actually earning her trust, had tipped the scales. She eventually relented, allowing me to drive to Wilmington and take the train up to the city. I spent the entire train ride wringing my hands together and staring out the window, wondering how it would be when we were finally in the same room together. I was an adult, finally. Freshly minted version, but still. He had treated me like his buddy or little sister for so long. What if that was all he ever wanted?

Talk about a culture shock! Pulling into the train station at noon on the day of his graduation, and seeing the mass of humanity everywhere, I felt like a mouse who was suddenly dropped in the middle of a maze filled with feral cats. The noise was unbelievable. Trains clacking by, people yelling, the stink of exhaust and stanky sweat filling the air. But it was worth it when I laid eyes on Jesse waiting for me. He had swept me into his arms and swung me around like one of those sappy romantic movies I always avoid. Seeing him at the ceremony in his cap and gown, he was the most beautiful thing I had ever seen.

It seemed the passage of two years hadn't hurt me in his eyes either. Things changed between us that weekend. He took me everyplace he could think of, proud of the campus and the city. We went out to eat with his huge family and I got to see him joke around with his brothers and sisters. He took me to MOMA. In front of The Starry Night by van Gogh he gently took my hand, entwining his fingers in mine, his thumb stroking my wrist as we walked through the rooms of beautiful paintings. We went walking around the Central Park Zoo, where he told me bizarre random animal facts. It was grand.

The train station is where Jesse finally kissed me the first time. Just as I was about to board the train. He hugged me goodbye, seeing the tears form in the corners of my eyes.

Reaching down, he brushed them away as they fell down my cheeks, then cupped his hand to my chin as he leaned in and softly pressed his lips to mine. I didn't want to leave.

Once I got back home, we were texting immediately. On the phone for hours at night whenever he could. We fell in love over technology. That fall when he got accepted to the University of Pennsylvania School of Veterinary Medicine, I was so proud. Once he started school, he was only about a two-hour drive away. So I was able to drive up and visit at least once a month.

By the start of his second year of grad school I'd moved up here to join him, sharing this tiny off-campus apartment. Helping with expenses by working in the University library during the day and picking up a few shifts waitressing at a coffee house. The worries Mom had that I was moving too fast have so far not come true. Being with him every day, even if his days are packed with classes and work, is wonderful. He is my best friend. We have horror movie nights at least once a week. Classic and new. He indulges my love of reading. Spending some of his precious free time with me scouring 2nd hand stores and book sales to help grow my collection. Patiently carrying my bags of treasures. I have become very addicted to old books. Antique. The older the better. They are often filled with surprises. Lost names, notes. Sometimes pictures. Once I found an incredibly old index card with the phrase, 'But I eat it. But I eat it. But I eat it one day.' Written in a child's box-like printing. It struck us as unbelievably hilarious. We still haven't figured out what it means.

I've become close with his family. All those siblings, I don't think one is under six feet tall.

Now here we are three years later. He's just finished grad school and was lucky to land a yearlong internship with a prestigious vet practice in Montpelier, Vermont. Jesse decided to specialize and become a large animal vet. This internship will give him the opportunity to gain a lot of the experience he will need when he starts his own practice.

I was fully ready to move right to Vermont with him when Mom called. She recently joined up with her best friend Talissa to open a bookstore. It's been her dream since I was a little girl. They found a place to rent in Georgetown, right on the main road people use to get to the beach. A great high traffic area. The grand opening is a month away and she begged me to come and help her get it off the ground. After a lot of back and forth with Jesse, late night conversations and adding up our finances and the cost of living in Vermont, we decided I would move back home for the year he is there. Letting him focus on work and I can focus on helping mom and maybe finding something I want to write about. I still love to write.

Mom even has room for me. She remarried two years ago after being a single mom since I was four. She and Tim bought a house outside of Seaford last fall. The renovation is pretty much done so I can easily park myself in the guest room. But, and this is the part I still can't believe; they bought the old house on the corner where Woodland Ferry Road turns right and becomes Woodland Church Road. The house less than a mile from Maggie's Bridge.

I've made my peace with what I saw when I looked out the back window that night. I never told anyone, not Toby, who would have been thrilled and dragged me back down there. Not even Jesse. At first because I was afraid Jesse wouldn't believe me. That he would think I was just a crazy little kid. But even as our relationship has grown, I've kept it to myself. Over the years I realize that it doesn't matter if I saw her or not. She doesn't matter to our lives.

I get up from the desk and crawl up the foot of the bed, curving myself again Jesse's side. I've been trying to write, to get out my feelings about having to leave. It's just making me upset. I run my fingers through the dark hair on his chest. Soaking in the smell of him, the feel of him. How can I not see him for a *year*? This afternoon I have to start packing. I have to load up my HHR with everything I care about, mostly books and music, and move, albeit temporarily, to the last place I ever intended to go.

My gentle movements wake him. He rolls to his side and pulls me as close as I can get. "Not much time now. You going to miss me?"

"Nah, you take up the whole bed. Besides, You'll be so busy chasing farm animals you won't even notice I'm not there."

"Tiny, that's the thing about you, don't even get it. You are impossible not to notice." He brings his face down and slowly begins to kiss me.

Chapter 6

Maggie

May 31ˢᵗ, 1880

Midnight

I convinced myself that I must have turned around somehow. It is a logical explanation. I need any excuse to make myself calm. I will find a tree to shield me from the worst of the rain and perhaps wait until the sun begins to rise. That should at least help me not to make more mistakes in direction and exhaust myself even further. The northern side of the bridge has trees closer to me, as this offshoot of the river grows more narrow as it goes north. The expanse of water is a bit smaller with less brush. I slowly work myself down the north bank from the edge of the bridge. It was easier to use the tussocks to pull myself up than it is to navigate around them as the ground slopes steeply down. I can feel myself pitching forward as I go and have to lean back and almost slide so that I do not tumble.

Once I reach the flat ground the going is arduous. The land so close to the water is far more difficult to transverse than the road had been. The muck rises above my ankles with each step. Using the trunks and low branches of the surrounding

MAGGIE I HAVE YOUR BABY

trees I pull out each foot as I move further away from the river's edge. The sleeves of my once beautiful dress are ripping into long shreds from catching on the thorny bushes pressing in all around.

My eyes have adjusted as best they can to the darkness, but it feels even darker in the woods. I must resort to relying on the lightning flashes to help me see which direction I should go next. After several minutes I come upon a large tree sitting somewhat higher than the level on which I am walking. It's root system lifting the base of the tree up. I sink wearily down and am relieved when I feel that the rain is indeed less underneath, the thick branches overhead stopping the worst of it. I wipe the wetness from my face and lean back against the trunk. Closing my eyes, I am so exhausted I soon feel myself drifting into an uneasy sleep.

I do not know how long I sleep. When I awake, I feel somewhat refreshed, but the sky is no lighter. The rain has not stopped, or even slowed. I am at a loss. What am I to do? Surely if Elias were expecting me, he would have tried to find me by now. Was this not the night we had planned to run away? I can remember our last conversation. He was determined that we leave Delaware altogether. We are clearly of age. He professes to genuinely love me and our baby. I love him, so I pray that it is true.

I rub the sleep from my eyes and peer around me. Wanting to see something, anything, that might help. Off to the left, something is different. There is a light! A dim one. Two! Now three! Moving off deep in the woods. They glow through the dark storm. My heart leaps in my chest. Is it Elias? I want it to be, but I think not as he would likely come alone to keep our secret pact a secret. Perhaps a search party my father has formed? From our surrounding neighbors perhaps, gathered quickly when I was not found in my room. Maybe they are working their way through the woods with lanterns.

"HELP ME! I am here!" I call out as loud as my voice will bellow. The lights do not find me. I cannot not let them get away! I struggle to my feet, ignoring the numbness that has started spreading from my toes to my heels. My fingers have also lost feeling. I begin to move. The trees are spreading out a bit as I get further into the woods. Away from the river. The ground is also a bit more firm, the walking easier. I chase the lights.

"HELP ME PLEASE! I AM OVER HERE!"

I cannot seem to get closer to them, no matter how fast I manage to go. I keep my arms out to protect my face from the low hanging branches. I yell as often as I can bear, needing my breath to make my way quickly in the dark.

My voice seems quiet in my ears. Muffled by the sound of the unending rain. The lights suddenly rise up together in the distance, higher into the air. I stop moving and stare at them. Trying to make sense of it.

The glowing lights begin to cross each other rapidly. Bobbing back and forth. I can see them moving excitedly around in one place as if they are dancing. Have they found something? It can't be me as I am still out of sight in the woods. They do not respond to my shouting. I have to reach them before they move away again.

"WAIT! I AM COMING! PLEASE DO NOT LEAVE ME!"

Mud? I look down. My shoes are sinking rapidly again as if I am near the river, yet there is no water this far out. I have left it behind. Yet the proof is at my feet. I push desperately through a large grove of bushes, scratching my arms afresh, and tumble headfirst into the river. It came up so abruptly. I have been distracted keeping my eyes on the lights ahead of me and didn't see it. I sputter and spit out cold, dirty water. I get to my hands and knees in the shallows, my feet such a tangle in my skirts that I cannot yet stand. I wipe the water from my eyes. Again, I am stupefied. I can see the lights clearly now. There is nothing between us now but the rain-soaked night air. They are moving on the bridge. And I am off the south side of it. In the water on the far edge. The lights are not lanterns. It is not a rescue party. The lights are floating, dancing, all alone. And I have somehow again returned to where I started.

Chapter 7

Claire

May 12ᵗʰ, 2023

Thank God it's not past Memorial Day yet. If it were just a few weeks later this drive south downstate through Delaware would be a completely different story. After the holiday, this road will be packed bumper to bumper on a Friday like this with people on their way to the Delaware beaches. Lewes, Bethany, Rehoboth. Even down to Ocean City in Maryland. The towns all line up like pearls on a necklace down the edge of the peninsula. Each wonderful in its own way, depending on what you are looking for. A peaceful day to relax on the beach and soak up the sun? A family friendly small-town experience? An LGBTQ+ embracing environment? A wild place to spend Spring Break? It's all here, along the shore. I *am* sort of glad to be back near the ocean. I can even smell it. You don't notice it till you've been away for a while. Funny thing, when I was a teenager, we didn't go to the beach all that often. I guess that's a local thing. You live here, you don't hit the beach too much. Especially during peak summer season when the tourists are here. May and September are the golden months for locals. We can enjoy the beach uncrowded. I've got to head to Rehoboth at least once before the end of the month. Get some saltwater taffy and margaritas. Always an excellent combination.

I turn off the highway into Seaford, and head for Mom's new house. I haven't been there yet. The last time I came down from Philadelphia with Jesse was last Christmas and they only moved in back in March. We were down just for the holiday afternoon so there wasn't a chance for us to drive out and see the house and its final renovations. They'd gotten it for a steal, but it cost almost as much to fix up. I'm interested to see the décor. Mom found someone to marry that's as eclectic and into Halloween and horror as she is. I half expect to see blood red walls and skulls everywhere. Maybe coffins in the living room instead of couches. We'll see. He's a writer. And a really nice guy. He's done several successful books on American History, with one just about to come out. He's researching a new book right now. Maybe he can give me some tips. But I'd prefer to write fiction. Nonfiction seems like so much trouble. Ugh. Still, it's nice to have a writer in the family.

I've not returned to Maggie's Bridge since that night. Toby tried to get me to go back a few times before I'd moved up with Jesse, but I always found an excuse. Even if the moon wasn't full. Even if it was daylight. I'm too freaked out by what happened.

I drive through town, taking a fresh look at a few of my old hang outs. My high school, my favorite pizza place, the library. I feel nostalgic looking at them but at the same time I get the icky sensation of being sucked back into the trap of small-town life. I spent so much time here. I haven't been to these places in almost three years. For some reason I'm disappointed that they look exactly the same as they always did. I don't know what I expected to see. I feel so different, I thought they would be too. I guess the only thing that has actually changed is the way I look at them. Now they are places. They used to be the whole world. My life revolved around these few square miles. Happily, I have discovered there is indeed life outside this small town.

Toby's parent's house is on the outside edge of Seaford, and I smile when I drive past. I haven't seen him for about six months, but we still talk a lot. He's living in Baltimore and teaching at a Montessori school in the city. He seems really happy. Last time I saw him he'd just gotten back together with his ex-boyfriend, and they are doing really well, living in Hampden. An eclectic little area just outside of the city. I'm glad. Part of me wishes he were still here. It would be nice to have an old friend nearby. He was one of the few people that I was close to in high school. I'll have to go visit him. Or convince him to come see me.

Slowing down, I turn left on the road through the woods that leads to the house. Driving around here is going take some getting used to. I've gotten used to lots more traffic than this. Beltways, highways, cars, busses. Horns honking, exhaust, and watching your car slowly overheat as you sit still on the highway like it's a parking lot. Not the threat of kamikaze deer leaping in front of my car in the dark, or box turtles trying to cross the highway then halfway across deciding to settle down for a rest. Here that's a real possibility.

It *is* sort of pretty. The leaves have fully come out. Everything is very green. I'm used to the sounds of city living. It's going to take a while to re-adjust to the quiet.

I finally reach the corner where the two roads meet. The corner where I'll be living for the next year.

The house was built in 1860, so it has stood by that corner for a long time. When I saw it at seventeen, it was empty. A faded relic slowly rotting into the ground.

It now looks alive. It's former drab grey color is a beautiful dark blue. The peeling window frames changed to a crisp white. The long side of the house that I'm facing is a large simple rectangle with four upper windows and two side doors. One in the middle and one at the back. The narrow side of the house is actually the front, with the main door facing the river. The sunroom the front door is a part of has been renovated into the "bird room". The new black roof glows like velvet in the sun. The house, the lush lawn, the new rose bushes, and multiple bird feeders all protected by a giant tree leaning its branches over from the neighbor's yard. They even have their own small dock in the river across the street. It was completely replaced. The new wood gleams in the sunlight. From the outside, this place is beautiful.

I pull into the freshly laid gravel driveway and can hear the birds already.

"Hello? Hello? Hello!"

"MA! MA! What you DOING?"

"Shut up potato!"

"AAAHHH, Aaahhhh. Are you gonna eat it?"

They are in fine form today. Probably enjoying their new space and the breeze coming in the windows from the water. That, or they are just excited for company.

Mom must have heard the car pull in because I see her face appear in an upstairs window, sporting a wide grin. She's out the door before I even make it all the way out of the car.

"My Clarity!" she screams. Yes, that's her nick name for me. She says that's what I give her.

If you want to know exactly what I will look like in about twenty-five years, Ophelia Ludlow-O'Brien is it. The same dark unruly hair, the same blue eyes ringed with yellow around the iris. The same aquiline nose and high cheekbones she swears are a gift from our Nanticoke Indian ancestry. Although by this point, our lone Nanticoke relative is several generations in the past. Her grandfather's grandmother. Blending with very pale skin and freckles, it's hard to spot. It didn't stop her from having a Nanticoke blessing and naming ceremony for me when I was a baby. I don't think she's missed the yearly Pow Wow in my whole life.

"Ahhh. I'm so glad you are here!" She wraps me in her arms and squeezes me tight.

"Mom," I can't breathe. "Please release me so I can continue to take in oxygen and live."

"Worry about breathing later, I'm dying for you to see the house. Let's grab what we can now, and Tim can come out later and help us bring the rest in. I'm totally excited for you to see your room. You're welcome to paint it whatever color you like except pink. We left the builders base color. Wait till you see the bird babies. They're about three weeks old now. We have another ten days or so before I take them to the hand feeder so you'll have to enjoy their cuteness as fast as you can. Of course, Finn will probably have another clutch after these leave. You know how they are." Her arms are still tight around me, and we haven't moved an inch. "Oh! And the store. It's getting there but there is lots left to do. I figured you could take a couple days to settle in and come over with me on Monday. Talissa is there putting out some stock this weekend, but she was fine with me taking a couple of days to see you. Seeing as how we are getting manual labor from you as a thank you. Do you wa-"

"*Mom!*" I said, interrupting her monologue, "Please calm down. I'm going to be here for months. You don't have to tell me everything in the first five minutes. Where's Tim?"

"Working. I mean hiding, in his office. I've been manic the last few hours waiting for you to get here. It was the smartest thing for him to do. Self-preservation for his sanity." She laughs and we walk up the newly made sidewalk to the step of the side door.

I step inside and my breath catches in my throat. They managed to retain the vintage feel of a really old house while keeping everything flowing and functional. Several cozy rooms, one leading into another. Beautiful dark, almost black, hardwood floors gleam under our feet. Offset by pale blue walls. The side door we came in through opens into the living room. Cozy burnt orange couches, chosen for comfort and functionality, sit facing each other in front of the large fireplace. The door to the sunroom is on my left. In front of it are stairs, leading up away from me, a giant flat screen against the side.

Across the living room is another door. Presumably to Tim's office, a room that sticks out from the main shape of the house on the far side. Off to my right is the entrance to the kitchen at the back of the house. As I suspected, bookshelves line every possible space against the walls. Stuffed with books, figurines, movie memorabilia, and skulls. I knew it. But it's cozy. Warm. Welcoming. I love it.

"Meow! Meow! Woof!"

"Quack! Quack! Wocka-Wocka!"

"I love you, shut up!"

Well, Rufus definitely knows I'm here.

Mom grabs my bags, and we start up. "Let me show you the upstairs and get these bags set down. There's a half bath under the stairs. The main one is right above our heads. We gave up the idea of a third bedroom in exchange for space for giant bathroom with a fancy stand up shower *and* a claw foot soaking tub. So Tim and I can both be happy."

"You'll be in the guest room here," she points, "Just at the top of the stairs. The bathroom is that middle door, our room is at the end of the hall. The whole back of the house. You'll be above the birds. Hope you don't mind. But you guys have the best view, an unobstructed look at the Nanticoke. If the sun is too much in the morning just tell me, we can order you some black out curtains. It's too much for Tim, he doesn't get up at dawn like I do, so we made our room in the back."

My bedroom has so many windows that it is bathed in light even in the late afternoon. The double bed and furniture are set up just as they had been in my old bedroom. Mom even put my ragged, stuffed wooly mammoth toy on the freshly made bed. The walls are bare.

I walk to the windows and look across at the river. From up here I can see so much. Sunlight gleams on the water. I see the ferry heading out, taking two cars across to the Laurel side of the river. Birds are everywhere. I can hear the seagulls calling. I have always loved seagulls. To me, their harsh calls are like music.

"Your closet is right over here," she said, "And lucky you, the pulldown to the attic is in there. So if you need to, we can store some of your things up there. Right now there's just our holiday stuff. Plus a box of papers and junk the builders found when they were doing the renovations.

"Can you believe they found stuff hidden in the *walls*? It's wild. I'm pretty sure they found some books in there too. I still want to go through them. Hopefully, there is a first edition Don Quixote. I could use an extra 1.5 million bucks."

"Let's hope, Mom." That's an exciting thought. One of my favorite things to do is dig though old stuff. Yard sales, estate sales, thrift stores, I love it.

"Hungry? I can make spaghetti," she offers, "I bet we can even lure Tim out of the office."

"Yes please. Feed me," I said. Most excellent. Not having to cook is another perk about being here. I plan to take advantage of that as much as possible.

53

Chapter 8

Maggie

May 31st, 1880

Midnight

I am on my knees, at the edge of the water, too frightened to move. Never, in all my life, have I seen lights independent of a candle or lantern. Fireflies, perhaps. But those would be small and would flash, the males dancing and signaling for the females waiting on the ground. Not glowing bright orbs, moving erratically in the rain. My mind tries to make sense of it. Are they ghosts? Spirits of the dead come to frighten me? I have never believed such things existed before, but it is hard to deny what I can see with my eyes.

Soon, the lights move off the bridge and travel down the west facing side of the riverbank. The very side where I am in the shallows of the river not thirty feet away. They stop, move to the ground and stay there. For several minutes I am perfectly still, holding my breath. I do not want them to see me. If they are spirits, I want to be far away from them. They suddenly rise up and all of them together move swiftly down the road towards the south.

I am alone again.

I wait a bit longer. Listening to my breathing and the sounds of the pouring rain, so like pebbles on the tin roof of our chicken coop. Once I am sure they have truly gone, I work to extricate myself from the mud. The skirts of my dress are twisted around my feet so badly that as I try to pull free I fall forward yet again. Dunking my head into the cold brackish water.

Reaching out to one side, I find I can grasp a fallen tree that is half submerged near me, and I use it to pull myself up. Sloshing through the shallows, I gain the riverbank a bit further down where the brush is less thick and finally stand again on solid land. Water is dripping heavily down me and mixing with the rain that will not stop.

Keeping the bridge in sight I work my way around the water but there is no way to cross back to it. I stop dead in my tracks, confused. This is nonsensical. It is a bridge over a narrow river. I should be able to just follow the shoreline of the water on this side till it meets back up to the bridge. Yet everything I see is mud banks and water. How can I get back there? I cannot swim. Even if I trust that the water is not deep, the storm is causing the water to flow so quickly I may be swept away though it is only waist high.

The tree! The tree I had used to pull myself out. How far does it go across the water? Does it reach the entire expanse? I turn and make my way back to see. And in fact, it does appear to make it most of the way. But am I able to cross it? Can I balance myself in the dark, in a waterlogged dress, across a slippery, half rotted tree?

I will have to find out. I scrape the mud off the soles of my shoes on an upended root and place my foot near the base of the tree. I stand up carefully as a new sound carries across the water. I stop still to try and understand it. It is a cry. Weak, soft, and pleading. Almost lost in the sound of the rain and the thunder. The cry is coming from the bridge.

The cry of a baby.

Chapter 9

May 15th, 2023

My phone beeps loudly at the crack of dawn. Pulling me out of a deep sleep. I struggle my eyes open, squinting in the bright light. Ahh, God. Remember when I had corneas? This is torture. My blackout curtains are on the way. It took only one morning of waking in the blinding sunlight before I caved and asked Mom to buy some. I grab for the phone with my eyes closed and pull it under the blanket with me.

Jesse: I pulled my first baby calf!

Claire: You pulled your WHAT? When??

Jesse: Just now. It was amazing. I won't gross you out but let's just say I need a shower. Pulled the baby right out of its mother. Helped her start breathing. It's the cutest little girl. A heifer.

Claire: OMG. I'm so proud of you Yeti. Have I mentioned yet today that I love you? And I miss you desperately?

Jesse: Oddly enough, no. But it is 6:20am. My feelings aren't too hurt. Day ain't over yet.

Claire: Well I do.

Jesse: I love you back, Tiny. Starting at the store today?

Claire: Yep, I'm excited to see it. It should be like the library, but with more noise and money. I've got to get moving. I'll text you later. Miss you... Go shower. XXXOOO

Jesse: Yes Ma'am. Be safe. XXXOOO

I sit my phone down just as the alarm starts blaring. Uggghh, time to wake up anyway. I have to get ready to head to "Dusty." Mom's name for The Dusty Bookshelf.

Settling into the house has been pretty easy. Rufus and Finn remember me. With them having babies in the nest box they are very protective of the mega giant cage they have that sits across the back of the sunroom. But they don't mind me coming in and checking out their sunny play area at the windows. Not a bad set up. Mom's going to teach me to handfeed. They have been having babies for several summers now. Happy as they can be. Mom's waiting list for adoptive owners is a mile long so she can choose exactly where each baby will go. She only picks the best, most experienced homes. She's had people fly in from all the way across the country to pick them up. It's crazy.

Tim has been great. I've spent hours already hanging in his office. He's been showing me how he does all the background research for his books. It's so complicated and intimidating. I'm definitely more interested in writing fiction. His office is amazing. Huge antique desk. Charts, maps, and tacked notes flow over the dark green walls like snakes. There are books on every available surface.

So far the bathroom is my favorite part of the house. I gather my clothes and stumble in, staring longingly at the deep tub I don't have time for. Later, my darling. But the shower is spacious and the water hot. Excellent. I'm starting to feel almost human.

Coffee is next on the list. I need help getting the fog out of my brain. Heading down the stairs I can already smell it. Mom and Tim are in the kitchen, kissing over their giant steaming cups. She is bright eyed and completely wide awake, it's ridiculous. He's still trying to get his eyes open. Just like me.

"Gross Mom." I said, "Do I need to see that?

She laughed. "You'll probably survive. Hungry? As you can see," waving dramatically at the table, "I've made a sumptuous meal of nothing. I have cereal, or some eggs if you are feeling ambitious, but I've been grabbing breakfast in Georgetown. There's a good place right near the store."

"Fine with me. As soon as the caffeine hits my bloodstream I'll be ready to go." I said. My typical uniform of jeans and a t-shirt is too casual if the store were open, but perfect for the day I'm about to have.

"Have a great day ladies. I'm off to try and be brilliant," Tim kisses Mom, refills his coffee, and heads for the office. He is dressed even more casually than I am. Old sweatpants, a paint splattered tee and tattered bedroom slippers. Wild hair and a messy beard. Working from home obviously has it's perks.

* * *

The drive from Woodland to Georgetown goes quickly. Mom can talk, that's for sure.

"Today we are starting on the Romance room. It's painted a pastel pink. Which I think is gross, but Talissa is totally into it. You'll probably love the Horror room, it's red." she laughs.

Mom and Talissa have decided that each of the rooms will have a different subject theme: Romance, Horror, Sci Fi and Fantasy, Cooking, Health and Wellness, etc. Even an Antique book room. The one I'm most interested in. I can't wait to get my hands on all those old books.

"Hunter will be in today; you haven't met him yet. Talissa found him at the gym. He's a great guy." She said. "He's setting up the security and POS systems. We're having cameras hooked up in every room. He's freelance so it's saving us a ton of money. I think it's partly because he found out we have a room for science fiction and fantasy. He's made some great title suggestions."

I love Georgetown. Only seventeen miles from the beach, it's got beautiful old historic houses up and down the streets surrounding the picturesque roundabout in the center of town. A courthouse, restaurants, banks, and shops in stately old brick buildings. My jaw drops when mom turns off the circle and a few buildings down pulls into the small parking lot behind a gorgeous corner Victorian painted a beautiful emerald green. A deep porch wraps around the two street-facing sides of the house. Gables, cornices and other stuff I don't know the names for give it unbelievable charm. It even has a turret! Ohh, I'd sit a chair right there.

"*This* is the bookstore?" I said, "You can't be serious."

"Oh it's serious all right." She looks mildly queasy. "And if it's not a success we are all in trouble. We have to get this place open in time to catch the tourists. We're going to really work to hit the Memorial Day grand opening." She grins, "Wait till you see the inside."

Holy crap. This place is going to be amazing. I follow Mom though the large front door. A polished counter is set up across the wide foyer, to the side of an ornate staircase. Several soft crushed blue velvet easy chairs sit in the front bay window in what Mom calls the "Let me read it a bit first" area. We walk through the ground floor rooms. Boxes of books are literally everywhere I look. It's like a maze. Or maybe a kids fort. Shoulder-high bookshelves line the floor and walls. The whole downstairs smells like new paint and coffee. I see that Mom's love of stuff has spilled over into her work. Each room will be an illustration of the genre it holds. Figurines, toys, framed pictures, all kinds of ephemera; sit waiting to adorn the shelves and walls. This morning, we will work in Romance. The pink walls in here are not as bad as mom thinks they are. A soft, dusky shade. Sweet.

This is where we find Talissa. Arranging books on a low, hot pink standing bookshelf. Her long box braids wrapped high on her head and falling down her back. When she sees me, a smile breaks across her glowing, golden-brown face.

"There she is! How's my girl? I see we finally came up with a good enough reason to get you back here." She stands and wraps her arms around me.

"Not forever. Just till Jesse is finished practicing pulling little cows out of bigger ones and chasing goats and horses around," I laughed. "But this place is going to be incredible! I can't believe it. I'm so proud of you guys."

"Come," she said, pulling me along behind her, "Meet Hunter, he's upstairs setting up a camera in the Horror room. Your mother's favorite place." She turns to Mom raises an eyebrow, gesturing towards the shelves, "I'll introduce her, Ophelia, you see if you like how I got started in here."

As we climb the stairs I can hear music faintly playing somewhere above me and the sound of a drill. We move down the hall to the large front room that overlooks the street.

The walls are indeed a dark maroon. I recognize several skulls that used to be in our old living room. Every foot of wall space without shelves is covered with taxidermy crows, bat skeletons under glass, and framed vintage Halloween themed Beistle die cuts. Fake cobwebbing has been stretched expertly across the top of the ceiling. The books are arranged perfectly on lots of black bookshelves. It is indeed my mother's taste. A blond guy is high up on a ladder in the corner with his back to us.

"This is the first room your mom got unpacked and decorated. I think if it were up to her, the whole store would look like this," she laughed.

"Hunter!" she shouts, "Turn that off and meet Claire!

The drill stops and he jumps down the three rungs all at once. Hitting the floor with an audible bang.

"Jeepers," he said, "Sorry. I gotta be more gentle with this old lady. If I don't pay better attention, I'm going to crash right through the floor."

"And you'll owe us money instead of the other way around. Hunter Gatewood, this is Ophelia's daughter, Claire Ludlow. Here to make this all work out."

"Right, no pressure on me at all. Thanks. Hi Hunter, good to meet you." I stick my hand out and he grips it firmly.

"Well, it's good to know the cavalry is here," He joked. He looks to be in his early thirties. Not bad looking. Kind of an intense face. Serious. "So this is the woman I've heard so much about."

"That doesn't sound good. Just know, stories of my sainthood may be grossly exaggerated."

"Duly noted," he slyly drops me a wink.

"We will be down in the Romance room if you need us," Talissa says.

"Will do. I've got a while still to go in here. Very nice to meet you, Claire." His eyes follow us as we make our way out the door.

We spend the morning moving books from one place to another. Dragging in boxes, checking books into inventory, alphabetizing, stacking. Trying to make it look good and fit everything on the shelves neatly, moving extra stock to the former pantry off the kitchen. Mom's right, it's hard work. Hot too. The central air is working hard, and we should be cool. But manual labor is... well...*labor*. By lunchtime I am sweaty and totally beat.

"Please tell me we are having food delivered and I can lay on the floor till it gets here." I drop to the colorful rug at the front counter. My back is killing me.

"You are in luck, my glorious offspring. Hunter went to procure sustenance. Just lay there." Mom said, tossing me a tapestry pillow off one of the chairs. I turn onto my belly and hug the plushness close, burying my face in it.

I am half asleep by the time Hunter is back with the food. Only aware of his return when he drops the take-out bag in front of my nose. The glorious smell of cheesesteak registers in my brain. Ahhhh.

"Come...rise my Clarity," said Mom. "We feast in the kitchen."

I manage to drag myself off the floor. Hunter laughs and catches my hands as I wobble unsteadily on my feet. Holding them firmly as he stares at me. "You have pillow lines on your face."

"Excellent."

"It adds character. Tell me we haven't broken you already." He jokes, "I...we have other plans for you. When you finish eating, you can help me adjust the camera views in a few rooms while I watch the feed. You are getting a state-of-the-art system in here. We want to make sure we can watch every inch of this place. You never know what you might need to see."

"Nourishment first..." I beg, "Please."

MAGGIE I HAVE YOUR BABY

He laughs, holding firmly to my hands.

We eat in the house kitchen. Last updated in the seventies, it seems. I'd heard of avocado-colored appliances before, but here they are in real life. It's a small space compared to the size of this place, but plenty of room for three to sit around a small table. It works well as a break room.

"Romance is coming along fine. It used to be the dining room, that's why the space is so big. Let's give it a break in there and move on to something else. The kid's room? What do you think?" Mom likes to do that, have many projects going on at once. It keeps her from getting bored. I do the same thing.

"I think I will stick with it," Talissa said, "I'm determined to make some progress before the day is out. Maybe I will absorb some romance through the books. Every book in there is more exciting than my actual love life."

"How about the Antique room?" I ask, "When can I get in it?

"Go! Help yourself. The small back room on the left, upstairs. We are having the hardest time setting up in there. Problem is, there are books from every genre. So it's tough to figure out the best way to organize them. You are welcome to take a shot at it," Mom offers, then adds, "We got a shipment of old books from an estate sale last week. It's up in there somewhere. There are some about Delaware. See if there is enough to maybe dedicate a local section."

"She promised to help me with the cameras," Hunter said quietly. Staring down at the remains of his lunch on the table.

65

He hasn't spoken during the meal. Mostly just watched us banter back and forth while he eats.

Talissa speaks up, "I can help you Hunter. No problem. It will give my back a break from lugging boxes. I'm not as young as I think I am. I'll finish Romance tomorrow."

Hunter does not look up.

"Great," he says, his voice flat, "Thanks."

Chapter 10

Maggie

May 31st, 1880

Midnight

Once I recognize that the cries are coming from a baby, I become frantic. Is it mine? Is that why I no longer feel the child inside of me? Have I lost more memories than I thought? Could I have already borne my child? Somehow lost him on this road while traveling? Were we travelling together?

What if he had been taken from me? Was I chasing someone that had stolen him? That would explain my leaving home on such a terrible night. Have I been I out here in the storm searching for him from the beginning? Was he dropped by the thief and is freezing alone somewhere in this terrible rain? Right now, all I can remember of this night is waking in the mud, and the living nightmare that has followed. What brought me to this place is still shrouded in darkness.

Climbing onto the log, I keep my knees bent to help balance myself. With my arms out I start to step across. Immediately, my feet begin to slip. The mud on my shoes and the waterlogged tree make taking steps and staying balanced impossible. I will never make it this way. I slowly lower myself and climb back off the tree. Picking up the front of my skirt into my hands I tuck the hem of the fabric into the waist. Baring my legs to the thigh. I must keep it out of the way to try this. I climb up again onto my hands and knees and start crawling out across the water. Feeling the way with my fingers, the sharp points of the uneven tree bark jab into my knees with each movement. Slowly I begin to make my way across the water. The tree has a straight trunk, so I at least do not need to climb higher as I go.

Halfway across the crying begins again. Louder now. I hear it clearly through the rain. A tiny voice plaintively crying out for help. He sounds so lost, confused, and so afraid. The pitiful sound splits my heart and raises a low helpless noise from deep inside me. I crawl as fast as I dare and at last reach the bank on the other side. The tops of the fallen tree's branches are mired deeply in the mud. I work myself carefully so I do not fall. The mud grabbing on to each foot as if it wants to drag me down. I reach solid land and pull my skirts back down. Climbing the bank again hand over hand, I am finally, finally, back on the bridge.

It is empty, and silent. The crying has stopped. I search as carefully as I can from corner to corner. There is no one here but me. I wait and wait but the crying does not resume. I sink to my knees with my head in my hands, giving in to my helplessness.

I weep until the last of my strength is gone. My tears mixing with the rain that continues to pour from the sky. What to do now?

What if I find a closer place to shelter under and try and gather my thoughts? Somewhere I can keep the bridge in my sight. Anything will be better than wandering around and getting nowhere. The lightning flashes and I look around me.

To the north side is an outcropping of land that reaches out into the water. I have not noticed it before. It is only a few feet from the bridge. The large tree at the tip has a trunk that leans gently out over the water. I can lay back against it and not have to place my aching head directly on the ground. The bank leading down to it is steep and thick with brush. Walking a few feet down the road reveals a small break between the bushes. Down to what almost looks like a narrow path. I pull my arms around myself and force my way through the break. Scratching my arms afresh. The path leads to the small spit of land. I settle myself down as comfortably as I can. From here I can hear the water rushing loudly beneath the bridge. Mingling with the rain and thunder.

I try to focus my thoughts and remember what I can. I can think of the first time I saw Elias, only last year. His dear face and kind eyes come to mind in an instant. A small sliver of peace washes over me. I block out the rain and the sounds of the storm and let my mind drift. I was a shy girl, not experienced in the ways of the world. It had started as any other morning. Rising, doing chores, having breakfast with my parents, before heading off to church.

September 1879

He is tall. With deep set, dark eyes and a large handsome nose. I am surprised when I see him in church. We do not often get new members. He's sitting across the aisle from me and my parents. I know he sneaks glances at me all through the sermon. Because I sneak glances at him. He seems older than my sixteen years. But not by many. Still a young man.

His mother and father are a formidable looking couple. His mother's stern face is watching him look at me. Her frown grows deeper each time I peek over. His father sits ramrod straight in his pew, staring straight ahead at our preacher, his eyes never flickering or looking away. His grey hair and long white beard framing eyes the color of ice.

At the end of the service the preacher calls our attention to them. "Folks, we have a new family joining our congregation today. They are new to the area. The Hastings family. Arba Hastings is a former ships cabinet maker and carpenter who has chosen to relocate to our community from New York. And aren't we lucky to have him? He brings with him his lovely wife Cora and their strapping son Elias. Elias is nineteen and finishing up his apprenticeship under his father. So soon we will have two talented cabinet makers local to our wonderful parish. Let's everyone make them feel welcome."

I see him blush. The tips of his ears turn a bright red, and he rubs the back of his neck. Embarrassed by the attention.

In the churchyard we stand with all the other families, waiting our turn to greet them. He is watching me. Every hand he shakes he glances back to see where I am. I feel as jumpy as a cat. No one has ever looked at me this way. It makes me nervous and excited. I do not know what to do with my hands. I clasp them behind my back and try to keep a pleasant smile on my face. I can feel my lips trembling and I bite down on them to make them stop. Finally my parents, Robert and Joan Bloxom, shake hands with his. "Welcome!" my father says loudly, "We are blessed to have you here!" Finally, Father introduces me, "Arba, Cora, Elias, this is my daughter, Maggie."

"Hello there, young lady," I smile politely as his father shakes my hand. I turn to face Elias. He grasps my hand with both of his.

"It is a real pleasure to meet you Maggie."

His voice is warm, surprisingly deep. He smiles at me.

We smile in silence at each other for several minutes while my father asks his father about New York state, and why they decided to come to this area.

I remember it all. This first Sunday.

Chapter 11

Claire

If I spent the morning in hard manual labor, I'm spending the afternoon reading till my eyes are dry. Surrounded by the dusty books that I stack in taller and taller piles around me. Some of these are amazing. Histories of Sussex County, ancient looking maps, an old book of local folk tales. Some are even wrapped in tissue paper to protect the covers. This is so much fun. I can't stop myself from flipping through every book, so it's taking longer than it probably should.

"MOM!" I have to show her some of this.

I hear her walk through the doorway. I can see just the top of her head above the books. She immediately bellows with laughter. Seeing the giant stacks of books everywhere and me sitting in the center.

"Are you creating an art installation?" she muses.

"Obviously. But you've got to look at this stuff," I said, "Some of these things are really, really old. They may belong in a museum instead of out for sale. At the very least, you need to list some of these on the store website. You could make much more money from them there than on a shelf here. Maybe eBay instead."

"That sounds like something you should research," she winks. "Maybe separate the ones that look particularly special, and you can look them up and check. By the way, it's time to go. Tim is making dinner. That's a good thing. We don't want to miss it."

She heads down the stairs. I've been so engrossed I didn't even notice the time. Out the window the sun going down. I check my watch...8:30. Geez, it's so late! As if in agreement, my stomach growls loudly.

I push myself up off the floor. My legs are asleep. I shake them both in turn and jump up and down to get the blood flowing again. Looking around, I just don't want to leave all this groovy stuff. How many of these could fit on the shelf in my bedroom? Overwhelmed, I grab the old book of folktales and legends. This looks cool. I'll read this tonight.

Hunter is waiting at the bottom of the stairs. "Found something interesting, did you?" he asked, glancing at the cover.

"Um, yeah. I was going to read it at home if nobody minds."

"Hey, the store's not open yet. I'm sure it's fine for you to do a little 'research' on the stock. He drops a wink, smiles and adds, "By the way, I enjoyed your dance just now."

* * *

Tim is a great cook. At least where tacos are concerned. The smell of sizzling ground beef and fresh onions is still strong in the kitchen. I have eaten my weight in food. I've had so many good meals here already, soon I won't be able to fit in my clothes.

"There's stuff enough for one last taco," Tim said, "Who wants it?" Mom and I both groan.

"I'm completely stuffed.' I said, "So hand it over." The hell with it, what's one more? I earned it today.

Dragging myself up the stairs to my room I collapse on the bed. The setting sun is lighting the sky beautiful colors, bathing my room in an orange glow. I pull the dog-eared, "Folktales and Ghosts: The Legends of Delaware" out of my bag, adjust the pillows under my head, and settle back to read.

This book is wild! I had no idea there were so many spooky things going on around this small state. I read through the story of The Legend Of Fiddler's Bridge, The Dark Magic of Old Mol, and then there she is.

Haunting of Maggie's Bridge.

On a lonely bridge in Woodland, not far outside of the township of Seaford, the spirit of Maggie Bloxom does not rest. Old folks in town will tell you of a young seventeen-year-old girl, cast out by her family for her unfortunate condition. She'd fallen pregnant with a bastard child. Hoping to better her situation and marry the father of her baby, she runs off into the night. A terrible storm caught her unaware and while crossing the sodden bridge, the horse was spooked and off the bridge they went. When the search party found her, so early the next morning that the sun had not risen, their lanterns illuminated her headless body. Lying in the broken wreckage of the buggy near the lifeless body of the horse. The head was found yards away by her grieving father, her face a screaming mask of agony. So take care when travelling that quiet stretch of road, you may just see the ghost of Maggie trying to find her way home.

Maggie had been only *seventeen*? She was unmarried and pregnant. Damn. Not a good situation to be in in the late 1800's. The fear of judgement must have been terrible. What was the reaction of her parents? Did they throw her out? Where were they going to go?

I remember being that age. For Pete's sake, that's how old I was when I took Jesse to the bridge. Seeing her myself that night, I was too busy freaking out at the sight of her headless corpse to have any idea how old she was. Imagine how Mom would have reacted if I were pregnant at seventeen! Angry, I'm sure. Disappointed in me sure, but... she never would have turned me away. I can't picture anything making her do something like that. Maggie must have been so scared. Who could she turn to?

I flip the page, and there is her picture. Adrenaline shoots through me and I recoil, dropping the book on the bed. I know her face. I recognize her.

Relax Claire. It's a picture, get a grip. It's not going to bite you. I force myself to pick the book up again and look at her. Here, she is beautiful. Long black hair mostly piled atop her head with loose coils hanging down her slim shoulders. She looks so petite. Even smaller than me. Her dark eyes seem sad.

In the six years since seeing her on the bridge, I've thought of her more times than I want to admit. I was absolutely terrified that night. It's the first and only time I've ever wanted to run in fear. I never want to see her again, or to feel that way. I've even tried to convince myself that it didn't really happen. That she was my imagination in overdrive, heightened by the dark and the bats. That her screams really came from some animal we never identified.

I've been lying to myself all this time. This is the face I saw that night. I had really seen her as we drove away. Her spirit is still out there.

Right now.

Why? What binds her to the bridge? Is she truly hunting for her lost baby? Do we frighten her? Have people been terrorizing her all these years? The idea is terrible, and I start to cry.

* * *

I wake up later in total darkness. Tears dried to my face. My phone buzzing with a text.

Unknown number: So, what did you find out?

Claire: Who is this?

Unknown number: You spent the day with me.

Huh? Who the? Oh, wait…

Claire: Hunter? How did you get my number??

Unknown Number: It's listed in the paperwork by the counter at the store. I've been logging the contact information into the system.

Claire: Well that's not creepy or inappropriate at all.

Unknown Number: Sorry, you got me curious about that book you took home. Checked it out yet?

Something makes me hesitant to share anything. I don't know this guy. It feels weird. I only met him today. He's older than me. Older than Jesse, even. Over thirty at least. And it's...12:15 am. Way too late to be texting relative strangers.

Then again, he does work for the bookstore. And he's friends with Mom and Talissa. He's probably trying to make me feel welcome. Showing an interest in things related to the store. I decide to cut him a break.

Claire: A little. There are some interesting stories.

Unknown Number: What kind of stories do you like? Are you one of those romance girls? Maybe sci fi? Fantasy?

Claire: Not really. I'm more into horror.

Unknown Number: So you like to be scared, do you?

Claire: Don't get any ideas. I like it in books and movies. Not real life.

Unknown Number: LOL. Don't worry. I'm just messing with you. Trying to get your vibe.

Claire: And why do you need my vibe at this time of night? We work in the same place.

Unknown Number: You seem interesting.

Claire: I'm a lot less interesting when I am exhausted. And I have a lot of boxes to lug around tomorrow so I'm going back to sleep.

Unknown Caller: I've seen you asleep, remember? You were passed out on the floor when I brought you lunch. You looked pretty comfortable. You can always take another nap there tomorrow.

Claire: Goodnight Hunter.

Unknown Number: I'll see you tomorrow.

I sit the phone back on the nightstand and roll to face the windows. I guess he's ok. A bit too friendly, but what woman doesn't have to deal with unwanted attention sometimes? I can be polite. I don't want to alienate him when Mom and Talissa need his help. It won't last forever. He'll do his job and leave. I can be nice.

As I snuggle into the blankets, I miss Jesse. His smile. The long arms he likes to wrap me in. His easy way of drawing me out when I'm too into my own head or calming me down when I get manic. Our conversations have never been awkward. Even in the beginning. I've grown up loving him. Sleeping alone isn't easy after being together every night for three years. I close my eyes, try to clear my head and relax.

In the quiet I can just make out the sound of Rufus downstairs, laughing menacingly from inside the nest box. He sounds like he's possessed. That's not much help.

Chapter 12

The past is becoming more clear to me. I am able to ignore the pounding rain, the thunder that never stops. Resting against the tree, I feel calmer than I have felt since I awoke in the mud.

If I can figure out how I got here perhaps I can figure a way out. Maybe I have hurt my head, slipped off the bridge while walking and knocked myself unconscious. That is why I did not know where I was when I woke up covered with mud. This confusion I feel may be easily explained away after some time healing. After some rest, the explanation with fall neatly into place.

The memories of Elias are bringing me comfort, and I welcome them. It is so easy to picture his kind face.

October 1879

After the first meeting I look for him every Sunday. It is not easy to keep my eyes from him during the service. I try to stare straight ahead. My parents, kind as they are to me, are very proper. Any attention that I give Elias will not go unnoticed. No matter what I do I still feel his eyes on me. I flush warm and my heart races the whole hour. I am surprised the other parishioners do not hear it. I wish for time to speak to him, but with our parents watching us there is no chance to say anything of a personal nature.

This goes on for three weeks. Three long, tension filled hours where I try to stay focused but can only think about him. Till the beautiful autumn Sunday I stand in the churchyard after the service looking at the brilliant colors of the changing trees.

"Miss Maggie?"

I turn, and Elias is standing behind me, his hand out to shake mine, "I hope you are having a pleasant morning." As he shakes my hand I feel the rough edges of a small scrap of paper. A note! He slides it discreetly into my palm and backs away.

My voice comes out shaking and soft, "Elias, nice to see you. I am...well. Thank you."

My heart pounds the whole drive home. After church I always help mother make supper before we sit down to our bible reading. Chores are done as swiftly as possible, as Sunday is a day of rest. I am not out of my parents sight for long. We spend the entire afternoon in silence. It is a struggle to sit still. There is no time to open the note until I settle myself into my bed that night. My hands are shaking as I finally unfold it and hold it up in the dim candlelight.

Maggie,

Please forgive my forwardness in writing to you.

I saw no other way to let you know of my feelings.

You are beautiful.

Your soft voice and kind eyes fill my thoughts.

Is there any hope that you could return my affection?

If so, please smile at me during the sermon next Sunday.

If not, I promise I will not bother you again.

Yours respectfully,

Elias

My heart expands with pleasure till I feel it press against my ribs. Never before in all my years have I felt the rush of emotion that comes over me. My whole body feels like it is humming. The feeling is still there the next morning when I wake. I spend the next several days confounded by how I should respond. Careening between joy and worry. What is proper? I have no experience. No friends to ask. I surely cannot ask my mother. She believes I am still too young to be concerned with meeting young men.

The next Sunday my nerves are high. I cannot bring my eyes to meet his as my family file into our regular spot. During the first hymn, I can hardly raise my voice to be heard, and I feel my cheeks redden as I sense his eyes on me. When the sermon begins I sit as still as stone. Trying to focus on the pastor's droning voice. The fear of what may come from accepting his attention is at war with the hope of the possibilities. I stare down at my lap as long as I dare. The sermon could end at any time, and I am still frozen with indecision and fear. This is the first time in my life I am considering deliberately disobeying my parents. I have always done as I am told.

Something inside me rises up. I feel a lightness fill my chest and I lift my head up high. Finally, I can bear it no longer. I quickly glance over at him. He is staring right into my eyes. I do what I most want to do.

I smile.

After the service I leave the pew, walk quickly outside and stand in the church yard watching the ferry moving across the river. My breathing has not yet slowed down. My parents have stayed inside for a bit to speak to our preacher. Father is donating one of our pigs to the revival our Church is having in April. Folks from surrounding towns will be coming in for the events and a lot of food will be needed.

Glancing back, I pretend not to see Elias coming down the church steps. Turning my back to him and studying the water intently.

"Maggie?"

I turn and he is standing before me. I open my mouth, and nothing comes out.

"Come next Sunday, there will be a note in the hymnal where you sit. It is just for you. Will you be able to collect it without being seen?"

I am still speechless but manage to nod my head at him. He reaches out, lightly touching my hand, then he is gone.

Chapter 13

Claire

May 16th, 2023

Morning sure comes early around here. Although I suppose my 6:30 alarm wouldn't be so bad if I had managed to go to sleep at a decent hour. After the messages from Hunter, it took forever to get back to sleep. Then this morning I was jolted awake by a nightmare even before my alarm had a chance.

I was having a dream about Maggie. Somehow, I was alone on the bridge in the dark, completely terrified. Searching the woods to see her. I tried to run back towards the house, but my feet wouldn't move. They were sunk deep into thick mud. I would pull and yank at my feet as hard as I could, but they wouldn't budge. As hard as I tried, I couldn't get off the bridge.

I tried screaming, realizing I must be having a nightmare. This trick had woken me up from bad dreams in the past. But the scream I heard didn't come from me, but from behind me.

I turn at the waist and look. I know I don't want to, but it happens anyway.

It was her. Right there. Not the terrifying thing I had seen that night on the bridge. But the sad eyed young girl whose picture I had found in the book. Tears dripped down her face and into her screaming mouth. She reached out for me and grabbed my arms by the wrists, hauling me around to face her, screaming and screaming.

That's when her head dropped off her neck and landed on the ground between us.

With such a fun wake up call, it's taking two giant cups of coffee before I'm ready to face this day. I sit at the kitchen table, my forehead leaning on one hand. I can do this. I intend to find a way to organize the mess I made yesterday.

"So I'm headed back in the Antique room this morning. Unless you need me to do something else," I tell Mom when she comes in, looking wide awake and chipper. "I think there is enough for a Delaware bookshelf. But have you thought about adding a separate area for local authors? It would be good to put those all together in the front room maybe. And hey, you could stare at Tim's books all day if they are out there."

"I've convinced him to do a signing for me when he gets back from the book tour. He claims signing books in front of me will make him feel like a...what did he say? Ah, a *douche-canoe*. I have no idea what that is, but it doesn't sound good."

"OMG," I laugh hard, "I'll get those books separated this morning so I can look them up online. We may have some valuable ones."

Mom looks thoughtful, "Think we need a locking cabinet in that room? For the pricey stuff?"

"I'll ask Hunter about it. He's still adjusting the cameras. Maybe we could put the shelf in an easily seen spot," I said.

* * *

Hunter is waiting on the porch when we get to the store. He looks up and smiles when we pull in.

"Good morning!" He calls out to us, "I got doughnuts."

"Well that's a first," Mom says, "We've been here three weeks and I've never seen him here before I get in."

We talk over the day's game plan as we eat. Talissa joining us at the table when she arrives. These doughnuts Hunter brought are amazing. I help myself to another chocolate frosted and try to pay attention to the conversation. I still feel out of it. I need more sugar.

"You're going to work with me today, right Claire?" Hunter looks hopefully at me. "I hear there are some books that we need to research the value of."

"Um, yeah. Maybe later, I guess," I said, surprised. Did I promise him that? "I still need to go through a few more boxes first. Maybe make some sense of what's in there."

He smiles, "Well, take your time. I'll be working on the system at the front counter."

MAGGIE I HAVE YOUR BABY

"I'll come get you when I'm finished. I may need some help moving the books around."

"Just look up and give me a smile." he said, raising his eyebrows, "Remember, I'll be watching."

What the hell? I frown at him, pick up my coffee and wipe the crumbs from the table. I turn without speaking and head out the door.

He calls after me as I leave the room, "It's a joke! The security system, remember? The cameras? That's why I'm here."

Oh right. I feel stupid. I wave my hand it the air to signal I understand and keep walking. Now I can't even take a joke. See what happens when I don't get enough sleep?

* * *

It takes a couple hours to organize and sort most of the towers of books I've stacked everywhere. I got several shelves set up and made a small pile of the books that may be worth a second look. I am covered with sweat and dust. My hair is probably insane. I can feel it grow bigger with every degree my body heats up.

I pull another box over and open it. It's filled with old paperbacks from what looks like the eighties. Flowing hair, ripped bodices, tight pecs, and row after row of abs on every cover. Well *these* are in the wrong place. The two boxes under them are filled with the same. These belong in the discount shelves of the romance room. I laugh to myself. I pick a few to read, of course. I may be a horror novel enthusiast, but I still enjoy a good steamy time waster. One of these will work well for a good long soak in the tub tonight as I try to sooth my angry muscles.

Enough. I can't finish in here until I get these huge boxes moved out. I pick up the small pile of the books that need checking out and head downstairs.

"What, you didn't want my help?" Hunter says as I place the books on the counter.

"There's some giant boxes of pulp romance that need to come down here. Can you get them?" I ask, "They're pretty heavy."

"Jeepers! Anything the lady wishes," he jumps up, gives me a crisp formal bow and quickly heads up the stairs as I laugh.

* * *

The rest of the day passes quickly. Mom leaves for an estate sale. Hunter works at the front computer, and I arrange shelves with Talissa. We work in the Romance room for a couple hours then move on to the Children's and Young Adult area for a change of scenery. It's the largest room in the back, painted a bright yellow.

"I recognize a few of Mom's old childhood toys on the walls in here. This is pretty cute."

"Isn't it darling? Most of my décor contributions are in Health and Wellness. The Sci Fi stuff is mine too. Your mom had nothing for those."

"Nah, she's not a Science Fiction girl."

I'm sitting on the floor, alphabetizing the fresh, clean-smelling new books, when the phone in my back pocket buzzes. I check it and smile.

Toby: Hey! You still alive down there?

Claire: OMG hey! Sorry, it's been a busy few days. I should have let you know I got here safe. I suck.

Toby: Nah, it's cool. How has it been? How's the store? How's Maggie? Go visit her yet?

Claire: Very funny. The store is going to be great; I think. Although I'm working so hard I may not live to see the opening.

Toby: I can't wait to see it. So really no Maggie? I'd have been down there so fast. Girl, you are RIGHT THERE!

Claire: I had an awful dream about her early this morning. I found this folklore book with her story. It's a lot sadder than I knew.

Toby: How?

Claire: She was only seventeen! And running away to her boyfriend when it happened. There is even a picture of her.

Toby: That's unbelievable. I want to see it. We have to go back. I can't wait to get out there with you. When should I come down? This weekend?

Claire: I really want to see you, but we are working pretty hard right now. What about next weekend? The 26th? It's still before the holiday, so you should be able to get through the traffic. We open the next day, sorta. Not the grand opening but the doors will be open. You can be one of the first customers.

Toby: Sounds great! See what else you can find before I get there. We can have an old-fashioned ghost hunt!

Claire: Um...we'll see. I better get back to work. I'm currently surrounded by children's books.

Toby: And I'm surrounded by children. LOL. Later!

I miss Toby. Since we live in different cities we haven't had much of a chance to spend time together the last few years. Just a few visits. Mostly me going to Baltimore. Toby loves taking me around the city. He's exactly the person I need with me this summer. Going back to Maggie's Bridge is something I would not want to do alone. Well, not at night at least.

I suppose I could walk down there in daylight this weekend. Just to prove to myself I can. It's strange, but I'm feeling guilty about my reaction to seeing her years ago. Toby had been right. She was a real person who had a horrible accident.

Before I can put it back in my pocket, my phone buzzes again.

Unknown Number: So you found a few good ones. Come see.

Claire: Is there a reason you can't walk ten feet down the hall and just tell me that? You aren't that old.

Unknown Number: Because this is easier. I broke my back carrying those boxes down for you.

Claire: Fine, fine. I'm coming.

Hunter has researched each and every one of the books I had set aside and had already listed most of them on the store's website that will go live on opening day.

"There's some here that are worth a few hundred dollars each, at least. Those, you should probably get professionally appraised and list on eBay. Or I can do it, if you want," he said.

"I'll ask Mom. This is great. Thanks," I say, and mean it. That was much faster, and probably better, than I could have done it.

By the time Mom comes back to pick me up, I've had it with this day. My back and feet are killing me. I climb in the front seat and collapse against the dashboard. "Let's stop for fast food. I'm too tired to cook and too hungry to wait for *you* to cook."

"Deal."

As we go through the drive through she says, "I'm worn out, too. I want to go to bed early tonight. Hope you don't need to be entertained."

"Mom," I said, 'I'm twenty-three years old. I think I can manage to amuse myself." Knowing I'll probably call Jesse, then soak in a hot bubble bath for an hour before I pass out.

* * *

Two hours later, I feel much better about life in general. Relaxed after the bath. That tub really is amazing. Mom was right to give up that extra bedroom. A bathtub like that is much more important.

I try calling Jesse. The phone rings and rings. He doesn't answer. I send him a text, but he doesn't reply right away. He's probably out on a hot date with a horse.

No, damn it. I am not going to be jealous of farm animals. I agreed to this, and I am going to stick it out. He is *working*. And so am I. Someday I will look back on this time and laugh at how much I acted like love sick teenager.

I really have to clean up this bedroom. I look around at the boxes of books and the trash bags filled with my winter clothes. There are bookshelves in the room but I'm really picky about how I arrange them. So for now, the books are still in boxes. Besides, I've been doing that all damn day. No more.

I can at least put the bags in the closet before I go to bed. I drag them over and open the door.

The closet isn't as big as I thought. These old houses have closets the size of a port-a-potty. If I unpack these and hang them all up I won't even be able to move in here.

My eye catches the pull-down ladder to the attic. If I put them up there I won't even have to look at them. I don't need them yet anyway. It's going to be hot and humid for months.

Reaching up I grab the cord and pull; the door comes down and releases the folding ladder. It stretches right to the edge of the closet door. Above me is a solid rectangle of darkness pouring out heat. There is obviously no air conditioning up there.

Well, this is going to be a hoot. I grab the first bag and carefully pull it and myself up into the dark attic. I drop the bag and fumble around in the blackness with my arms out until my face literally smacks into the light cord. Brilliant.

I pull it and the room fills with light. It also turns on the fan in the ceiling. The blades slowly start to rotate, and I feel a slight coolness as the downstairs air starts rising up here. Only the front half of the attic is finished. A wall with a closed door separates the finished half from the part over Mom's room that I'm told is just open beams and insulation. I can see the plastic tubs labeled with names of different holidays. There are literally twice as many Halloween tubs than every other holiday put together. This doesn't surprise me at all.

Back next to the door is a lone cardboard box. Curious, I go over. I wonder if that the stuff the builders found in the walls?

I opened the first box, and my eyes grow wide

Chapter 14

Maggie

May 31st, 1880

Midnight

Sitting under the tree, as the never-ending storm continues its assault on my body and my mind, I continue to think of Elias. The images of him have slowed the pounding of my heart.

October 1879

We file into our regular pew on Sunday. I am self-conscious now of my every movement. As if the whole of the congregation is watching me. When in truth, there is only one set of eyes on me causing this feeling. I sit between my parents, so I am the person that holds the hymnal up for us to sing. Before every service I look up the songs so I can easily find them when we are called to sing. It is not difficult to find the small slip of paper wedged in about halfway through. I heard that Elias offered to clean the sanctuary during the week since his family is only a few houses down from the church property. So it is easy for him to place the note here.

I slip it into my hand. I glance down at the page where the note was tucked and see the hymn is titled, "What Wondrous Love Is This?" I feel myself blushing, the heat creeping up my neck. I duck my head down to hide the color on my cheeks and tuck the note into my cuff.

I hastily slip the note under my bed pillow when we arrive at home. I feel it up there the rest of the afternoon and evening. What will he say now, knowing that I return his feelings?

He seems like such a kind young man. And to me, he is very handsome. Any girl would be proud to have caught his attention.

No longer able to wait, as soon as darkness falls I sigh loudly and rub my temples.

"Maggie girl, are you feeling alright?"

"Not really Mother, my head aches a bit. If it is alright with you, I would like to head up to bed. I will be right with a little rest. I am sure it will be gone by the morning."

"Of course my dear, sleep well."

Finally alone in my room, retrieve it from under my pillow and bring it into the glow of the lamp.

I open the note…

My dearest Maggie,

Your smile filled me with such happiness.

I will work very hard to be worthy of you.

Your sweet face, your beautiful eyes.

Could you write to me?

Leave a note in the hymnal next Sunday.

In the place of this hymn that made me think of you.

'What wondrous love is this.

O my soul! O my soul!

What wondrous love is this!

O my soul.'

Yours, Elias

I clutch the letter to my chest. Filled with excitement, I do not sleep the entire night. I lay in my narrow bed in the dark and stare at the beams in the ceiling above my head. My heart racing too fast to rest. I can feel the beating even in my fingers. My eyes filling with tears I cannot explain.

This is how it begins. For several months we exchange notes every Sunday. I fall in love with him through letters. All through that fall and winter we communicate back and forth. He is funny. He is sweet. He is always respectful. He loves stories as much as I. I send him passages from my favorite books. He in turn sends me quotes from Shakespeare. And once, the most beautiful sonnet.

When in disgrace with fortune and men's eyes,

I all alone beweep my outcast state,

And trouble deaf heaven with my bootless cries,

And look upon myself and curse my fate,

Wishing me like to one more rich in hope,

Featured like him, like him with friends possessed,

Desiring this man's art and that man's scope,

With what I most enjoy contented least.

Yet within these thoughts myself almost despising,

Haply I think on thee, and then my state , Like to

the lark at break of day arising from sullen earth:

sings hymns at heaven's gate.

For thy sweet love remembered such wealth brings,

That then I scorn to change my state with Kings.

Chapter 15

My eyes are wide as I take in all that is jammed in this box. At least a dozen old books, what looks to be a huge, old leather bible, a net bag of beautiful glass marbles, a small leather teddy bear giving birth to horsehair stuffing from a rent in his side seam. There's a handmade wooden chess board, the beautifully carved pieces in a small burlap sack, and what appears to be a block of wood about the size of a brick. It's ornately carved with pearl inlay in some sort of abstract design. It is caked with dust. I sneeze hard three times in quick succession and wipe my nose on my sleeve. Ok, *everything* is covered with dust. But the wood is in beautiful shape. Someone took a long time and a lot of trouble to carve this.

I set it to the side and begin to look through the books, piling them up next to me. Once I get them in a stack I pull out the bag of marbles.

"Claire?"

I scream and the bags drops from my hands to the floor. The old fabric rips and marbles begin to roll in all directions.

"Mom! SHIT," I yelp, "Are you trying to give me a heart attack?" Geez, I almost wet my pants.

"Sorry love," she said. "I was hearing strange noises above my head, so I came to check that it wasn't some wild animal trapped up here going crazy. You didn't answer my knock, so I figured you were the wild animal. What in the world are you *doing*?" She watches as marbles roll into every corner of the room. "Well at least you've determined the floors are level. Tim will be so relieved."

"I was moving my winter clothes up here and the lure of other people's stuff sucked me in," I said. "As you can see, we have toys."

She walks over and looks at the stack of books. "I should have Hunter check these out. They look in pretty decent shape for having been sealed up in a wall. These are really old." She reads a few titles. 'Ooh look, the complete works of Shakespeare," Pulling the largest book from the bottom of the pile, "This is for me. One can never have enough copies of Hamlet."

Hamlet is one of her favorite things. And not just because of her name. She actually loves it. She has at least a dozen copies. Some over one hundred years old. She's watched the four-hour Branagh film God knows how many times. I've always been a Macbeth girl, but to each their own.

"This will be in the bookshelves downstairs, should you decide to give Hamlet another shot. Although maybe one of my newer copies would be easier," she laughs. "This thing is gigantic."

"Not tonight. My adventures are finished for now." After getting the crap scared out of me, I'm ready to go to bed. Enough of today.

I grab the large family bible out of the box. It is beautiful; old and ornate. With a tarnished clasp on the front. I'll start my exploring with this.

We make our way carefully back down the ladder, and she kisses the side of my forehead, "Good night, my Clarity. I'm so glad you are here. It means so much to me that you were willing to help me out."

"I love you, Mom. I'm glad I could help. I think it's going to turn out great."

I climb into bed and reach down for the charging cord to plug in my phone. As it lights up I see I have messages. The first one is from Jesse. Sent about twenty minutes ago. Just about the time I was screaming in the attic.

Jesse: Sorry I missed your message, Tiny. I just got back from working. I got to do pregnancy checks on a whole herd of cattle. It was amazing!

Eww. So far to me it seems being a large animal vet is just sticking your arm in parts of a cow that should be left alone. But he's obviously so happy.

Claire: Um, congratulations Yeti! Should I be jealous? You are spending a lot of time with the ladies up there. I'm going to bed now. I love you so much it makes me nauseous. I'll talk to you tomorrow. Get some sleep. XXXOOO

I check the next message.

Unknown Number: So what's up?

I put the phone down, turn off the light, and settle into my pillows.

* * *

By Friday we have most of the books on the shelves in several of the rooms. Horror is done, so is Romance. I've made sense of the Antique room. At least as good as it's likely to get. It's starting to really come together. It doesn't surprise me as we are working ourselves half to death. There are seven days left until we open the doors and less than two weeks till the grand opening. I think we are all starting to get nervous. If no one shows up it will be a disaster.

I'm really happy Toby is coming next weekend to see it. I'm starting to really love this place. The stack of books next to my bed keeps growing. I think Mom intends to pay for my help partly with novels. I've stayed up late the last couple nights reading.

To be honest, I've been trying to put off going to sleep. The nightmares about Maggie happen every night. It is always the same. I'm stuck on the bridge, trying to get away and can hardly ever get my feet to move. In the rare instance that I can, every way I try to escape just leads back to the bridge. Like a weird Mobius strip. Then she appears. I jolt awake every time. It's awful. It's starting to wear on me. I'm tired all day long. Yesterday I fell asleep with my head on the table in the break room. I can't remember the last time I fell asleep during the day.

I'm going to walk down to the bridge tomorrow. I need to get some fresh air and sunshine. I've been cooped up in this store all week. Maybe seeing the bridge again will help the bad dreams settle down somehow; like breaking down and listening to that song you just can't get out of your head.

* * *

Ok, I can do this. I have the sample order form next to me on the counter. I'm trying to navigate the system we will use to special order books when I feel, rather than see, someone next to me.

"Need any help? I was just about to run a system check, but I can certainly rescue you first," he asks. Leaning against the counter and dropping his hand on my shoulder.

"Yes, but I'm trying to figure it out myself." I answer, "I have to eventually, you aren't going to be here forever."

"I'm here till the fall at least. Your mom asked me to stay on a couple days a week to make sure the system is set up right and troubleshoot any problems that pop up in the first few months," he gives me a sideways glance, "And you know you can text me anytime. I'm always available to answer any questions you have."

"Oh. Thanks, but I'm not really *confused*, just slow. I need to practice. So I'm cool right now. I'm just practicing the procedure so I'm ready when we open the doors."

Talissa joins us at the counter, a smile on her face that's not quite reaching her eyes.

"Can I watch you, girl? You are already better at this than I am. And I'm one of the women running this place. Your mom has it already figured it out. One day you'll be leaving us, and it'll just be me and her. I have to be up to speed." She glances at Hunter's hand, still on my shoulder.

"Hunter can help you," I said, backing away from him and heading for the stairs, "I'm not good enough to teach anyone yet. I'll go ahead and keep working in Health and Wellness. When you are ready to learn about TikTok, call me."

* * *

"Mom, really, I'm so full I can't move." I push myself away from a table; the remains of an epic lasagna spread out around us. The last of the evening light coming through the kitchen windows is gleaming on the giant row of new cabinets. When Mom isn't opening a new business, she is a big cook. I'm going to be so spoiled this year I'll never want to cook again.

She is determined to teach me how to bake. That's her favorite pastime, especially in the fall. Her gingerbread is legendary. She's also a great cookie maker and cake baker. So all these cabinets are necessary for her gadgets and pans.

I carry my dishes to the sink, yawning as I go. "I'm heading up to bed. Unless you want my help loading the dishwasher."

"Honey, we are fine. Are you ok?" she frowns at me, "Am I working you too hard? You seem awfully tired out and you've only been here a week." Concern is all over her face.

"I'm ok. It's just an adjustment. Sleeping in a new bedroom. Not having Jesse around. It'll get better," I said.

She gets up and hugs me. "I can make some chamomile tea if you like? Tell you a bedtime story? Sing you a lullaby?"

"It's ok," I said, laughing, "I'm going to read for a while," I kiss her cheek, yell goodnight to Tim, who has already snuck back to his office, and head upstairs.

I change into my sweats and a t-shirt, stop in the bathroom and brush my teeth, then stand over the pile of books stacked by the bed. What to read tonight? My eyes fall on my desk under the front windows facing the river. On it sits the old, ornate bible I found in the attic. I've yet to even open it.

I pick it up, brushing off the dust with one hand and sit it on the foot of my bed. The clasp is tricky. Age and disuse have sealed it shut. If I pull too hard I may break it.

It takes a few minutes, but I get it open without damaging the latch or the cover itself. I open to the first page.

This thing is at least a hundred years old. The pages are thin and delicate. The inner cover is beautiful, the colors faded but still bright enough for the beautiful floral designs to make me draw in a deep breath. I immediately sneeze from the dust.

Turning the page I see what looks like a family tree. Names fill the page. The branches on the top go back through generations, all leading from the name written large across the bottom in an elegant hand.

Hastings.

Chapter 16

Maggie

August 31st, 1880

Midnight

How can the night last so long? How can the rain continue to fall so hard? Surely it must stop . It cannot rain all the time. Eventually the sun must rise. It has to.

The numbness in my feet and hands has spread up through my arms and legs. Even my face is numb. I cannot feel my own skin as I touch it. It is only the ache in my heart that keeps me anchored to here and now. That, and remembering falling in love with Elias.

I lean back against this slime covered ancient tree, remembering our time together. Dreaming of every moment that I had with him. While I am thinking of him I am no longer trapped.

February 1880

Who knows how long we would have continued to communicate solely through the hymnal, if my mother had not wanted new cabinets in our kitchen. Ours were old, sorely in need of repair. She had been gently pestering my father for months. Now that we had not one, but two cabinet makers living just down the road, her complaining had reached an all-time high. She wore my father down. After church one Sunday he spoke to Arba, Elias's father, and bartered an exchange. A supply of fresh chicken eggs and several young pigs for the replacement of the cabinets. We would provide all the materials. His said his son would be happy to do it.

He is coming to our house today! How should I behave? I have such strong feelings for him, and yet we have exchanged no words out loud beyond polite greetings in the churchyard. How will it be when he is right here in my own home?

I study in our house as I do not attend a formal school. There is a school in town, but it is miles away. Too far away to travel every day. Father also believes I would be too influenced by the outside world. I place my books at the table on the far side the kitchen and try in vain to concentrate.

I am reading about sentence structure when I hear his horse ride into the yard. My heart jumps into my throat and I keep my eyes on my book, waiting for his knock on the door. When it comes, I jump. I do not look up as my father opens the door.

"Good morning, Sir."

"Hello there young man. So you are going to build us something beautiful, eh?"

"I'm going to do my best, Sir."

"Fine, that's fine. Come on in and we'll get you set up."

His eyes fall on me, "Good morning Miss Maggie, Mrs. Bloxom. How are you? Good to see you."

I nod as Mother smiles, "I am happy this morning. These cabinets will be the death of me. I do hope you are as talented as your father claims you are."

"I hope so too. Would you like to tell me exactly what you are looking to have made?"

For a few minutes he stands talking with my mother. Measuring, taking notes as she flings her arms wide and gestures here and there. We have already removed all of the food and dishware and set them in the back pantry. Soon he sets to work pulling the old wood shelving down.

Father goes to the barn to work while Mother sits and watches with mute fascination. After the old cabinets are finally removed Elias begins to measure. After an hour Mother finally gives up and goes to the front room to work on her loom, making fabric. It is the first time we have been alone together.

He leans to me and whispers, "Maggie, I am so glad we are finally together. Even like this. I would have done anything to see you outside church. My father told me about this, and I saw it as my chance to be close to you."

"I'm glad to see you too," I murmur, "It's nice to be able to talk to you, even if I have to whisper."

"This is going to be the best work I have ever done. The longer it takes, the more time I will get to spend near you." He turns to face me, looking me right in the eye. "There is something I would like to talk about with you. When I finish the cabinets, I would like to ask your father for permission to court you. If that is something you would want."

The floor drops out from under me. My head swimming with the possibilities, "I think that I would like that very much."

It gets easier, after that first day. He becomes familiar to my parents. I can speak to him without disapproving looks from my father. Only about appropriate things, of course. My mother begins to give him food while he is working. Eventually inviting him to take his noon meal with us.

He has a wonderful sense of humor, making my mother laugh. I can see that she approves of him. She sees what a fine young man he is. My father is more reticent. I sense he understands Elias's intentions and has withdrawn the warm side of his personality in favor of cool detachment. My father is very proper. He does not believe in a girl marrying so young. I fear he will reject Elias's request to court me, or at the very least, make us wait till I reach my eighteenth birthday. Elias may not want to wait that long and move on to some other girl, someone older and more ready for marriage.

On a beautiful early morning about a week into the build, Elias arrives at our house to find both my parents gone. Our neighbor to the south invited my parents to come to town and see their Sholes & Glidden typewriter. It arrived the day before at the neighbor's law office, and they wanted to see the new-fangled contraption.

I stay at home to tend to the animals. Father told me very sternly before they left that I am to tell Elias that he cannot come in, as they will be gone most of the morning.

"I'm sorry, the folks are away. You cannot work today. They will be gone till noon, maybe longer. I am not allowed to let you in the house."

His eyes darken, "I understand. I'll go," he turns to walk away, "But maybe…could you take a walk with me? It is a beautiful morning. For a few minutes? Just to take the air?"

"I wish that I could, but I cannot leave the property. If any neighbors were to see me on the road…"

"Of course. You are right. I'm sorry. I'll go," he turns immediately and heads back to collect his horse. I just cannot let him leave.

"Wait! Um…would you like to help me collect eggs?

It is nearing the middle of March and the weather is beginning to warm. The hens eggs will be sparing, if any, but I am obliged to check. It is the first thing I can think of to delay him that isn't directly disobedient to the promise I made.

"I would like that very much," he backs away from the door and allows me to lead him to the back of our property where the chickens are kept. The enclosure is weathered wood framing surrounded by chicken wire with a small shed in the center. Hens march up and down the narrow ramp leading to the small entrance. I lead Elias around and open the narrow back door. A long row of roosts stretch across the left side with poles across the right for perching.

Inside, the air is damp and warm from the hen's bodies. I begin to gently feel under each downy bird. Elias helps me. "Do they not get angry that you are taking their babies?"

"If they are, they have never said it to me."

He laughs out loud and walks to the opposite end of the row. Gingerly sliding his hand under a bird, I see the smile grow on his face and his eyes light up. He pulls out an egg and holds it up triumphantly.

"Success!" he steps closer.

Working inward we neither one find another egg. Each check bringing us a step closer to each other. I smile into his eyes as I reach under the last hen and feel a jolt race though my body as our fingers touch underneath. He gently grasps my fingers and I feel his thumb caress the palm of my hand.

The hen, indignant at being so disturbed, squawks angrily and flies to the floor. I jump back, feeling a tingling race up my arm. He does not release my hand. My eyes lift to his. He steps closer and whispers my name.

"Maggie." His other hand comes up and he gently runs his fingers around the curve of my cheek. Slowly leaning his face to closer to mine. My eyes close without thought and I lift my face. Waiting.

I feel his lips brush gently back and forth across mine. The faintest contact. The softest touch I have ever felt. I exhale my breath and hear him breathe in. Taking in the very air from my lungs. The thought makes me weak, and my lips drop open. He takes that moment and presses them more firmly to me. I hear a soft sound between us but do not know if it comes from him or me. The inside of his mouth is like silk.

His lips and hand suddenly disappear. My head spins. I open my eyes again, he is gone. I stand, shaking, in the coop, holding the egg he somehow placed in my hand, as I hear him mount his horse and ride off down the road. My knees are weak, and I feel myself start to sway. Reaching out, I grab the edge of the roost for support, cracking the fresh egg in my hand. My heart filled with joy.

Chapter 17

Claire

May 20th, 2023

I'm hanging the damn blackout curtains today. I should have done it last night, but I was too worn out. Ugh. This sun is ridiculous. It's right in my eyes as the sun comes up. Groaning, I roll away from the windows and bury my head underneath the pillow. I can't really breathe under here but at least it's dark. It's Saturday, and far too early for the whole 'being awake' thing. We are taking the day off. Thank God. My back and feet need a break. Even my arms are sore. Hopefully working in the store will actually be easier when the store is open. Setting a store up is rough. It's exciting, but I think it might be killing me.

"MA! MA! Are you gonna eat it?"

"I wanna come OUT!"

"Go night-night?!"

"Ha! Wanna make a baby? Haaaa…"

Good grief. I love the birds, I really do. But being above them when they talk to get attention at the crack of dawn does not help a body sleep in. This is proving hard to get used to. Jesse never started screaming for food the minute the sun came up in the morning. I laugh to myself under the pillow and drift back to sleep.

Fear permeates my entire body. I'm surrounded by darkness and rain. I know she is here somewhere. I will turn and see her when she screams. I can't stop myself. I can't run. I can't get away from her. There is no way out of here.

Jolting awake; I sit bolt upright in bed. Groaning loudly at the bright light flooding my eyes. I flop back down. I have got to get myself together. This is getting ridiculous.

Well, I'm awake now, no question.

Rolling over, I pick up my phone to check the time. It's after nine already. I've missed another message from Jesse.

Jesse: Good morning angel face. It's been a week and a day since you left, and I miss you so much. Your good heart, the way you tease me, your beautiful eyes, even the shape of your arms. I've got it bad. I'm doing farm calls all day today, but I'd love to talk to you later.

Tears well up in my eyes. Overly emotional, anyone?

Claire: Oh Yeti, don't make me cry. Is it crazy to do this? I don't know if I can make it the whole year without you. Maybe I could come visit after the summer season? Or you could come here? I love you. Call tonight whenever you can.

I hug a pillow to myself. I miss him so much it feels like a hollow place inside me. I remember the first time I ever saw his face. How I felt the first time I heard his voice. Waiting months to see him again in person is going to drive me crazy. And that's a short trip on a good day.

Maybe going down to the bridge today will help me feel better. He held my hand for the first time on that bridge. Maybe being there will help me feel closer to him. I know he's busy working. He has always had a heavy schedule. But when we lived together I was there at night when he came home. I was there to see his sleepy face in the morning. He could spend his bits of free time with me. Being without him sucks. I wipe the tears off my face and rub them on the sheets.

I smell coffee. The final motivation to drag myself into a standing position.

Mom is sitting on one of the couches in the living room, a giant mug of coffee in her hand. Laying across her lap is the large book of Shakespeare we found in the attic. She smiles as I come down the stairs.

"My Clarity! I see you managed to resurrect yourself. I've been alone down here for three hours. Birds don't believe in weekends." She laughs and points with her free hand to the kitchen.

"Go caffeinate yourself and come back. I'll read you sonnets while you wake up. We can pretend we are exceedingly intellectual," she says to my back as I head into the room, my nose following the glorious smell.

Grabbing the biggest mug I can find from the cabinets; I fill my cup. Adding an obscene amount of sugar and cream, I stir it and head back with it to the living room. Dropping down on the couch opposite her.

"I'm pulling the babies today," she said, "Want to watch me handfeed later? I'm not taking them to Stephanie till Monday."

At this age, baby macaws look a lot like some weird dinosaur porcupine hybrid. With their feathers almost grown in but not out of the protective sheath that covers each one. They are covered in quills. They are so ugly that they are cute.

"Sure," I answer, "But first I'm going to take a good long walk after I wake up. I need some fresh air and sunshine."

"Let me give you some culture first." She smiles and turns a few pages, reading lines here and there.

"In black ink my love may still shine bright."

"Summer's lease hath all too short a date."

"All days are nights to see till I see thee, and nights bright days when dreams so show thee me."

That one makes me groan, "Mom, you aren't helping me. This just makes me miss Jesse even more."

"Sorry honey."

She flips another page, and lifts a single eyebrow, "Someone wrote in here. With pen and ink. Nice handwriting, really. How cool. I wonder how long ago that happened?"

"Really?" I tipped the coffee mug up to get the last swallow, "What does it say? Is it directions to the lost city of Atlantis?"

She laughs. "No, it's just a name," she answers, "Maggie."

It takes a beat for the name to register in my head. When it does, I sit up straight on the couch, my eyes widening.

"Maggie??" I get to my feet, "Let me see." I sit down next to her on her couch and pull the book into my lap. Following her finger as she points.

There, right in the margin next to sonnet twenty-nine, written in flowing letters, the name "Maggie." Adrenaline shoots through me. It couldn't be, no way. I mean, there is more than one Maggie in the world.

But to find that name here. In a book found hidden in the walls of this house, so close to the bridge. The odds are high that this could be the Maggie I had seen there. The one who's photograph was right in the folktales book on my desk. The one plaguing my dreams at night. A chill goes through my entire body.

'What year was this book published?" I ask.

She flips to the front, turning the first few pages till she finds the date.

"1870," she said, and flips to the title page.

There, at the top, I see another name.

Elias W. Hastings.

* * *

An hour later I'm out the side door, determined to make it down to the bridge. This late May weather is beautiful. I hold my face up to the sun, soaking up the rays. Birds are singing everywhere as I start walking. Thankfully, they're not shouting profanities like Mom's. The day looks like a postcard. The Woodland Ferry is a few lots down across the narrow road from our house. A couple cars are lined up waiting for the ferry to make it back to our side. They have their windows down and wave to me as I pass by. Up on the right is the church. A sweet old white building with a tall, peaked roof, and a more modern long, low extension jutting out from one side. Wrapping around the side of the church and across the back is a cemetery. Filled with old sort of half round headstones. So worn away by time that the names are no longer clear. Mom told me the original part of the church is even older than our place.

There are few houses, and the road soon passes into the woods itself, the tall trees pressing in on each side of the paved road. The woods sound alive. The breeze rushing though the leaves, the birds talking to each other, insects buzzing loudly everywhere. Dragonflies with buzzing wings swooping back and forth across the road in front of me.

It smells wonderful out here. Like earth and green. The sun warming the dirt. I begin to relax, slowing my pace to enjoy it more. The road is fairly straight. Curving to the right only just as you approach the bridge and back to the left after. So I won't see it till I round the corner.

Is it really possible that Elias Hastings knew Maggie? He must have lived in the house all those years ago. Those are very likely his games and books found in the walls. But how had they gotten in there? Had he put them in there to protect them or to keep them from being seen? Why would he hide them? Who was he hiding them from?

117

The bend in the road is ahead of me. I'm getting close. The woods open up as I round the corner. The off shoot of the river is wider to my left and becomes narrow and more muddy off to the right. The brush surrounding the river just as thick as it was six years ago. Enough to keep anyone from attempting to enter. I certainly won't be trying today.

I take my first steps onto the bridge itself. Graffiti is everywhere. Clashing with the surprisingly beautiful marsh all around me. It's so green! The water is still and reflects the sky and treetops above. A chorus of bullfrogs is competing to make the loudest croak. I take a deep breath and look around, waiting to be afraid. It doesn't happen.

I walk to the very spot I stood before, looking out I see the tiny finger of land I noticed that night. In the daylight, it's less appealing. The ground looks dangerously soft and partially covered with thorny brush.

Graffiti marches up and down both guardrails and is sprayed across the ground from one end of the bridge to the other. Interspersed with lots of blacked out squares which must be the places the city has covered over. Across the left guardrail, the messages, "WHERE'S MAGGIE?" and "I HOPE YOU FIND HIM" are sprayed crudely in black paint.

I pull my phone out and shoot a few pictures to send to Toby. Including a selfie with the bridge behind me, proof that I have been brave enough to come back down here alone.

Maybe Toby is right, and this is just a place where something bad happened a long time ago. But why had we seen lights? Heard those terrible screams? Why had she appeared to me as we drove away? Was she trapped here, unable to move on to whatever was next? Was she lost and confused? Did she understand what had happened to her? Had she seen us as we are, or where *we* ghosts to her? Where the visitors who came at night and called to her just as scary for her as the lights and her screams had been for us?

Is she in a nightmare she can never wake up from?

The walk back from the bridge to the house is nowhere near as nice as the walk out. The idea of Maggie being stuck in a world of confusion for such a long time is really getting to me. I head upstairs to my room and sit at my desk. I shoot a text to Toby, including the pictures I took. I wait less than a minute before I get a response.

Toby: Girl…YES! I'm so proud of you. How was it?

Claire: Beautiful. Lonely. Not as creepy as it is at night. You'll never believe what I found in the attic.

I wait. I enjoy taunting Toby.

Toby: WHAT? A gorilla? A pot of gold? The Easter bunny? Strippers covered with whipped cream? Come on, don't be evil. You know I have less than no patience.

Claire: You know how I told you they found stuff in the walls when they renovated? Well, there's a book of Shakespeare with the name MAGGIE written next to a sonnet.

Toby: CHRIST ON A BIKE! You think it's her?

Claire: Could be. The age of the book is right.

Toby: Any idea who's book it is?

Claire: Someone named Elias Hastings. There's more stuff too. I haven't been through it yet.

Chapter 18

I am leaning against the tree, remembering the feel of Elias's lips pressed to mine, when I hear voices. Muffled. I strain to make out any words. Is this my rescue? Pulling my feet under me; my arms and legs are so numb that I cannot feel them at all. I lean, bracing my body against the tree. I scream out, *"Hello? I am OVER HERE! Please someone help me!"*

The mumbled voices continue. The sounds carrying over the pounding rain. I can hear several together. Shouting something out into the trees. Is that my name?

Before I can even understand what is happening, or get my legs to move, the sound cuts off. I stand in stunned silence. There is again nothing but the noise of the rain. Joined every minute or so by a booming crash of thunder and flash of lightning.

I sit back down under the tree. I do not understand. If people are trying to find me, why can I not see them? Why can they not see me? The voices came from the bridge right in front of me. They should be easily seen, even in the storm.

The numbness in my body is total now. Even the burning my chest has gone away. Yet I am not cold. I have been soaked with water for so very long that I should be freezing, but I am not. There is no sensation left in my body at all. The only thing that I can feel, is fear. Fear and an ache for Elias filling my head.

March 1880

The last day arrives. Elias finishes the cabinets. They are masterful. The quality of his work is far above an apprentice level. I can see that my father is very pleased. He stands silently, admiring them. They are strong and even, each door carved with a beautiful matching rose design. Polished with oil to a beautiful sheen. My mother is beside herself with excitement. Practically dancing around our kitchen. Twittering like a bird.

"Maggie dear, help me. I want to see how well all of our things fit." She is racing back and forth from the pantry to the new shelves. Trying to have everything back in all at once, so that she can see it finally finished. I help her, though I am embarrassed for Elias to see me running around the kitchen.

"You dear boy, this is just wonderful. You are a very talented young man. You are going to be very popular around here." My mother is gushing with praise.

"Come young man, let's walk to the barn and you can choose your livestock. You earned it."

After they go outside my nerves grow tight. Elias gave me a meaningful glance as he left the house with Father, and I take it to mean he is about to ask permission. My stomach flips over.

I wish desperately to be able to hear the conversation, but I have to sit, inside, while my fate is decided.

We wait for what feels like hours. The meal is prepared and growing cold on the table.

"Whatever could be keeping them?" Mother wonders. I can only shake my head.

Finally, they return. Elias looked resigned and my father is stern and silent as they take their places around the table. Neither of them look at me. I squeeze my hands together under the table to keep them from fidgeting.

They both speak pleasantly to Mother all through the meal, talking of the upcoming church revival and pig roast happening in just a few short weeks. Neither one saying anything about what had been discussed outside the house. I sit silent, hardly eating, with my stomach in a knot. Trying to avoid catching my father's eye. Worried about what I will find there.

When the meal is finished I rise to clear the table.

"Maggie, sit down. It seems that we have something to discuss." I sit, staring down at my lap.

He turns to Mother, "This young man here has requested my permission to court Maggie. Now I have explained to him the rules of our house. Maggie will not be ready for anything of the sort until she reaches her eighteenth birthday. I have also told him that for me to consider him worthy of her he must finish his apprenticeship and secure a home for himself. I want to be assured that she will be properly taken care of in the future.

"Now, he has agreed to all of these things. He has also agreed until the date of her birthday there will be no solicitous behavior. He should focus only on making himself ready. I wish to see nothing that might tarnish either of their reputations. If he can accomplish these things, I have allowed he may then court her with the intention of making her his wife."

I am stunned. He has agreed to everything father wanted.

I do not look up, but I hear my mother's intake of breath. The excitement she is trying to temper. Elias has already won her over.

I sense Father turning to me, waiting for my reaction.

"Maggie? What say you to this? If you are not in agreement here, there is no need to go further."

I finally lift my eyes and find Elias smiling at me from across the table.

"Yes Father, I am in agreement with everything."

Chapter 19

Claire

May 26th, 2023

This is going to be a long day. The store opens tomorrow so we have a ton of final prep work to do. Plus, cleaning up after ourselves. Dusting everything, cleaning the floors. Stocking the front counter with bags, etc. All the super fun stuff we've ignored in the frenzy of getting the shelves arranged and the rooms decorated.

I must admit, it was worth it. This place looks incredible. Like something out of a book lovers fantasy or a fairy tale. The reader in me wouldn't mind just living here. Convert the attic, no problem. It's finished. It has a real staircase. The old servants rooms were up there, I'm guessing. It has a nice open middle space. There's even a bathroom with an actual clawfoot tub. Some spackle and paint, a few new fixtures, and I'd be all set.

I hope we get the store clean in time to have it looking good when Toby arrives. I can't wait to see him. He's leaving work early and should get here by the early afternoon. It will be a relief to see his face. It sucks not having a friend my own age to talk to. Everyone around me is over fifty. Except Hunter. He is thirty-two. Ask me how I know? He's quite prolific with the word vomit. Talk, talk, talk. He's been a big help with stocking the shelves and toting all the books around. I don't think those tasks are in his contract but it's good to have another set of arms. Working next to him, you don't even have to talk. He is perfectly happy doing all the talking at you. In the last week I have probably heard more about him *from* him than I know about my own mother. Ok, that's an exaggeration. But it feels like it. He also likes to talk close. He's not one for keeping his distance. I've known a few people like that. I usually try and take a step back. I like my personal space and don't want people in it. Really tall veterinarians are the exception to this rule.

To his credit, he's really gotten me trained well on our computer system. Taking the time to walk me through literally every possible scenario I might encounter when the store opens. I feel emotionally ready for tomorrow, whether customers come in the door or not.

He is still texting me at night. At least every other day. Nothing inappropriate. Just casual banter. I haven't answered any of them. I don't want to encourage him. It's best to keep to a strictly professional relationship. He'll be working at the store for a few more months and I don't want to make it uncomfortable by getting friendly outside of work.

* * *

"Claire! Company!"

I'm dusting in Health and Wellness when Mom calls me from the front counter. I drop the feather duster with a grin and head to the front.

There stands Toby, a huge grin plastered on his face. He swiftly crosses the room and wraps me in his arms.

"GIRL! It's so great to see you! Damn, I've missed your face! You look great!" He's squeezing the breath right out of me.

"I missed you too," I try to say. "Let me give you the tour."

"Please do. This place is the bomb. Do I have really to wait till tomorrow to buy stuff?" he laughs.

"Come, let's start upstairs and work our way down," I pull away from him and we head for the stairs, discovering Hunter blocking the staircase.

"And who might this be? The alleged boyfriend?" he says with a half-smile on his face.

I frown. "No. This is Toby, my best friend from high school. He's visiting from Baltimore for the weekend. Toby, this is Hunter."

"Hey," Toby eyes him warily.

"Well, it's a pleasure to meet you…Toby," he says to our retreating backs as we head up the stairs.

"So who's the creep?" Toby asks as we enter the Horror room.

"Our security guy. You don't even know," I said, "I think he's got a thing for me."

"Of course he does, who wouldn't?" he remarks loyally. "So, what room is this?" he looks at the crows and skulls, "There's no way to tell."

* * *

By six o'clock that night we are sitting around the kitchen table, comfortably nursing our 2nd glasses of wine; Toby entertaining us all with stories of the kids from his class.

"So Mark comes running up to me, 'Mr. Toby, Mr. Toby! What hand is better to write with?'

"So I, of course, launch into a story about being left-handed myself and how it's no different than being right-handed and he goes, 'NO! It's neither. It's better to write with a pencil!'"

We all groan, and I stand and load the dishwasher, leaving the casserole dish in the sink to soak.

"Alright kids, I'm done." Mom turns to Tim, "Darling, retire with me up to the boudoir and partake in viewing of the latest episode of "Watch Your Wife Sleep."

"Most excellent! I love that show. Although I always end up falling asleep before the end." They head up the stairs and leave us sitting at the table.

"Ok, let's go. I've waited long enough, show me the books," Toby says, taking our wineglasses and directing me out of the kitchen and towards the stairs. I'd left everything on my desk but haven't looked into anything further since he had asked me to wait. I was excited to get back to them.

"Here's the book I found her picture in. Her story is marked," I hand it to him and flop on my bed as he sits in the desk chair and begins to read. He whistles when he gets to her picture.

Pretty girl. It sucks that she was so young. Can you image how bad it would be to turn up pregnant back then? Damn. To be that young, and have to run away from home?

"It's hard for me to picture, really. Mom would never have made me feel like I had to run away. But I am lucky."

"Yes, you are," he looks up and smiles ruefully, "You know, your mom was more accepting when I came out than my own parents were. They came around, but it took a while."

I smiled. "I'm really glad you're happy, you know, you deserve it."

He leans over and hugs me, "Stop the mushy stuff before we get all sappy," he joked, "Show me the Shakespeare."

I'd brought the book up from Mom's bookshelf this morning and I spread it out in front of him, opened to the 29th sonnet.

"Oh wow," he said, running his finger lightly over the name, "Look at that! So you think this Elias guy wrote it?"

"Who knows? It's his book. I'd say odds are good though. This thing is old, really old," I said.

I had a sudden thought.

"Hey, let's check the old bible I found. It's has a Hasting's family tree in it." I reach down to the pile on the floor and grab the big heavy book. Laying it across the end of my bed I flip to the tree. Scanning down the names, I find him. The third and next to last generation in the book, Elias William Hastings.

"Born on September 22nd, 1860. He married a woman named Ellen Callaway in 1887, when he was...um... 27 years old. They had 2 children, a daughter Joan in 1889 and a son Albert in 1892."

"Well he didn't marry Maggie," Toby scoffs.

"Of course he didn't, she died," I replied, "That doesn't mean he didn't know her," I notice more dates and my heart sinks, "And oh, God, both Ellen and Albert died in 1903. I wonder what happened to them? That had to be terrible. To lose a child, and a wife together? He already had enough tragedy in his life."

"He sure waited a while to get married. Isn't 27 a bit old for back then?"

"Maybe he was so brokenhearted losing Maggie it took him years to get over it. You'd be that way. Moony as you are over Jesse," throwing himself on the floor and covering his eyes with the back of his hand.

"I happen to love him, you jerk," throwing one of my pillows at his head.

He sits up abruptly. "I just remembered, I bought you something," he jumps up and heads down the stairs. I can hear him digging though his suitcase that's sitting next to the couch Mom made up as a bed for him.

When he gets back to the room his hands are behind his back. He pulls them out with a dramatic flourish.

"This ought to help," he said, in his palms is a small black device that looks kind of like a big, thick cellphone.

"This," he said, "Is a spirit box. With an EVP recorder. It uses radio frequency sweeps to give any entity around the power they need to be heard. I thought we could go down to the bridge and see if Maggie has anything to say. You up for it?"

"Oh good god, Toby. Are you serious?" I give the idea a moment to sink in. It might help me answer some questions. What if I could be brave enough to actually go down there at night. Could we actually talk to her?

"Yeah, I was thinking tomorrow night we head down there when it gets dark. It's not a full moon but I thought we could give it a shot. It's got a memory card so we can capture as much as we want."

"At night…I don't know. It's a nice idea but I don't know if I'm up for that."

"I have all day tomorrow to convince you."

"Good luck with that. You have your work cut out for you. But first I better sleep, I have to open a store tomorrow morning."

"You'll be great doll," he leaned over and kisses the top of my head, "Get some rest."

* * *

The Dusty Bookshelf opens the doors for the first time at 10:54 am. Six minutes before the sign on the door claims. There are a few people standing on the front porch waiting and Mom can't stand the suspense. I'm stationed at the front register, and I hope to God I remember how to ring people up. I can see the nervousness on Mom's face as they come through the door.

"Welcome! Come on in! I'm Ophelia and this is Talissa. Feel free to look around. Let me know if you have any questions."

The customers slowly search the entire house, marveling at the colors and decorations on the walls. They leave with a couple books each. I check them out myself. Surprisingly, I do it perfectly. An auspicious start. Mom is glowing. Talissa looks ecstatic. I'm relieved. The morning goes on, we get into a rhythm. Mom greeting people at the door and running the front, me and Talissa wandering the rooms, answering questions, helping people navigate the house to find what they want. Hunter sits in front of the cameras, keeping his eyes on everything.

Toby amassed a literal stack of Manga and is sitting in a chair in the bay window reading, lost to the world.

There's a pretty steady stream of visitors all morning and into the early afternoon. By the time 4 o'clock rolls around I have relaxed. This is much easier than setting up the store had been.

"Get ready," Mom said, peeking out the window at the road, "Early bird tourists will be heading past for the beach any minute."

She wasn't joking. Traffic picks up and the parking lot begins to fill up. There is an influx of people in the door. Customers in each room. People talking, walking up and down the wide staircase, arms filled with books. People laughing and taking pictures of the décor. We answer question after question after question. The bells over the door begin to sound like a song. Ringing every time it opens. For the next few hours I don't have time to think. I can't imagine what it will be like in here when we have the grand opening being advertising everywhere. Yikes.

"Let me help you guys clean up. This is insane," Toby looks around at the shelves with books laying sideways on shelves, and dirt all over the floor from people shoes. The rush really hit us.

"Please do. You're young and strong, you can help Claire carry these books upstairs and put them away," Mom is all smiles.

By the time we close the doors at eight o'clock I am more than ready to call it a day.

At home Tim is broiling steak for everyone, "How did it go? When you didn't respond to my messages, I figured you'd either been abducted by aliens or it went really well."

Mom is incandescent, "It went *fantastic*! I'll tell you all about it while we eat." She rushes up and kisses him hard on the mouth.

"Tim, that smells amazing. Please feed me," I plunk myself at the table, dog-tired.

We stuff ourselves while Mom catches Tim up on everything. I don't say much. I'm too busy eating. I'm not sure when was the last time I finished off an 10oz steak. My appetite is too damn big here in Delaware. We load the dishwasher and Toby and I settle in the living room to relax.

"We are heading upstairs," Mom smiles wearily at us, "I want to watch a movie, but I can no longer remain vertical. Will you guys be ok?

"Of course Mom, go ahead. Congrats on the success today."

Mom and Tim head upstairs to watch TV in their bedroom, so Toby and I have the downstairs to ourselves.

"You need coffee before we leave? I hope you aren't too tired." Toby said, tipping his head back into the couch cushion and staring down his nose at me, "You know where we are going, woman."

"I'm not so sure about this," I can feel my palms start to sweat, "I know I said earlier that I would try but I'm really not feeling it."

"Hon, even if she rises up out of the ground and hovers screaming right in front of our eyes like a demon released from the bowels of hell, she can't hurt us."

It's on the tip of my tongue to tell him that she had once done *exactly* that. But I can't. Come on Claire, you're acting like a baby!

"As long as you drive, I'll be ok. Nighttime and the bridge are not a fun combination for me." Fear has been creeping up on me since we arrived back home.

We grab the spirit box and head out to Toby's car. The night is full of stars. There is very little light pollution here, so the sky is bright with tiny lights. The moon is waxing. So a bit more than half of it is shining above us. Crickets are chirping loudly across the road by the river.

It takes no time at all to get there in a car. In less than ninety seconds we pull over on the far side of the bridge. Toby's car is small enough that I can get out and around without falling into the brush. I smile to myself; of *course* I can do it when there's no one to impress. I stand next to him at the edge of the bridge.

"So what do we do? We can't stand on the four corners, there's only two of us," I ask.

"Let's go to the middle and stand back-to-back. Call out to her and see what happens. Even if we don't hear anything the box may pick it up," he walks ahead, and I follow. We get to the middle of the bridge. Toby has evidently practiced using the spirit box. He handles it easily. He switches it on and presses the record button. We stand back-to-back.

"Let's call out to her the way we're supposed to first," Toby said.

I'm not super keen on that idea; as I know exactly what happens when you do that, but I'm not about to show Toby how scared I actually *am*. Coming here in the daytime is one thing. It's kind of nice. At night it's a whole other deal. There are no streetlights. We don't have any kind of flashlight. The stars and the half-moon are all we have to light up the woods and the water. It's just damn creepy. I gather what wits I have. I can do this. I *will* do this.

"OK," I said, and we call out.

"Maggie, Maggie, I have your baby!"

"Maggie, Maggie, I have your baby!"

"Maggie, Maggie, I have your baby!"

The woods are eerily quiet. It's almost the end of May. There should be crickets. There should be frogs croaking everywhere. I hear them every night out by the river across the road; but here at night, there's nothing. Just the sound of our voices and the slight breeze rustling the leaves in the trees above our heads. We wait. Nothing comes back to us but more silence.

"Maybe we should separate and stand on either end," Toby said softly. "At least try and get as close to the rules as we can."

"OK, if you say so," I said, hearing the tremble in my voice. We step apart from each other maybe ten or fifteen feet. I feel much more afraid when he is not next to me.

Toby calls out to me, "I'm going to start asking questions. You should too."

"Maggie, are you here?"

"Maggie, are you lost?"

"Maggie, can you see us?"

"Maggie, how can we help you?"

"Maggie, talk to us please."

The night stays silent. All I hear is my breathing. It's so silent I can even hear Toby's breathing from across the bridge. But there's nothing. No lights, no screams, nothing. I'm frozen in place, waiting.

We are standing in silence at each end of the bridge when suddenly the blinding bright high beams of an oncoming car curve around the bend and shine right into our eyes. Shit! We scramble out of the way; the spell broken. Toby starts laughing and I join in. I feel the tension leave me in a rush.

"Well that was a whole lot of nothing," Toby laughs, 'I didn't hear anything, but maybe we caught something on the spirit box. Let's head back to your house and I'll see if we can hear anything."

"Works for me." I admit and turn to head back to the car.

Chapter 20

The Church's annual revival begins on Saturday night, the 25th of April. Along with donating the pig for roasting, my mother and I are responsible for cooking all sorts of things to take for the church supper on Sunday afternoon. Pies are baked, canned vegetables brought down from the attic. I spend hours preparing a large basket of muffins with the last of the blueberries I canned last Autumn. I keep wetting the sleeves of my shirtwaist with repeated wiping's of sweat from my forehead. Mother and I are constantly racing back and forth across the kitchen.

During all of this, it is hard not to stop and run my hand along the cabinets; knowing that they had been made so beautifully by Elias. The two weeks since he kissed me I have thought of little else. The sensation of his lips on mine. The feeling of having him so close to me. I want him to do it again. And again. My body grows warm every time I think of him. I don't know what to do with these feelings. At times I feel like I am going to burst open.

My studies have suffered. I cannot concentrate. My mother, who is my instructor, smiles and indulges me my moodiness. For she understands the reason why. Never questioning why I linger so long at the chicken coop in the morning. I often stand at the place he kissed me and imagine his breath on my face.

The first night of the revival is thrilling. This is the first year I have been allowed to attend. I would not normally wish to go, but Elias will be there. I cannot miss any opportunity to see him. The fervor that comes over the people is rousing. I feel such a stirring in my heart. My heart thumping in time with the music. Even my taciturn father is swept up in it, singing loudly and clapping his hands.

Elias is not so moved. At least not by the sermon or the singing. I feel his eyes on me. I am attached to him by a tether that only we can see. When I glance over he is always watching. His face remains solemn, but his eyes burn with a heat that I can clearly see. In every other way he is as well-mannered as any father could have wished for. But he continues to watch me. I sense it even when I do not see it.

The morning of the church supper is hectic. We awaken early, as we usually do. I am helping fry breakfast when my father calls from the yard, "Joan! Maggie! Come quick!"

I move the eggs off the heat and follow Mother out the door. We find father standing in the barn door, looking distraught, "One of the sows is having trouble farrowing. I need you both to pitch in and help."

We follow him into the pen and kneel next to the animal. Father hands us each a rag, then reaches into the sow and carefully pulls each piglet out. Mother and I are charged with caring for each one as it emerges to stimulate it to breathe. We clean out the mouth and rub it vigorously. Putting each squealing baby into the pile to keep them warm together before moving on to the next one. Nine piglets emerge alive; we do not lose a single one. After everyone is breathing and safe we look at ourselves. Blood and mucus are all over our clothes, hands, and arms. Cleaning ourselves up and changing into our Sunday best takes a long time. Making us quite late as we head for the churchyard.

The look on Elias's face when we drive up is one of open relief. I can see it all the way across the lot. He is biting his lip to suppress a smile. Obviously, he has been waiting for me to arrive. Father stops the horse and buggy at the far end of the church yard. It is quite full; many buggies and single horses tied to posts. Obviously, many people from nearby towns have come in to attend the supper. Mother and I gather our food from the buggy and head over to all the women; my father hurriedly joining others seated at the tables where men are waiting for speeches to begin.

* * *

I am stirring a large bowl of stew in the makeshift kitchen when my mother comes up to me, her face a mask of worry.

"The pies are not here!"

We are responsible for a dozen of them and in our hurry, we forgot to get them from the pie safe. She looks close to tears.

139

"Please Maggie, go home and get them. The others will notice if I leave. I would be so embarrassed. Take the buggy and bring them back before the speeches are over. Go quickly but do not let them see you rushing. We eat little more than an hour from now. Please Maggie."

Everything in me wants to stay, but I am an obedient girl. "Yes Mother. I will leave right now, do not worry." I pull my apron off and walk slowly towards the collection of buggies. I glance at the group of men as I pass, hoping to see Elias, but he is nowhere to be found.

I climb into the seat and drive out of the Churchyard. I have been driving the buggy for several years. I trust Roger, our horse. I urge him on as best I can as I do not want to be away from the supper any longer than necessary. Now that Elias finished the cabinets the only time I get to see him is Sundays at church. Out of sight, I urge Roger to go faster, I don't want to waste any of the opportunity the day has given me.

The small wooden bridge is the halfway point between our home and the church itself. As I drive over it I see dragon flies alighting on the water. I hear the rush of the water underneath the boards as I ride over. Roger is not wearing blinders today and can see the drop-off from the bridge to the water below. He doesn't like it. He is a sweet old horse that has been around most of my life, and I smile as I encourage him forward.

Finally our farm comes into view. I turn Roger down the lane intending to stop him by the front door. I can quickly grab the pies and secure them in the back of the buggy.

As Roger comes to a stop and I pull the buggy brake, I look up. Elias Hastings steps out from behind our house, hidden in the shadows, but I can see him clearly. He has a grave expression on his face. I freeze, and my mouth drops open. My hands are tingling. I am in shock. I cannot believe he is here. At my home. Alone. And so am I.

I climb down from the buggy, opening my mouth to speak but say nothing. I simply run to him.

He reaches out for me and lifts me clean off the ground into his arms. Our mouths come together without hesitation. He carries me toward the barn; his mouth still sealed to mine.

Inside the barn, he carries me back to the far stall, where we store the hay for the horses. Setting me down, he spreads out one of the horse blankets we keep there on a shelf. He drops down on it and reaches out for my hand.

"Maggie, will you sit here with me just for a few minutes? I've thought of nothing but you for such a long time."

I am still reeling, "How are you here? How did you know?"

"I heard your mother asking you to come home and couldn't waste the chance. My father believes I am feeling unwell. If I could just be here alone with you for a while. Maybe hold your hand. Please?"

I quickly drop to the blanket next to him, and unable to stop myself, I put my arms around his neck and pull his face to mine once more. I am hungry for his kiss.

A low sound issues from his throat as he tightens his arms around me, my head tips back and he trails kisses softly down my throat. Gently easing me down flat, he runs his fingers down my cheek, staring into my wide-open eyes.

"I love you, Maggie. We are going to be married one day. If you will have me."

My eyes fill with tears that begin to spill down the side of my face.

"That's what I want Elias. More than anything, I would love to be your wife."

He drops his head, taking my mouth again, filling my body with a feeling I do not understand. All of me reaching out, I wrap my whole body around him. Pulling him to me. Wanting to be as close as possible and not feeling like I can. I have thought of nothing but him and waited so long that I cannot believe I am actually here. That it is really him pressing his body down atop me. Elias begins to run his hands up and down my sides, caressing me. Soon putting his hands in places that before I did not know a man could touch. I feel a frenzy inside of me growing bigger and encourage him to touch me everywhere. I put my hands on him, learning the feel of his body. In the next few minutes I learned the secrets of what a man and a woman do together that my mother had never told me about.

Once our breathing slows, I once again become aware of the barn around me, the sounds of the animals in their stalls, the smell of the timothy hay in the rafters, the sunlight beaming through the upper window. I remember what I was supposed to be doing. How long have I been gone? I sit up quickly. Panic suffuses my limbs. I try to arrange my dress and check my hair at the same time.

"Let me help you." He picks several stray bits of straw out of my hair, and a tiny piece of chaff from my sweat beaded upper lip.

"I have to get back. They will miss me!'

"Go. Go quickly. Maggie, I am sorry. I never meant for it this to happen. Or for us to go this far. I only intended to spend a little time alone with you. You must understand, I intend to marry you, but we should not risk this again. It could ruin everything."

He is right, of course. We may have spoiled it already. I allowed myself to get carried away. It is a wonder how quickly the body can overrule the mind.

"I will not be coming back to the supper. I will go back through the woods to my house. There's a path in the trees beyond the bridge. It is how I got away from the church when I overheard you were leaving. It won't due for us to be seen coming from the same direction.

I kiss him swiftly and race out of the barn, my heart in my throat. I gather the pies and rush a startled Roger out of the barnyard at a run.

I make it back to the church yard and the speeches are underway. I jump from the buggy and take a moment to check my hair and straighten my skirts. I pray there are no more bits of chaff in my hair to give my actions away to the crowd. Smiling politely, I carry the basket of pies over to the long tables the women have loaded with food.

"Maggie!" my mother calls, "Bring them here, dear."

She takes it from my shaking hands and places them on the table loaded with fruitcake and cookies. Smiling at me with a curious look, "Whatever was the trouble? I was starting to get worried. You've been gone quite a while."

"Roger was disagreeable, Mother. He wanted to eat before he would cooperate and come back."

"Is that what that smell is? You smell odd," she looks at me with a dour expression, "A bit like a barnyard. Best go wash your hands and face at the pump. You are quite flushed.

Chapter 21

I make breakfast for everyone Sunday morning. I cook a mean omelet. I pack it with cheese and bacon. Nothing healthy about it whatsoever. It's absolute heaven.

"Ok, sleepyhead, time to face the world again."

I pull the pillow out from under Toby's head as he sleeps on the couch, and gently smack him in the face with it. He groans and his eyes open.

"You sadistic freak. I can ignore the birds, but I can't ignore a physical assault."

"Oh yeah, this pillow is soooo dangerous." I laugh as he sits up and rubs his eyes. His bedhead is spectacular.

"Come on, Mom and Tim are already in the kitchen. You could sleep through a parade walking past you. Let's get it moving, I cooked."

"All the more reason for me to stay right here. You remember of course, the lobster incident?"

"Shut up! How was I supposed to know you boil the poor things alive? I'd never made them before."

"You're lucky your generous boyfriend was able to stop laughing long enough to help you out. I thought we were never going to eat."

"Remind me how you take your coffee. You prefer it *with* spit, right?" I turn my back on him and head for the kitchen.

Seeing how there is no lobster murder involved, breakfast is delicious. Tim is on a roll with his book, so he grabs his omelet and heads back to his office with it. It's just the three of us around the table.

"So what did you two get up to last night?" Mom asks, "I heard you heading out late."

"I took her down to Maggie's Bridge," Toby told her, "We were trying to communicate with her spirit. I took the EVP recorder I bought Claire, but not a thing happened beside us almost getting run over. I can't hear anything on the recording either. I tried it late last night. Claire, you need to listen. Your ears are better than mine."

"Oh fun!" Mom said, "I did that a bunch of times when I was in high school. I never saw or heard anything. But we freaked ourselves out pretty good. I suppose that's the point, anyway.

"Of course, we didn't follow all the rules. We just went whenever we felt like it, blue moon or no blue moon."

"Blue moon?" I'm confused. I haven't heard that before.

"Sure, if you want to communicate with her you should try to go on a blue moon. You might see or hear her during a normal full moon, but it is said to have happened on a blue moon so somehow it is supposed to work better then. At least that's what my grandmother said when I was a teenager."

Toby pulls his phone out immediately. "Well, let's see what that will happen," he searches briefly and exclaims, "August of this year!"

"Cool, you can have another chance," Mom said, "I'm off to the store you two, thanks a bunch for breakfast. I'll see you at lunchtime."

We will be open the longest on Sundays. So starting today we are working staggard hours. I don't go in till one o'clock. Toby is leaving for home around noon. So we have a few more hours together.

"Let's go through the rest of those books you found. Maybe it has Maggie's direct phone number tucked into the pages of one," Toby laughs.

"We can look at the books, but I don't guarantee she has cell service where she is."

The rest of the books that were found in the box are still in the attic, so I walk into the closet and pull down the ladder. It's not so foreboding today. I look up and see light spilling across the ceiling. Heat begins to pour out like oil. Climbing up the ladder I see the sunshine streaming through the small window the faces the river. There's only the one, but up here that's plenty. I turn on the light anyway to activate the fan.

We need it. I pull the box over to the middle of the room and Toby and I sit on either side of it.

"Dig these old toys. Do you think that these belonged to Elias too?"

"It's possible," I said. "Mom says the builder found all of this stuffed in the same spot. The back of the house used to be two more bedrooms and a small bathroom. When they tore down the wall to join the two rooms they found all this stuff plastered in between.

Toby pulls out the small ornate block of wood.

"This thing is so cool! It looks homemade. The hand carving is incredible," then he frowns, "Oh, uh maybe we should be careful. What if this is a dybbuk box?"

"A what??"

You know one of those boxes that they trap demons and evil spirits in and when you open it all hell breaks loose. Although there is no latch or hinges. You can't open it even if you want to. Maybe not. Probably just a craft project to practice carving.

"Why not set that aside for now," I smirk, "I'm not really in a demons causing havoc kind of mood… but thanks, maybe later."

Toby digs around the bottom of the cardboard box.

"Hey there's a picture in here. Wow. Check out these two," holding the photo out to me.

The picture is amazing. The couple, obviously from the 1800's, are quite a pair. The woman looks like an angry schoolteacher; frowning face, hair pulled tightly back into what I assume is a bun at the back of her head. But it's the man that really draws my attention. Even in a black and white photograph his unbelievably light eyes are striking. They are the palest I've ever seen. He has thick gray hair and a long white beard. They both look tired. I can't determine their age, but life wore deep lines in their faces by the time this was taken.

I turn over the picture and can see writing in very faint ink. I get to my feet, walk to the window, and hold the photograph directly under the sunlight to see if I can read it more clearly.

The handwriting is difficult to make out. The script is very ornate and old fashioned. I tilt the photograph to catch the sun's rays. Studying it, I suddenly recognize the names that are written.

Cora and Arba Hastings.

"Oh my God Toby, these are his parents! I saw the names on the family tree that's in the Bible."

"That's wild! I wonder if there are any more," Toby say, and reaches into the box, pulling out everything.

We spend the next few minutes sorting through what's inside. Setting the games next to the box. There are several schoolbooks, a few boy's adventure stories that I've never heard of, but we find no other loose pictures.

"Let's flip through the books," I said, "maybe there's something stuck inside." We each take a few and begin to search. We are about halfway through our respective stacks when I find it, stuck in the final pages of what looks to be an

American history book. Another picture. The young man is dressed formally, with a high starched collar. His hair appears a light brown or very dark blonde, He has a large nose and deep-set eyes. An intelligent face. I flip the picture over. This name is much easier to read.

Elias William Hastings.

I can hardly breathe. Could this the man that Maggie loved? The one she was running away to on the night that she lost her life? There is no real way to know, but the idea is thrilling. In all the years I've known the legend of Maggie's Bridge no one has ever mentioned who the father of her baby was. Where were they planning to go? Did he love Maggie? Were they intending to get married? I know from the family tree that Elias does get married eventually. But was Maggie his true love? Did he really mourn her for years before being able to move on? If it's true, that's terrible.

"Toby, it's him."

Toby stands up, walks over and takes the picture from my hand.

"Wow, so you really think that the name Maggie written in that book is *this* guy talking about the Maggie from the bridge. Really?"

"Well it's the right age. We're close by. This house is directly down from where she must have lived. She could easily have been on her way to *this* house. I just have a feeling."

"What a trip!" he checks his phone, "Damn, listen doll, I gotta hit the road. Besides, we are going to pass out if we stay in this heat much longer. It's sweltering up here. You want me to help you carry some of this stuff down?"

"Yes please, that would be great. Let's bring the whole box. I'm gonna miss you, you know. Promise me you'll come back down again soon. I'm hoping to get Jesse back here for a mini vacation or something. You should try to come back then. We can all do something together."

"I know that Aiden wants us to come down during the summer and see the beach, even with all the tourists. So we'll see."

The air is blessedly cold as we come down the ladder. I peek into the mirror and see the hot air has caused my hair to practically double in size. I grab a clip and twist it into a high knot, feeling the cool air hit my sweaty neck.

We stick the box in the corner of my room, and I walk Toby out to his car. He gives me a giant hug and I squeeze him back.

"Thanks so much for coming. It's great to see your face. I'm sorry we didn't have anything happen on our little excursion."

"Not nothing! We got scared by a car. Don't forget to check the EVP recordings. I left the spirit box on your desk."

"Really? That's awesome. You know, you're not a bad guy."

"Well it's a gift for you, I told you. Anyway, you've got better ears than I do. Too many rock concerts. That or the constant chatter of small children is getting to me. Get some headphones and listen really well. Maybe you'll catch something I missed. Love you."

* * *

151

I pull into the parking lot of the store just before one o'clock. I'm glad to see it's almost totally full. Thank goodness we have designated employee parking spots. Otherwise I'd be in trouble. Inside there are customers everywhere. People wandering in and out of the different rooms. The chairs in bay window are taken by customers reading in the sunlight. There's actually a line of three people waiting to check out. I drop my bag and swing behind the counter to help out Talissa. She looks really happy to see me.

"Good afternoon, young lady. Nice to see you are punctual," Talissa smiles at me, "Your mom is upstairs in the horror room with some customers waxing lyrical about Stephen King. So we may not see her for a while."

"Figures. So what do I need to accomplish today?"

"Some of the shelves are getting empty in the Children's room, besides the fact that it looks like a hurricane hit it. It needs restocking. The boxes should be marked in the stockroom. But they are pretty heavy.

"I'll get Hunter to help me bring them out."

"Great. Um…listen Claire, about Hunter, is he uh…hassling you? He seems really *attentive* when you guys work together, and I just want to make sure that he's not crossing any lines."

"He seems to want to be friendly, but nothing I can't handle," I answer.

The late-night messages have stopped but he is pretty damn friendly when we work together. Hopefully, he'll behave himself until his contract is up. I really don't want to have to talk to Mom about it. The store seems to be running pretty well. We have had a couple computer issues and he's been able to sort them out in no time. It would suck if Mom had to find someone new this close to our grand opening on the 31st.

Around 1:30 the bells above the door herald the arrival of a well-dressed young woman and a photographer. She smiles at me, "Hello there! My name is Marlow Smith, I have an appointment with Ophelia O'Brien?"

"That's my mother, hang on," I rush to the back room, "Mom! The lady from the paper is here."

"Oh God, please don't let me say anything stupid," she squares her shoulders and heads out to greet her. Marlow sits in the bay window to interview Mom and Talissa. They pose for pictures on the big deep porch in front of the bay window. I spend the entire time sitting behind the counter doing busy work, hoping it makes me look remotely professional. Good luck with that. A good article in the paper should bring in even more business. It's nice to watch Mom's dream come true.

* * *

I sit at my desk, the spirit box in my hand. I've pulled out my old headphones from the pile of stuff in the back of the closet. Yes, I stuff everything I'm not using back there, sue me. I want to find out if I can hear anything on this recording. I'm also half hoping I don't hear a thing. Toby has already messaged me asking if I have listened to it. I have to get it over with.

I plug the headphones into the side and begin the recording.

At first I just hear the two of us talking. God, I hate the sound of my voice. For someone who loves a good voice I sure got stuck with a bad one. Then we call her. Nothing.

"Maggie, are you here?" Silence.

"Maggie, are you lost?" Silence

"Maggie, can you see us?"

There is a faint sound. Static crackles out of the device, making me jump. There's also something like a humming. Rising and lowering in pitch. That's odd, I remember there was total silence. No crickets, no frogs, no wind. No sound at all.

"How can we help you? Talk to us please."

In the moments after our voices stop I hear it again. I can't make it out. I turn the sound up as far as it will go and push the headphones tight against my ears. I start the recording over again, wincing at the loud sound of our amplified voices.

All at once I know what the noise is. Once I identify it, it's impossible to ignore.

It's unmistakable. It is a woman crying.

Chapter 22

The next few weeks pass in a blur. I move through my life as if watching it from a strangers point of view. I am shaken to my core by what I did. I knew it was wrong even as it happened, yet I could not help myself. If I had it to do over again I would do each and every thing exactly the same. It was the most wonderful thing that has ever happened in my life.

I try to behave as though all is normal but inside I am shaking. If my parents were to find out my father would disown me. He's a good man, but a morally rigid one. I have not seen him be affectionate with my mother ever in my life. He would not understand nor would he be able to forgive me.

So far they think nothing is amiss. I am behaving much as I did before. I am trying to, anyway. Sleep is difficult, however. I toss and turn most of the night. I find that I am tired quite often.

I woke up swimming with nausea this morning. The thought of trying to eat breakfast making my gorge rise to the back of my throat. Standing at the stove frying eggs, the gelatinous runny white is more than I can bear, and I run into our backyard to vomit into the bushes. Thankfully, Father is in the barn tending to the animals. Mother, however, witnesses the whole thing.

"What's wrong with you, girl? Are you ill?" She comes to me and runs her hands over my face, feeling for a fever. "You seem alright. You need to lay back down?"

"I am alright. Perhaps my dinner did not agree with me. I will be fine in a few minutes."

I vomit again the next day… and the next… and the next. It must be nerves. A reaction to fear. I have never done anything so deceptive before. It is not sitting well on my conscience. At least I have been able to hide the sickness from my mother after the first day. Vomiting behind the chicken coop when I go out to collect eggs. I put on a brave face each time I go back inside.

* * *

I am in church, sitting close between my parents, when the thought comes to me. How long has it been since my last monthly course? It's regular arrival is not something I talk about with my parents.

The first time it happened I was convinced I was dying. Waking up to find the bed beneath me stained with red. Terrified, I had screamed out in the early morning light. It took my mother some time to calm me down and explain this aspect of womanhood. Why she had not chosen to do so before, still baffles me.

Since that day several years ago, I take care of my own linen for it each month. My mother would not think to question me. I count through the weeks in my head and realize the last time was almost six weeks ago, around the time of my birthday.

My stomach drops, and a sour taste fills the back of my mouth. I struggle to remain composed while surrounded by the entire congregation. I know what it means when a woman misses her course. Mother explained at least that much on the morning I awoke, laying in blood. If it does not arrive soon, I will know I am with child.

During the greetings after the service I can sense Elias looking at me with his typical concealed hunger. I cannot bring myself to even speak to him. I remain silent and stare at the ground as everyone around me speaks happily about the beautiful day and the sermon. I cannot engage. I am not myself.

I am filled with dread.

May 31st, 1880

Midnight

I sit under the tree, wet to the skin from the ceaseless rain. The memory of discovering my pregnancy is so clear in my mind that I am overwhelmed with sadness. Why has the baby gone? I know he was here. I had felt him inside me, like a secret. He must surely be here somewhere, lost in this endless nightmare.

As if summoned by my thoughts, the crying begins again. The soft, tiny, pitiful voice calling out. I have to find him. I make my way off my little spot of land and back up to the road. I am being soaked afresh by the downpour, now that I am away from my shelter. I have been here for too long. What must I do to escape this place? If I could just find my baby and somehow get away from here. My determination returns. I tighten my fists, set my jaw, and push my shoulders back.

The crying draws me to the center of the bridge. The wooden boards are soaking and slippery with mud. I stop and listen carefully. Trying to discern exactly where the crying is coming from. I hear a hollow echoing sound to the cry. Could it be...underneath me? But only water flows there. How could a baby survive in the rushing water? I drop to my knees, place my hands to the boards, and lower my head to the ground.

I hear it, directly under me. Frantic, I stand and work my way off the bridge, trying to get down to the water's edge. Ripping my skirts away from bushes that grab onto me as I pass. I teeter just at the edge of the water, next to side of the wooden boards. Peering underneath, all I can see is darkness. There is a broken branch laying on the riverbank and I grab it to support myself as I lean in. The lightning flashes and I momentarily see I see what appears to be a small dark wrapped bundle amongst the rushing water. Is it my baby? Has he somehow remained alive and unharmed under the bridge all this time? To find out I must do the one thing that I fear most of all. I have to enter the water.

The storm has been so ferocious that the river has risen quite high and is rushing wildly past me. It is terrifying. If I don't stay balanced I will be sucked away in the rush. But I cannot just ignore it when there is a chance that it is my missing child. Using the stick forced down into the muck to hold me steady, I move slowly and carefully, pushing back against the force of the water. I am but a few feet away from the dark bundle when the current begins to catch me. Grabbing and swirling my wide skirts and wrapping them tight around me. Pulling me hard upriver. In a panic I blindly throw my arm up and find the underside of the bridge just within the reach of my fingertips. Bracing myself against it I manage to stay upright. The water is only as deep as my shoulder. Carefully I work my way across the middle and reach out for the bundle wedged underneath the bridge. I drop the stick and scoop the round object in my arm. Holding it tightly against my chest, I work my way back, struggling to remain upright as I no longer have the stick to help me fight the current.

I am just about to step a foot onto the bank of the river when my shoe catches on a root underneath the water and I trip. The bundle flies from my arms and lands on the riverbank in front of me. I crash down on top of it. The hardness of it slams against my chest as I hit the ground and I yelp in pain. I lift myself up. My God, what if after all this I have crushed my own child? At that moment lightning brightens the sky and I look down and see what it is that I rescued. A helpless terror fills me and I drop helplessly to my side on the ground; scrambling to get away from it. The bundle is not a baby. The rain washes the tangled knots of long dark hair, spreading them out onto the riverbank and uncovering a face. The eyes are open and pleading. The mouth is stretched wide in a screaming grimace of pain.

But that is not the worst of it. It is my face; it is my head.

Chapter 23

Claire

June 25th, 2023

Mom smiles at the three of us standing around the front counter, "If business keeps up, I'm thinking we will need to hire more employees. We are all working too hard. We can use a couple part time people. Plus, Claire won't be around forever."

"It's true, I saw the grim reaper next to my bed just this morning."

Everyone laughs, "You know what I mean honey."

We are having a staff meeting. I am trying hard to stay awake. All I need is a couple toothpicks to prop my eyes open and I'll be set. So far, The Dusty Bookshelf is a great success. The location is perfect for people on their way to the ocean. It's proving to not be too far inland to attract tourists already at the shore either. We get a lot of people driving in from the beaches to check us out. Mom advertised in as many places down there as she could. If we can the word out enough and get established it should continue to be a success even after the summer is over. Which is important. Summer season is only a few months out of the year. Local customers are vital.

Mom wraps it up and I leave the counter.

I'm working too hard. I can tell. I'm tired all the time. I've started napping in the kitchen on my lunch break. I'm heading there right now. Laying a pillow right on the table, I drop my head on it. The stress is even upsetting my stomach. I feel queasy sometimes. I'm hiding it from Mom. I don't need her worrying about me when she already has so much on her plate. Tim is leaving today on a month-long tour for the book he wrote about the Whisky Rebellion of 1794 and its implications in current society. Ok, that's what he said, don't ask me what it means. It came out this spring. She's going to have to take care of the house, and the store both. I don't want to be even more stress. I'm supposed to be here to *help*.

I've listened several times to the EVP recording. I don't know whether to be afraid or sad about it. I'm afraid because let's face it...it's a ghost. On the other hand, the crying is so heartbroken, so unutterably sad that part of me wants to run down to the bridge and just *be* with her so she's not alone.

My phone rings, a video call from Jesse. I touch the screen and his beautiful smiling face appears. At the sight of him, everything hits me all at once: the stress of the store, not getting enough sleep, the disturbing thoughts about Maggie and what is or isn't real, and the loneliness of being away from the man I love so much. I do the thing I've been working hard to avoid. I burst into tears.

"Claire! What's wrong!? Did something happen?"

"No. Not really. I just...just...miss you. This is really hard. I can't sleep well without you next to me. I even miss your dirty socks all over the floor."

His face falls and he softly laughs. "Oh Tiny, I miss you too. I get lonely when I wake up at night and you aren't snuggled up next to me, arm across my chest... snoring."

"I don't snore!" I laugh with the tears still wet on my cheeks, "And even if I do it's rude to point it out."

"You are right. I would never accuse you of snoring like a breeder hog. I'm far too much of a gentleman."

"Ugh, you're lucky I love you."

"Yes, I am. I think about it every day. Listen, Dr. Schwartz is taking his vacation at the end of August and the other vets will be running the practice for the week he is gone. So he's giving me that time off. Can I come down? It's not for long but I really need to see you."

"YES!" I squeal loudly, forgetting where I am. We have customers all over the store. I drop my voice, "Please come. I need to touch you. Know that you are real and not just a face on my phone. This is worse than when I loved you long distance while you were at NYU."

"That's because now you know I give a mean foot rub and I'm an amazing singer."

"You wish you were an amazing singer. I love you in *spite* of your singing voice."

Mom comes through the door of the break room and sees Jesse's face. "Dr. Mumford! How's the barnyard?

"Great Mrs. O'Brien. I was just asking your daughter if she'd mind a visit from me at the end of August."

"Well, I'm sure she would, but even if she doesn't, I'd love to see you. Get yourself down here." She blows him a kiss, grabs a soda from the fridge and heads back out. "You almost done Claire? I'm sorry, but it's getting crazy out here."

"Ok baby, I'll let you get back to work. I'll call you again soon. I love you. I can't wait to see you."

"I love you too, Yeti. I'm so glad you are coming."

I shut off the phone and sigh. The end of August is still two months away. It's turning out to be a long ass summer.

I go and find Hunter who is sitting, as usual, in front of the TV monitors showing the video feed from all the cameras.

"Hey there," He sits up straighter, turning the monitor slightly away from me. Tapping quickly on the keys in front of him, "Have a nice break?"

"Too short. But hey, the money is coming in. Can't complain."

"So, um… did you drive today? Talissa and I were thinking of heading down to Rehoboth for dinner after we close up. Want to come with us?"

"I did drive today, actually, but Tim is leaving late tonight for his tour, and Mom probably wants to have a family dinner on his last night at home for a while." I don't really want to spend any time with this guy outside the store. That's a plausible excuse.

"You really don't think your mom would like a few hours alone with Tim before he goes?"

I pause, he has a good point. Damn. Technically she's still a newlywed. They have been so kind and accepting of me moving into their space. It might be nice to give them a little bit of privacy before he leaves for a month.

Hunter sees the look on my face and holds up his hands in mock surrender, "I promise, just friends. I'll be a gentleman. I've been dying to try out this new restaurant. My treat and everything."

I'm still hesitant, "Let me run it by Mom and I'll let you know."

I find Mom in Mystery and Thrillers. The walls here are covered with ornate masks. There's an antique candelabra with old wax dripped all over it, sitting on a high shelf. And tiny apothecary bottles on the windowsills. The walls are a dark eggplant.

"Hey Mom, how would you feel about an evening alone with that guy you married?"

"What are you talking about?"

"I'm thinking maybe I skip dinner at home tonight. Go out to eat with Talissa and Hunter after I close up. Maybe catch a movie. Try not to be home before midnight, if you know what I'm talking about. Hint, hint."

She smiles, then her face twists and I swear she looks like she's about to cry.

"Honey, would you? That would be so sweet. We have been working so hard, it would be nice to have a romantic dinner and spend some time with him before he leaves. I'm going to miss him so much. I'm used to having him around."

"Don't forget, I'm the person who actually understands. Starting tomorrow we can be sad and miserable together. Eat ice cream, watch sappy movies. Cry our eyes out. We will do it all, I promise. Go on, get out of here. Go home to your man."

She laughs and hugs me, "You're a good kid. I think I'll keep you.

Hunter looks up and smiles when I return, "That looked like a yes. So you like seafood?"

* * *

Culver's is not what I thought it would be. I was expecting a family style, touristy seafood restaurant. I figured it would be bright, loud, and filled with loud vacationing families. I'm sort of underdressed for the small dark room we are seated in. The murmur of voices is low and pleasant. The small tables have thick pristine white cloth that drapes to the floor, candles, and elegant crème-colored menus. I'm dressed decent for work, of course, but most of the people in here are clearly dressed for date night.

"So are you enjoying your time back here on the shore? I hear you lived in Philadelphia for a while" Hunter says to me, "Nice city. This must be quite a change."

"It's different. Actually it's turning out to be kind of nice," I crunch down on a crusty bread roll slathered in cinnamon butter. "The area, I mean. I guess I didn't appreciate it when I was here."

"I know your mother is thrilled to have you back," Talissa smiles, "We heard about you every day since we first got into the store."

"Oh great."

"It's true. Every day it was more stories about the magic that is Claire." Hunter sounds just this side of sarcastic.

The server appears at the table, 'Welcome to Culver's. What can I get you folks to drink this evening?"

"I think I'll just have an iced tea, thanks." I still feel a little queasy, and I don't particularly want to lose any coherency or focus while I'm out with Hunter.

"Oh come on," he teases, "One little drink won't hurt you."

"No thanks, really."

"I'll have a Scotch on the rocks, sweetie."

The server looks down at him, and I catch a quick flash of irritation cross her face before the professional smile returns.

Talissa tells her, "I'll have a dirty martini."

"Perfect, I'll be right back with those for you."

* * *

Dinner isn't helping my opinion of Hunter. He's kind of a creep. It's becoming more obvious as he drinks. The Seafood Ceviche is delicious. I would have enjoyed it more if I hadn't had to listen to Hunter bragging about all the clients he's had and how incredibly important his job is.

"So what's it like living with your Mom again?" Talissa asks, trying to change the subject, "It must be quite a change from living with Jesse for what…three years?"

"The house is amazing. I love it. It feels so *historic*. But sleeping over the parrots can be a challenge."

Hunter speaks up, "What? Like birds? What's the big deal?"

"The big deal is they like to wake up with the sun. Asking for breakfast at the crack of dawn."

"They talk?"

"They talk a lot. You have to be careful or they will pick up anything you say."

"Far out."

It's still kind of early to go home so we move over to the bar. Taking three ornate, velvet covered stools at the mahogany counter. Hunter downs another drink, fast. A shot of some kind, and gestures immediately for another. I rest my feet on the brass footrail and look around at the other customers. I am the youngest person here. This place caters to an older, more sophisticated crowd. I don't know which of these painted up older women is wearing the gallon of perfume, but my eyes are beginning to water from the stench.

"So Talissa, how's the dating scene?" I ask.

"A nightmare. I'm over 40. So the only men interested in me are old farts who want a last roll in the hay before it stops working forever, or young guys who want me to teach them how to do it and take care of them financially."

"Well that sounds like a great time."

"Yes. Any man my actual age is either married, has so many deep-seated issues I wouldn't go near them with a Sherman tank, or they are only after women half my age. I don't recommend it."

"I'm feeling very dedicated to Jesse right now."

"I would be. Speaking of being old, I'm going to hit the road kids. It's getting late for an old lady. You'll be alright Claire?"

"Uh…yeah," I only have a bit longer before I can leave. I don't want to head home and hear or see something that might traumatize me for life. "I'll be heading out soon myself."

"You want me to wait?"

"Nah, I'm ok. You take off."

"Thanks for dinner, Hunter. I'll see you guys tomorrow."

Hunter lifts his hand in a farewell and looks at me as he says, "You're welcome. Don't worry about Claire, I've got her. We will be just fine."

Hunter throws back his fourth drink and his words are beginning to slur. He slides into Talissa's empty seat and leans into my personal space. I lean back.

"So your boyfriend is coming to pay you a visit?"

"How do you know *that*?" I certainly hadn't told him. Mom could have, I suppose, but why would she?

"Uh...well...the break room is right down the hall from the front counter. I heard you yell." He's smirking at me. Oh. My face reddens.

"Yes, he's getting a break at the end of the summer season. It will be nice to see him again." I sound formal, like an old lady.

"Well if I had a female as sexy as you, I don't think I'd be able to spend any time away. You're quite sumthin..."

I slowly turn my head and stare fixedly at him. Speechless. He did not just say that out loud. Go on buddy, keep going. I dare you. Unbelievably, he actually does.

"Older females are so insufferable. Bossy, set in their ways. Picky, full of themselves. Younger girls like you are so much more, *receptive*. Malleable."

Oh dear god. He can't be serious. I check my watch, 11:25. Close enough. I can sit in my car for a while. I am getting the hell out of here right now. I stand and grab my bag off the bar. "Look Hunter, I think I've had enough for one evening. Thanks for dinner, but I'm going to head out now."

He winks, "I got you babe, let's go."

The dude can't even walk straight now. I cringe in embarrassment as he trips on the doorjamb and stumbles through the front door of the restaurant. I duck my head and follow him out. I hope nobody saw that. I scan the parking lot to see if by some miracle Talissa is still here. She only just left the bar a few minutes ago.

"Hunter, let me call you an Uber, you're drunk."

"No way pretty girl, I'm not leaving my car here. I'm fine...I can drive. I do this all the time."

"That doesn't make me feel any better. I'm calling a ride for you. I'm serious. Just sit yourself down or I'm calling the police."

"Geez...*women*." He frowns like I smacked his puppy, throws his keys to the ground and sits on the curb in front of his car. Look at this asshole pout! His lower lip is actually all pooched out. Like a child. Alcohol brings out the loveliest side of people.

The sky is clear and warm. I can smell the ocean only a mile or so away. I breathe in deep to try and clear the perfume stench out of my nose. I pull out my phone and order the ride. While I wait for it to arrive I stand next to him and check my messages while he sits on the curb. I missed a text from Jesse. A quick flash of guilt goes through me. I didn't mention I was having dinner with Hunter tonight. I guess I consider it a nonevent. He's really kind of a jerk. And Talissa was here. It's just a work-related thing.

I begin to type a reply to Jesse when I feel a hard and sweaty hand slide up the back of my leg and squeeze high on the back of my thigh. I react without thinking. Swinging around and smacking Hunter hard across the face. With the hand holding the phone. I hear an audible *thwack* as the edge of the phone case catches him right under the eye and bashes his cheekbone. His head reels back as he slips off the curb and lands in the gutter.

I am instantly, powerfully, pissed off. "Touch me again, you asshole! *I dare you!*" I stand over him, screaming, "Who the hell do you think you are?? Lay one finger on me *ever* again I will have you arrested so fast you won't even have time to piss down your own leg." People are running up behind me as we've attracted the attention of everyone within earshot. I hear their comments and laughter as he lays in the dirt, holding his face.

"Damn girl. Good for you."

"Did he assault you, Miss? Do you need me to call the police?"

"Well, that fool won't mess with you again."

I am mortified. All these elegantly dressed people, watching Hunter try to get his brains back on straight. I've never hit another person in my life.

It's right at this moment the Uber driver pulls up. A big hulking guy. I've never been so happy to see anyone. A couple men help him load Hunter into the back seat as I say, "His address is on his license."

The driver gets behind the wheel. "I'll get him home, don't worry."

"I don't care where you take him, as long as it's away from me." I head across the parking lot to my car and quickly lock myself inside. I'm shaking. I cover my mouth with my hands and rock back and forth in the seat, trying to get a hold of myself. This was an evening that will not be repeated. I hope at least Mom had a good time. I turn on the radio and sit by myself for a few minutes, just breathing slowing and letting the adrenaline melt away.

When I pull in at home, the house is dark. Mom has obviously gone to bed. Tim's SUV is gone, he already left. I'm still trembling, and I wish Jesse were here. But if he were here I would have never been in that situation in the first place.

* * *

I can't settle down. I have been reading in bed for over an hour, but I can't get sleepy. Adrenaline is still running through me. I give up and drop the book to the floor. This is ridiculous. I might as well do something. I'll try and clean up my room as quietly as I can. Maybe it will help me work off the shakes and calm down. Anything is better than laying bed feeling my heart pounding in my ears.

I turn on the overhead light, looking around. There are several boxes of stuff still piled up in the corner. Just odds and ends. Crap I thought I might want while I was here. Maybe I can get a couple of these unpacked. I sit on the floor next to the box and pull out a framed photo of Jesse and me, dressed as the twins from The Shining. He looks adorable in a little blue dress, his hairy legs looking about five feet long. I find my fuzzy winter slipper socks, my favorite coffee mug, and a half empty package of tampons. As I hold the tampons in my hand, a hollow feeling of dread grows inside me. Wait. Why have I not needed these yet? How long have I been here? I count the days in my head. It's June 26th. I arrived on May 12th.

Grab my phone and pull up my menstrual tracker app. It says my last period started April 27th. Oh no. Oh no. Oh my God. The sleepiness, the tears, suddenly all make sense. Everything has been such an upheaval in my life that I hadn't even noticed it's a whole month late.

I'm pregnant.

Chapter 24

I stare at my face for a long time. It all came back to me in the instant I recognized myself. Every moment of how I came to be here crisp and clear in my mind. I am dead. This must be purgatory. I have been doomed to wander here because of wrongs that I committed. Is the punishment of unsanctified love damnation to a living hell? What did I do beyond a lapse of judgement with the man I love? The man I intended to spend my life with? Are all such souls trapped in a nightmare?

Where is my child in all of this? He is an innocent soul. He has done no wrong beyond his illegitimacy. Is that enough to damn him? Is that why I hear his cry? Is being a bast-

The sound of a whinny cuts sharply through my thoughts. A horse? It sounds close by. As it comes again I hear the desperation in it. The animal is afraid, or in pain. I lift up my poor head by the tangled hair; I cannot bear to touch my own face. I climb back up the riverbank and return to the center of the bridge. There are marks across the wood. They were not here before. Deep gouges across the planks and off the edge.

At the far side of the bridge I look down and recoil in horror; it is all visible to me now. Laid out in a horrible tableau. The buggy is here. Mangled and destroyed in the water below. The buggy top is snapped off completely. The wheels are twisted and broken.

"Oh God help me, NO!" I scream, for there, tangled in the bridle and reins, half submerged, and wedged partly under the bridge is the body of our pinto Roger. The black and white patches on his body clear even through the rushing water. His neck twisted back at a horrible angle, his front legs barely visible, disappearing beneath the wooden planks. The horrible noise of fear and agony is coming from him. I cannot see this. I cannot hear this. A shudder moves through me and I back mindlessly away from the sight. I drop my dangling head onto the bridge and climb down the riverbank. I wade without hesitation into the water. I must get him free. When I reach him his wild, terrified eyes turn to me. Begging me for help. I pull at the bridle, trying to move it. It will not come. Broken planks from the buggy press across his neck and hold it tightly. I pull with all my strength. The seams of my sleeves ripping under my arms with the effort.

He screams again. Why is he also in this horrible place? Must his spirit be trapped here as well? He did nothing in his life but try to please my family. Try as I might, I cannot free him. I am not strong enough. I work my way back to the buggy itself to see if I can shift some of the wreckage and loosen what is trapping him. The inside of the buggy is twisted right through the center. The iron stays of the buggy top broken off at wicked sharp angles. Fabric billows out from the seat across the water. Moving the fabric aside, I stop short. This is too much. Too terrible a sight to bear. I break down and cry. My poor, waterlogged, headless body is wedged into the buggy seat, hands still tightly gripping the reins.

May 24th, 1880

Elias,

I must speak to you.

Please come to my house tonight at midnight.

Meet me in the back stall of the barn. Be very quiet.

It is imperative that I see you.

Maggie

I walk quickly ahead of my parents into Church on Sunday, slipping the note into the hymnal as they pause to talk to our neighbors in the chapel foyer. I see Elias watching my every movement. All through the service I do not look up. I cannot meet Elias's eyes for fear he will read them in an instant.

I am certain now that I am with child. There can be no mistake. My belly is hard. Gently rounded. So far my skirts hide all trace of it. My parents have not yet figured out the truth. I must tell Elias about the baby before it becomes known. There is going to be such a scandal; I have to prepare him. How will he take the news? He will be shocked, surely. Will he still love me?

All during supper I look at my parents. Will they still want me at home? Will they send me away? I know places exist for unwed mothers. Will my father's anger be so great that he throws me to the streets? He is a very proud man. Even if we could be married before anyone finds out, my father will never forgive either Elias or me for breaking our promise to him.

At bedtime I climb under my blankets. I know I will not sleep. Worry knots up my insides. I lay awake and listen to the chiming of the grandfather clock in the living room. My parents retire at ten o'clock and I listen for them to quiet down in their room. When they have been silent for at least an hour I rise and quietly wrap my shawl over my nightclothes. Slipping silently down the stairs I tiptoe to the backdoor. Turning the knob gently, I ease it open and slip out into the night. Racing across the cool grass in my bare feet. The gentle breeze blowing my loose hair away from my face.

Elias is already waiting for me as I enter the barn. His horse is nowhere to be seen. He must have walked here from his house.

I feel tears prick my eyes as he runs up to me in the dim light. He has a lantern glowing softly, hidden in the shelves of the stall. The light is just bright enough to see him. I had not seen the light from outdoors. It will not be seen from the house.

He pulls me into his arms and kisses me all over my face. My eyes, my forehead, my cheeks, my lips. Running his hands down my body I hear his deep inhale as he feels the thinness of my nightdress against his hands. They curve around my shape. I push him away.

"Maggie, what is it? What is wrong?"

"Do you truly love me?"

"You know that I do. What have I done to make you doubt it? What is this all about? Don't be silly."

"Elias, everything is ruined. We are in trouble. I am in trouble. Can we sit down?"

He has already spread the blanket back out onto the ground. He helps me to sit down and takes his place across from me, holding tightly to my hands. I stare down at our clasped hands and try to decide the best way to say it. This moment should be a joy. A time of celebration. Not a hidden, hushed conversation in a dark and quiet barn.

"The last time we were together...here...we made a baby."

His eyes widen as his mouth falls open. For a moment he does not speak. His hands squeeze mine tightly, "Are you sure? There can be no mistake?"

"No, I have not had my monthly since that night. And here, feel."

I place his hand on the small swell of my belly. His face lights up in wonder. In the next instant he pulls me tightly against his chest. I twist my head to the side just to snatch a breath as he rocks me from side to side. I feel him swallowing repeatedly against my head. His voice comes out choked, "My sweet girl, why have you not told me before?"

'I wanted to be sure. Now I am. I'm so afraid. What are we going to do now?"

"This is what I wanted for us, just not so soon. But God works in mysterious ways. We will accept what he gives us. What do you want to do? Should we tell our parents?"

"No! They will never let us be together. We went against my father's wishes."

"You're right. Well then, will you leave with me?"

"And go where? Where can we go? What will happen to us?"

"Give me a chance to send a telegram to my cousin. He works for the railroad in Salisbury, Maryland. Perhaps we can stay with he and his wife for a while. Salisbury is but twenty miles or so away. We can journey there on my horse. We can be married."

"But my parents! Your parents! We cannot just leave everyone. What will they think? What will they say? Will they not try to find us?"

"Maggie, you were right. If they find out they may send you away from me. I will not be apart from you. You promised to love me. Will you not do ask I ask? We can settle in Salisbury, be married, and have as many children as you like. My cousin will keep our secret. Once we are wed there will not be anything they can do about it."

My relief is all consuming. I wrap my arms about him, suddenly joyous. All will be well. Perhaps not in the way we had originally thought. But we will be together and wed before our child is born.

"If we are really going to run away together, I should bring the buggy, I have things I have been saving for us. Put aside to help us get started. I can move the things out to the barn this week. I can fit them behind the seat."

"That will be dangerous. Can you hitch up the horse alone? In the dark?"

"I will have to. I am sure I can do it. Roger is a gentle horse. He trusts me," I smile, "When should we leave? How long do you need?"

"A week perhaps. To give me time to reach Alan and hear back. Come next Sunday night. As soon as you can sneak away. I'll be watching for you. The moon should be full again, it will be easy to see the road. We can take the back way to Reliance and travel south from there. Anyone looking for us will likely stick to the main roads. We can be out of the state by morning."

Reliance is on the state line, only four miles away. Even in darkness we can make it out of Delaware quickly. I will need to pack food for the trip, and anything else I can find to take.

"May I hold you Maggie? Both of you?"

His smile warms my heart and I settle myself into his arms. I am content that the future, while unknown, will at least be met together.

Chapter 25

Claire

June 27ᵗʰ, 2023

I hardly slept at all last night. I laid awake for hours checking and rechecking the dates in my tracker app. How could I not have realized? I feel so stupid. I've counted and counted, and it still doesn't feel real. I need to get out of here and get a pregnancy test. I have the day off today. I was looking forward to spending the day on the couch with a good book. That will definitely not be happening now.

I hear Mom head into the bathroom. She's leaving for work in a few minutes. It wouldn't be unheard of for me not to go down to breakfast. She'll expect me to try and sleep in on my day off. Especially since I was out late last night.

Oh god. What will Hunter say to her? Did I mark up his face? I had to have done something. My phone smacked into it so hard he's sure to have a black eye. She'll ask him about it, I know. Should I tell her before she goes in? She'll fire him, no question. But what will we do after that? We still need his help. The store is so important to Mom, and we are doing so well right now. I don't want to rock the boat. Maybe I tell her after he's finished the job. As long as he can keep his mouth shut and behave. Hopefully, he learned a lesson last night.

She's going to look at my face and see something is wrong, I know it. She can read me with one look. I've never been able to hide anything important from her.

There is a soft knock on my door. Crap. So much for hiding. I plaster a smile on my face. "Yeah?" the knob turns, and the door softly opens.

"Honey, you awake?" She looks so sad. Her face is haggard, like she didn't sleep either. Oh damn, in my worry, I completely forgot Tim left last night. It looks like everybody is having a rough morning. I don't have a corner on the market.

"Hey Mom. I'm up. You ok? Want me to come down for coffee?"

"Would you? It's silly, he's been gone for nine hours and I'm already sad. I feel like a ridiculous teenager. I'm an adult, I'm supposed to be happy for the free time. That's what all the books tell me."

"It's love Mom, it sucks sometimes."

She's already brewed the coffee by the time I make it downstairs a couple minutes later. I fix her and myself a cup. I can play casual. Relaxed. Even though I'm screaming on the inside. I paste a sympathetic expression on my face as I sit the coffee down in front of her and take my seat.

"It's hard, Mom. But I promise it will get better. It's only a month."

"I just thought it might help in I wallowed in self-pity for a bit. Get it out of my system instead of repressing it. I have been so consumed with the store that last few months, and he's been busy working on the book. I only see him when I wake up in the morning and like an hour before I go to sleep at night. You'd think it would be easier than this. But those few minutes matter a lot. He keeps me grounded."

"I can help with that. You're grounded. Go to your room." I point towards up above my head.

She laughs and rolls her eyes, "Honey, that's a terrible joke. Grr, I'll be fine. Enough of this, I'm going to go kick some ass today. I do not need my man velcroed to my side. I raised you by myself for years. I can handle this," she pauses, her face drawn, "Just remind me of this statement later, ok?"

"How about we have a movie night? Something gory? Some good slashers should cheer us up. When are you getting home?"

"That would be great. I open. Talissa is closing. Hunter is on all day. So I should be back by 5:30 or so. You line 'em up and get 'em ready. Want me to pick up dinner?"

"Yeah, sounds perfect." I stand and hug her.

* * *

I wait approximately four minutes after she leaves before I throw on some clothes, grab my keys, and head out. Another ten minutes after that I'm in the drug store grabbing three different brands of pregnancy tests, trying hard not to have eye contact with the cashier.

Does Jesse really want to have kids? Does he want to have kids with *me*? We have talked about our future together, but only in the…'It's so far away it's a nice dream'…kind of way. A baby right now could be a disaster for both of us. He has to focus on what he's doing. Who knows where he will get a job? He knows I'm willing go wherever he wants. But how will he feel about having a baby in tow? Will we be able to afford it? He may absolutely freak out when I tell him.

He could leave me. Oh my god.

I pull up in the driveway, go in the house, and drop my bag on the coffee table. My phone buzzes in my purse.

Toby: What you up to girl?

Claire: Oh wow. You don't want to know.

Toby: ???

Claire: I'm getting ready to pee on a stick.

Seconds later, my phone rings. I don't even have to check the caller ID. Toby, of course.

"Hey."

"What is God's name are you doing down there, young lady?? Who knocked you up?!"

"That's not funny. Who do you think? Jesse! There's never even *been* anybody else."

"Haven't you not seen him since…what…the beginning of May?"

"Yep. I should have noticed sooner. I'm kind of an idiot."

"GO! Go pee on a stick. Let me know what happens. Send me a text, I have to get back in the classroom.

"Oh, and the reason I wrote you, Aiden and I are coming down for a few days. We'll be there Saturday, the 2nd of July. We are leaving at the butt crack of dawn to try and beat some of the traffic. Let me know if you are up to hang out with us."

"I am. You should come straight here. I need the support! Oh god, I have to go do this before I lose my nerve."

I grab the paper bag and head to the bathroom. Setting up all three tests on the countertop. I decided peeing in the actual cup included in one of the tests is the best idea. Then I can use it for the other two tests as well. This should let me know one way or the other.

The job done; I sit on the floor with my back to the counter to wait it out. Two very long minutes that I count off one by one in my head. I try and keep my breathing slow and steady.

116…117…118…119…120.

I stand.

All three tests are positive.

Oh my God. I feel terrified and excited at the same time. Just like the day I moved up to Philadelphia to live with Jesse. I reach down and cover my belly with my hands. I can't believe there's a little somebody in there. I grab my phone.

Claire: Hey Uncle Toby.

Toby: OMG Claire! You're going to name him after me, right? When are you going to tell your mom? What about Jesse?

Claire: I'm telling Mom tonight. There's no way I can keep it a secret from her. We are having a movie night and she's going to want to have cocktails.

Toby: Good luck. What about Jesse?

Claire: This is a big thing to tell a guy over the phone. He's coming down in August, maybe I'll wait till then. I haven't decided yet.

Toby: Hey hon, congratulations. You will be a great mother.

* * *

By the time Mom gets home I'm gotten my mind around the idea of being pregnant. I've thought about nothing else all day. I'm twenty-three years old. That's not too young to have a baby. I'm not a teenager anymore. I'm a grown adult. Mom can't totally freak out, right?

She comes in close to six, her arms filled with take-out bags.

'How do you feel about Chinese?"

Ugh. "Ahh, ok. Sounds good." Sounds like that might make me throw up. It doesn't sit well in my stomach on the best day. And this is not the best day. "How is the store? Did I um…miss anything?"

"Oh yeah, wait till you see Hunter! I don't know what happened to him last night, but he was a mess today. He has a *huge* black eye. The whole side of his face is swollen. I sent him home early; he could hardly keep his head up."

I'm surprised he made it in at all, with the face smack/hangover combination he's dealing with.

"He didn't tell you how it happened?"

"No, he just brushed it off…flat out refused to talk about it. Let's eat in front of the TV. What are we watching?"

"I thought we'd go with the 1974 classic, 'It's Alive." I smile, "Sound good?"

"A mutated killer baby ripping apart unsuspecting humans? Who wouldn't want to see that while eating Kung Pao Chicken and fried rice?" She drops the bags on the coffee table and heads for the kitchen, calling back over her shoulder, "Want a Riesling? I got some to go with the food."

"Maybe later," I stammer, trying to stall her, "Let me eat something first."

I eat a little. Not doing much more than picking at the food. I can't swallow past the lump in my throat. I'm so nervous. This is big news. It's going to change everything. At least I'm not Maggie. Mom's not going to throw me out for being unmarried and pregnant. I'm not worried she will never speak to me again.

I wonder if Maggie parents found out or if she kept it a secret from them before she ran away. Can you imagine them finding out after she died? Having to know that if they had not been so judgmental she would still be alive. That would be a guilt I would not want to live with.

We watch what has got to be the freakiest baby I have ever seen tear into people. It's ridiculously awesome. But I picked this movie for another reason, and it's about time I get to it.

"So is this how I was as a baby?"

"This? No, this baby is a pleasant walk through a meadow compared to you. HA!"

"Right, my kill count was obviously higher, but was I a good sleeper? Was I fussy? Did I give you a lot of trouble?"

"Oh sweetie, you were a baby doll. The prettiest little thing I'd ever seen. So adorable that I wanted to bite you. You were the very best thing that ever happened to me.

"Of course, when you were a toddler you stuck a kernel of corn up your nose; I had to take you to the emergency room. We get you checked in, and you sneeze. It shot right out and hit the nurse in the face."

I laugh. "So you liked me."

"You could say that. You should hurry up and marry Jesse and give me some grandchildren to love."

"That's important to you? Being married first?"

"Not really. I mean, this isn't the Fifties. I wouldn't make you feel guilty if you-" she stops, taking in the look on my face, my barely touched food, and my glass of water.

"Claire?"

I smile, shrug my shoulders, and sigh.

"CLAIRE??"

"I took a test this morning."

She screams. Literally screams, then jumps off the couch to grab and hug me; beer bottle flying out of her hand and dropping to the rug, shooting Riesling all over the new hardwood.

* * *

We are up late. Mom has pulled out every photo album she has and spread them all out over her king-size bed. Going over every baby photo of me that she can find. Sharing every story about how I was the most wonderful baby in the world and mine will be the same way. She is blissful.

"I hope the baby has dark hair like us. Poor you, you were born so bald. You stayed that way so long I was afraid you'd never have hair. You were almost three before I could even give you little pig tails."

"Well, once it came in, it's given me nothing but trouble." I try to keep it tamed, but in the summer humidity, I look like an angry witch.

"When are you going to tell Jesse?"

"I don't know. I hate to tell him over the phone. Is it bad to wait till he comes down here?"

"You do what you think is right honey. We will call tomorrow and see about getting you into the doctor for an official blood test. You better get yourself to bed. I'll clean this up."

"Thanks Mom. Listen, don't tell anyone, ok? I told you, and Toby. But I'd rather other people didn't know till I tell Jesse."

"I won't. It will kill me, but I won't. Listen honey, I'm so proud of you. You are a strong, smart young woman. This is going to work out great, you'll see." She hugs me and kisses the side of my head.

I climb into bed, marveling at how radically the world shifted in the last 24 hours. Having Mom on my side means everything. I know that no matter what, she is here for me. The fear I felt this morning has been replaced by a simmering excitement. This baby is going to change everything, and I am ready for it.

June 28th, 2023

Arriving at the store the next morning, I'm feeling much better. Having crackers instead of coffee has made me a bit more sleepy, but a lot less nauseous. I walk up the steps, squaring my shoulders and holding my head up high. This is my mother's store. Hunter is an employee. I'm not the one who screwed up here. I unlock the door and head inside.

I'm standing at the counter with Talissa when Hunter arrives at lunchtime. He greets us without making eye contact. I can see the kaleidoscopic shine all around his eye. Mom's description hadn't done it justice. Holy shit. I really did a number on him. The whole underside of his eye is a deep purple. The lower lid swollen so much he can hardly open it. The bruise leaching color almost all the way down his face. And this is almost 2 days later. I can't imagine how much that hurts. For a moment, I feel guilty. Was what he did *really* that bad? He copped a feel of my leg. He didn't kidnap me and tie me up in his basement to be his sex slave, for god's sake.

Maybe that will be the end of it. We can just move on from here.

I'm upstairs a few minutes later, alone, in the Health and Wellness room fixing the shelves when there's a noise behind me.

"Claire?"

Hunter is standing in the doorway, arms above his head, holding onto the frame, blocking the exit.

"I, um, just want to make sure there are no hard feelings about the other night."

I take a deep breath, "As long as you understand Hunter, I am not interested in you. And even if I were, what you did is not the way to go about it. You never put your hands on a woman like that. Not without an invitation."

"Jeepers Claire, I noticed that. You sure know how to get your point across. My head has been splitting for two days."

"I'm sorry Hunter. I probably overreacted. I was just surprised."

"Don't worry about it. I can get a little obnoxious and handsy when I drink. Thanks for helping me get home safe. You're a good kid."

"So are we ok?"

"We're ok. I'm heading out for subs. Want one?"

* * *

I go back to work, relieved the discussion is over. We can both just move on from here and work together without animosity till his contract is up.

What doesn't occur to me till later, is that Hunter did not, in fact, apologize.

Chapter 26

I feel nothing but despair. The feeling, I am now sure, that our vengeful God wishes me to feel. There is no hope. There is no way out of here. The night will last forever. The rain will never stop. I will be trapped between this world and the next forever. My precious baby is lost, somewhere out there. The only things I have for solace are the horrible sounds of my suffering horse, and the terrible gruesome countenance of my own severed head. I cannot save my baby. I cannot save poor Roger. I cannot even save myself.

How long shall God keep me here? One might ask, how long is eternity? No one is coming to save me. There is no one to help me.

How much time has passed? Is time longer here? Is it truly not yet morning? Must I suffer for what feels like eons but in life is but only a few minutes? Like a broken clock, stopped just before the last chiming of midnight.

Or is the opposite true? Has what felt to me like weeks actually been months, years, even decades of time? Have Elias and my parents finished mourning me long ago? Am I now just a memory? A brief life cut short, that they think of less and less?

Elias may have married. Brought forth other children. Thinking of me now only as something unfortunate that happened a long time ago? Or perhaps as a mistake he was lucky to get free of? Does he think of me at all? Does *anyone* think of me when they pass over this bridge? Am I just an unfortunate lesson in the value of listening to your parents and doing what you are told? A cautionary tale?

There is nowhere to go. Now that I am aware I am no longer mortal, the land is not as difficult to transverse. I wander. I lose track of myself. I will sit down underneath a tree to rest, and when I open my eyes again, suddenly find myself deeper in the forest. I head off in whatever the direction I am facing to get back to the bridge.

It does not matter which direction I travel in anyway; I end up back at the bridge. Purgatory is a circle. All roads, all paths, lead back to the same place.

I am sitting under the tree, on the land jutting out into the river when the voices come again. I look around and try to place the sound. I'm surprised to see that the night is not as dark as it was. It is lighter right now than I have seen it thus far. Though the rain still pours, and the thunder still rolls overhead. The voices are louder, and more clear. They are coming from the bridge. I jump to my feet.

They are calling my name.

I scream out to them. Hoping to somehow break the veil between our realities. To reach them. If I can hear them, perhaps they can hear me.

The voices call out again.

I close my eyes and pray with everything inside myself that I can connect with them somehow; before they leave, and I am left alone again. I feel a rolling storm inside me. Rising up from the bottom of my belly and forcing its way out of my mouth in a vicious primal scream. When I open my eyes I find myself no longer under the tree but in the middle of the bridge. I see them. Diaphanous shapes of people retreating into the darkness. Running.

Running away from me.

May 26th, 1880

Supper time is the most difficult. Sitting with my parents. Looking them in the eyes. Making polite conversation. Talking about my father's upcoming fishing trip. Discussing the state of the garden with my mother. Knowing I am about to deceive them. In a few days, I may never see them again.

What will that be like? I have spent every day of my life under the watchful eye of my parents. The idea of the two of us young people being on our own, not having to answer to anyone but each other, is exhilarating.

Elias is so skilled at his trade that it will not take us long to become established in Maryland. I have no doubt he will be a good provider for this child, and the others we will have. I have always dreamed of a large family. Being the only child of my parents, I have often felt lonely. The reasons for that are shrouded in mystery. They have not shared why, and I do not ask. I only know that my parents were older than what is typical when I was born. They had been childless for a long time before me.

I sometimes see a wistful look on my mother's face as she stares at the large boisterous families in church. While we sit silent, just the three of us. I knew long ago that I hoped for something different. I shall love to watch our many children grow up together. Loud, rough and tumble, and chaotic. With happiness always seated at our table.

I am sure my mother is suspicious. I can hardly manage to eat my breakfast, yet I eat the share of two people for supper. I have seen her watch me as I eat. She sees me retire early every night, too tired to stay awake a moment longer. I try to focus on my studies when we are together. I read the passages she puts me to but remember nothing of what I am supposed to learn.

I am hiding things in the barn. Pulling them from my dowry chest when I get the chance. Slipping them out in the mornings when I gather the eggs before my mother even rises from bed. The quilt I made, my clothing, my books. I cannot bear to leave my books.

Sunday is coming quickly, although the days themselves feel long. I am beset by worry. I toss and turn in my narrow bed at night. What if my father should somehow stumble upon the small pile of things hidden in the barn? What if the weather is bad? What if I am unable to hitch Roger to the buggy? What if Elias changes his mind or cannot get away from his house? That would be a disaster.

I try not to let the thoughts consume me, but it is very difficult. This is my life's happiness. It all hinges on this.

Chapter 27

Claire

July 2nd, 2023

I swore to myself I wasn't going to go to the beach during the summer season. But when I step out of Toby's car and the smells of the ocean and the boardwalk hit my face, I know it was a good idea. This salt air is incomparable. Technically, you can smell it all over Delaware, but here in Rehoboth, the scent is concentrated to something that is almost a perfume. I'd wear it if I could.

Yeah, this is my favorite beach. The breeze coming off the ocean always makes the summer heat less oppressive. I'm a Fall and Winter girl. Give me cozy sweaters and hot chocolate. I hate hot weather; I always feel gross and sticky. I thank God and Willis Carrier for air conditioning every year.

"First, I want to see the ocean. Then we need to ride the bumper cars. And the Paratrooper! We have to go through the Haunted Mansion!" Toby is bouncing on his feet, exuberant. He may actually still be twelve inside.

"Absolutely the Haunted Mansion," I said, "You know my mom rode that the first year it opened, in 1979. She was seven years old. I rode it when I was a kid too. It's practically a rite of passage."

Aiden is from Texas, so he has not experienced the wonder of the ocean front amusement park that is Funland, or even Rehoboth beach at all.

We managed to find a parking spot only three blocks down from the boardwalk, right on the main road. So we quickly make it to the wide weather-beaten boards that span the shore a half mile in either direction. The sun is blindingly bright. People are everywhere, laughing and talking. Families of all ages and varieties crowd everything. Looking at the ocean, running up and down the boards, washing the sand off their feet at the little cleaning stations, standing in lines for the huge variety of boardwalk food, that they eat while slowing wandering around. The experienced ones shielding their food from the seagulls flying overhead. The birds have no qualms about dive-bombing you in an attempt to get your food. I lost many a fry when I was a kid.

The arcade is lit up with flashing lights. Happy shrieks and laughter echo out from the rides at the back. The ever-present ocean breeze lifts my hair and spins it in crazy circles.

"Mother of all that is good and pure, *where* is that pizza I smell?" Aiden is sniffing the air like a bloodhound.

Toby giggled, "That my love, is Grotto Pizza. We will be eating there, trust me. It's heaven. We are going to give you the classic Rehoboth beach experience."

Two hours later the sun is going down, we have played Skee-ball where I lost, Whack a Mole where I kicked their asses and the basket toss that we sucked at as a group.

"What's next?" Toby chirps, still bouncing up and down.

"The bumper cars!"

"OMG, yes." I am excited. "They are one of my favorite rides. It made me feel so grown up when I was little. Like I was really driving."

"Not so fast, young lady. That might be just a bit much for a woman in your delicate condition." Toby said.

"You can't be serious. It's basically people driving around in a circle. There is very little bumping, you party pooper!"

"Nope! Your mother would kill me if I let anything happen to you. You can practice being Mom. Stand over there and watch us and cheer appropriately."

I stand placidly on the sidelines. Watching them pummel each other mercilessly. I'll be surprised if they don't get whiplash. Maybe he's right. I have to think about my safety. It's not just me anymore.

We ride the Paratrooper together. Grandpa Toby agreed it was safe enough. Whooping and hollering as it spins gently up through the air, giving us a view of the lights of the boardwalk spread out all the way down.

Finally we sit down to a giant pizza at Grottos, with an ice-cold pitcher of Birch Beer. A soda I love, but only seem to drink when I'm at the beach. Now the trip feels official. I'm finally relaxed, the worries of the past few weeks forgotten in the fun of just playing. I needed this. I should bring Jesse here.

"Mmmm. Omg. OMG. This is amazing. I can die happy, right now." Aiden is in some sort of Italian heaven. Grease and cheese dripping down his chin. Toby hands him napkins, then gives up and wipes his face for him.

"Eat up doll, we can take a walk on the beach after we hit the spooky ride," Toby said.

The Haunted Mansion at Funland has been a staple for decades. Now on its third generation of fans, no trip to the beach is complete without it. It's basically a haunted house ride. Individual cars move one by one suspended on an overhead track that spans two different floors. We all squash in one car together, me in the middle. The car takes off with a jolt and we bust through blood red doors and rise straight up immediately into the darkness. It's a maze of small rooms with locally made monster displays and jump scares. All in pitch-black darkness.

Toby and Aiden are squealing and laughing the whole way through. Enjoying every moment. It's fun, but I'm getting an uncomfortable feeling. I'm not sure what's wrong with me. I feel lonely and sad. There's a tightness in my chest. I'm on the verge of tears, and I don't know why.

We round a dark corner and come abruptly to a screaming, desiccated corpse, it's arms reaching out to us. In a flash, I see her in my mind, Maggie. Is she, right at this very moment, still lost? Is she real, or just a memory of a bad moment? Like the pictures you take for the insurance company after your house burns down. If she *is* real, could there be any way to help her? The car busts out through the exit doors.

"YES. That was awesome. Just like I remember it," Toby is smiling as he helps me from the car.

"I was doing fine but that loud truck with the skeleton freaked me out. I wasn't ready for that," Aiden laughs.

"You're kidding? I never would have guessed. The high-pitched screaming didn't give it away at all."

Toby sighs as we walk back out onto the board walk. There are a million lights and sounds coming from behind us and a wonderful view of the dark beach in front of us. You can see the waves crashing against the shore a few dozen yards away. It's so familiar. A core memory. I feel so at home here. Very little has changed in the last twenty years.

"God, it's beautiful. Come down to the ocean and make out with me under the stars. We can be a walking cliché," Aiden says as he walks away.

I glance at Toby, "I'm pretty sure he means you."

He smiles and follows him. I lag behind. I don't want to ruin a good moment. This is a romantic spot, regardless of the noise and lights close by. We walk onto the sand; they head down to the water's edge, and I stay above the tide line, trying to walk straight in the loose sand. My feet sink in it like quicksand. I'll be taking some of the beach home.

I wish Jesse were here. This would be so amazing if he were here. He arrives the 27th of August. A mere fifty-seven days away. Will I be able to keep the secret that long? It's quite literally growing inside me.

The guys wander back up to me, looking happy. I'm glad for them, and more than a little jealous. I've made a decision. Something I want to try while I have reinforcements.

"Do you guys have plans for tomorrow night?" I ask them.

"We are having dinner with my parents, but they always go to bed by nine. What did you have in mind?"

I look up at the moon overhead, just about to be full. "How's about tomorrow night we go try and talk to Maggie again?"

July 23rd, 2023

"So I get to meet the boyfriend tonight, huh?" Mom asks, "I heard so much about him from Toby the last time he was here."

She was at work when they arrived yesterday, scooping me up from the house and dragging me down the beach. The parking lot had been full at the store when we had driven past, not the best time for introductions.

"They are so cute together, wait till you see them." It's Talissa's night to close, so Mom and I will be heading out together later this afternoon. Hunter has the day off.

He's been behaving since the night I decked him. He'd better. Actually he's been pretty standoffish. Like it was my fault he's a disgusting pervert.

We've implemented a frequent buyers program. With club cards that track purchases to qualify for discounts. It meant yet another computer program for Hunter to install and troubleshoot. Along with teaching us mildly computer literate women how to run it.

"So what time are they coming?"

"9:30, I think. We are going to have another go at Maggie's Bridge. There's a full moon tonight."

"Fun! But you be careful down there, little lady. No shaking my grandbaby loose. You already rocked him around on the thrill rides."

"Yes, mother dear. I will be careful, but I don't consider what's at Funland *thrill rides*."

"Now what can I feed you, my spawn?"

Mom has been nothing but supportive since she found out about the baby. She's great to have nearby when I'm sick in the mornings. So far I have not thrown up, but the nausea is there from the minute I wake up until lunchtime. I hope it eases up soon. The pre-natal vitamins I get to choke down are the size of cough drops.

Also, seriously, I have to pee every five minutes! I thought that happens at the *end* of the pregnancy, when I look like a beached whale, not at the beginning. These last few days I've been up every few hours all night and running to the bathroom ten times a day at work. I'm seriously considering wearing a diaper. It'll give me practice for when the baby comes.

* * *

The car pulls up later as Mom and I are sitting on the matching orange love seats watching Psycho. I love this one. Anthony Perkins was yummy. Sadly, I was born too late to ever *not* know it was Norman dressed as his mother.

Mom jumps off her couch and flings the door open. I swear, she's like a puppy when company comes over.

"Toby! Come here and give me a hug," she wraps her arms around him while eyeing Aiden over his shoulder, "And who is this hunk of burning love you have here with you?" She releases Toby and reaches out, taking Aiden's hands in hers.

"Claire," Toby calls out to me, "Did she embarrass you this much the first time you introduced her to Jesse?

"Worse! She whipped out her phone and started showing him a video of the macaws having sex. For scientific educational purposes, she claims. The worst part is, he was into it! Sat with her for an hour taking about gestation, cloacas and nesting schedules. I thought I would die of embarrassment."

"Hello Mrs. O'Brien, "I'm Aiden Allen, nice to meet you. Please do not show me bird porn. I am young and innocent and wish to remain that way."

"Yeah, right," Toby snickers.

"Come sit down. You can finish watching the movie with us while we catch up. Claire, move over here with me and let them sit together."

We finish the movie. Me resting my head on the back of the couch, Mom and Aiden chatting about Tim's tour, the bookstore, and Aiden's job as a sous chef at a restaurant in Baltimore's Inner Harbor.

Mom stands and stretches when the movie ends.

"All right kids, I'm off to bed. It was great to finally meet you Aiden," She points a finger at the two of them, "You both better take care of my girl tonight. Or I'll hunt you down."

"Yes ma'am."

"We have less than an hour before midnight," I say, "I want you guys to listen to what was recorded on the spirit box. See if you can hear it too, or if I'm imagining things."

"Ooh, what did you hear?" Toby said, "All I could hear was nothing, plus a little static."

"Ah yes, but it's the static you need to listen to."

Toby flops across my bed, the headphones jammed into his ears. I press play. He listens closely but I don't see that spark of recognition that I had. "I don't hear anything. But my hearing sucks, you know that. Aiden, you try."

I start to feel disappointed. I'm *sure* I heard crying. It's faint, but it's there. It's not my imagination. I watch Aiden take the headphones as Toby replays it.

At first, Aiden's face stays the same. Then I see his brow knit a little, a puzzled expression coming over him.

"Wait, play it again." He turns it up as far as it will go, "I can hear you guys really loud, but Claire is right, there's something in between your questions. It sounds like a woman far away…crying?"

207

I smile triumphantly. "Told ya."

"That's crazy. Was anyone there with you?"

"Toby and I were alone. That's why I want to go back. I don't know how we can possibly help her, but I want to try. There are only three of us, but the moon *is* full. We may be able to pick up something else. Are you in?"

"Let's hit it. Grab the box." Toby is up and heading for the door. He glances back at Aiden who looks anxious.

"Um, I'm not really sure about this. I know I said last night I was up for it, but this is a little...real. I'm not super into being terrified."

"Hon, even if she is there, it's not like she's going to come out of the darkness waving her severed head around. I've been there a dozen times and I've never actually seen her. Never been hurt. Yeah, we've heard some stuff, but that's all that happens. I promise, I'll protect you."

I laugh, Aiden has a good five inches and forty-five pounds on Toby's slight frame. I'd like to see how that would go.

"Yeah alright, but if I die, it's all your fault."

One of these days I'm going to have to break down and admit to Toby that I actually did see Maggie that night. Right now is not the time. Aiden would absolutely freak out, and I really want him to come with us.

Five minutes later we pull over just past the bridge. The full moon is amazingly bright. It really makes the difference on being able to see at all. Toby and I get out of the car. Aiden hasn't moved from the passenger seat, staring out the window into the woods.

"Babe, come on. It's ok. I promise, I won't let her take you without a fight."

"Toby, that's not even a little bit funny."

"I mean it, we can sacrifice Claire first. I'll just chuck her right at the screaming ghoul. You'll be perfectly safe. Just come on out here with us."

Toby likes his humor on the obnoxious side sometimes, but it does the trick. Aiden climbs out his door and comes around to join us.

"Let's line up down the center. Claire, you stand between us and hold the box. We will spread out on either side of you."

"Ready guys? Let's call her first," I tell them. I press record, and we start.

"Maggie, I have your baby!"

"Maggie, I have your baby!"

"Maggie, I have your baby!"

We wait in the silence. Thankfully, no bats attack my head this time. Although the mosquitoes are having a feast. I slap one dead against my face. Yuck. The humidity presses in. It's like I'm breathing hot water.

There's a noise, very faint. An animalistic noise. Strangled. Desperate. Coming from somewhere under my feet. "Do you hear that? What *is* that? Toby? Is it a trapped animal?" I kneel to the ground.

Aiden looks gob smacked. He starts peering into the star lit woods in every direction, looking for something.

Toby gets on his knees with me at the center of the bridge. "I hear it. I don't know what the hell that is. It's not a woman crying, that's for sure. Could it be the sound of the water moving underneath us? There's so little room, isn't it just a pipe running under the road?"

The noise cuts off abruptly. The night is silent. Aiden walks over to join us, "I know what it was," he whispers, "I'd know that noise anywhere. I grew up on a farm. It's a horse... a horse in pain."

"Oh my god," I can hardly speak, "How could a horse be underneath us? *I* couldn't even fit in that pipe, let alone a full-sized horse..." my voice trails off. The air feels heavy around me. It can't be a living horse. Maggie's? God, was he trapped here too? I hadn't considered that at all. I speak out louder now, "Maggie! Are you here? Let us help you! What do you need?"

I have a sudden inspiration and start calling out questions to her, "Maggie!"

"Did you love Elias Hastings?"

"Are you here waiting for him?

"I found his picture! I know what happened to him!"

"Talk to me! Let me help you!"

"Is he the father of your baby?"

Nothing comes back to me but the sound of our rapid breathing.

"Would it be alright with you guys if we got the hell out of here? I don't like this; I don't want to be here anymore. At all." Aiden is visibly upset. He's breathing so fast I'm afraid he might hyperventilate.

Toby looks guilty, "Of course babe. Let's go. Besides, maybe we caught the horse sound on the recording." He walks Aiden, who is visibly shaking, back to the car.

Aw, now I feel like a shit. The whole idea of Maggie is a lot to take in on the first night you come here. I picture Jesse frozen, staring off into the water, unable to move over to where we are all huddled together. Only able to when her scream pierced the silence. He's spent years trying to explain away the experience.

We are silent on the short drive back to the house. We pull into the driveway. Toby reaches to turn off the ignition, Aiden speaks up, "Babe, can we go back to your parents? Right now? No offence Claire, but my anxiety is getting the best of me, and I need to not be here. I want to get away."

"Hey sure. It's late anyway. I have to work tomorrow, and you guys need to rest if you are going to see the fireworks in Ocean City. Just call me before you head home. Let me know you're ok." Toby smiles apologetically as I climb out of the car and watch them back out and drive away.

Inside the dark house I head up the stairs, spirit box in hand. I flip on the bedroom light and shut the door. Snatch the headphones from the blanket and plug them in. Already

211

turning up the volume. As before, it starts with our voices. There is nothing, no sound, in between our shouting. I hear us talk about hearing a noise. I hear talking about what it might be. I can't hear the horse at all. That's a disappointment.

Then I hear me ask her the questions. There is static, oscillating in and out. And there! There is a voice. It's not crying, it's speaking. I sit in stunned silence, listening.

"Did you love Elias Hastings?"

"endless"

"Are you here waiting for him?"

"trap"

"I found his picture! I know what happened to him!"

"nowhere"

"Talk to me. Let me help you!"

"nothing."

"Is he the father of your baby?"

"lost"

Shaken, I drop the spirit box. She is trapped. She sounds so sad. I'll never know how far along she was in her pregnancy when she passed away, but I know how much I have come to love my baby in less than a week. If I were to lose him it would devastate me.

There has to be some way to help her. I grab my phone and pull up Google.

Chapter 28

Maggie

May 31, 1880

Midnight

I am losing track of myself more and more. The times when I am alone are so long that feel I have floated away. I can remember my life. I see the images vividly in my mind. Moments with Elias, living with my parents, playing with the animals on the farm when I was a young girl. All of these more real to me than the place that I now am.

The people come. When I hear them calling, I mostly cannot see them in the darkness. They are just voices in the rain. I scream into the storm, but nothing happens. They do not help me. Why would people come and not help me? Do they come just to taunt me? To tease me with what I can no longer have? In life, people were not so malevolent. We looked out for one another. We took care of each other.

There have been a few occasions when I can see glimpse those who come to the bridge. The rain seems not as loud, the woods appear brighter. At those times I can hear the voices clearly.

In the brief moments when their shapes appear I scream as loud as I am able, but all I do is make them run. Sometimes they are laughing as they go. How do I reach them? I am not a joke.

The longer this goes on the more I change. I no longer feel any of my body. The numbness is complete. I cannot make my legs move, nor my arms. Not the way I did before. I learned that anger and despair alone move me. It can not only move my arms and legs, but it can change where I am in this place. When I let the emotions overtake me I will suddenly find myself somewhere else nearby. On the bridge, in the trees, in the water. But never away from here. Always, I am here. The bridge and these woods. It is my prison.

I spend endless stretches of time laying under the trees, cradling my own head, letting desolation overwhelm me till I fall asleep.

The sleep of oblivion. The sleep of the damned. I do not dream anymore.

May 31, 1880

Morning

I wake with a start, gasping for breath. I was dreaming of water. My head was trapped under water, and I could not breathe. I rise quickly from bed and slip down the stairs to get a drink. I look around the kitchen. Today is the day! This is the last day I will be in this room, this house. I run my fingers along the cabinets, caressing the wood. They are so beautiful. Mother had all her friends in to marvel over them. Every woman leaving with the intent of hiring Elias to redo their own. I will miss these.

I laugh to myself. I am taking the craftsman with me! Surely I can have cabinets like this in my own home. As many as I wish. Elias can build much more than cabinets. Furniture, toys, anything made with wood. He is skilled in so many ways. Someday our home will rival the nicest houses in town. I smile, eager for the day to pass so my adventure can begin.

Everything I do this morning is something I do here for the last time. I made my bed, for the last time. I will soon collect the eggs, for the last time. How I wish I could take some of the hens. I love them so. Their fussiness. Their indignant look when I retrieve the warm eggs from underneath their soft feathers. Their little skirmishes and disagreements among themselves always amuse me.

Will our parents look for us? My father trying to hunt me down to drag me back home by my hair? I doubt it. Once he deduces the reason for our secret departure he will be only too ready to cast me aside. It hurts that his love is so conditional.

"Maggie, dear, how are you this beautiful morning? Feeling alright?"

"Mother! I am quite well, thank you," I smile, determined to act normal and be pleasant. "After I gather the eggs, and get myself dressed properly, may I help you with breakfast?"

"Of course, child. What would you like to do tonight? Your father is leaving for Georgetown after church. We shall be on our own. Oh! Shall we play checkers? We haven't done that in so long!"

"He..is?" Dread steals over me. "How long will he be gone? Is he taking Roger and the buggy?'

"Of course he is dear. They will be home Tuesday; we will get along just fine here for two days. He is boarding at the hotel. He has a meeting with a lawyer. Something about getting his last will and testament together." She sees my worried face. "Not to worry love. Your father is not ill. I believe it is all to set things up for you. He may be gruff, but he knows Elias and you will need to make a home together in a couple years. I believe he just wants to be ready. He and I are not young anymore."

I grab the back of a kitchen chair to steady myself and sit weakly down. If the buggy and Roger are gone…how will I leave? I do not trust our other horse to ride. He is young and freshly broken. Very spirited. I am not experienced. Roger and I have grown up together. I learned to ride on his back.

I will tell Elias that we must wait. At least a few days. We cannot wait long, any day my condition will be too obvious to hide. Perhaps I can send him a note at church. Will he know to look in the hymnal?

Resigned, I go to dress in my room. Combing my hair into a high bun at the back. I'm wearing my nicest dress. It took me such a long time to make. I am a good seamstress, but slow. This is the first dress I have made all on my own, a beautiful polonaise. Using the fabric given to me by my parents for Christmas. I toiled many hours with the fine dark blue cloth.

Setting in the many pleats, ruffles, and gathers so they hang perfectly around to the bustle in the back. Once dressed I hastily write a note to Elias, hoping he can read the words. My hand is shaking.

Father is silent as we ride to church. I too am silent, too full of nerves to speak. The note is tucked into my sleeve. What if I place it in there and he does not see? What if he does not check, confident that our plans are set? Sure that I will be coming to him as soon as my parents are asleep for the night? Will he think I changed my mind. Will he be angry?

As we mount the church steps; I am determined to catch Elias's eye as we sit. So he knows I have left him a message.

My eyes go immediately to his usual bench, and the empty space next to his mother where he should be sitting.

Chapter 29

Claire

August 14th, 2023

Remember how I said it was ok, because I had only felt nauseous but hadn't actually gotten sick? Well, those days are long gone. Three months along now and the morning sickness changed from a general queasy feeling most of the time, to straight up barfing every morning. This pregnancy business is no joke. I'm glad the bathroom is close to my bedroom.

Mom hired some additional help at the store already. Two part time workers, both in their forties. They each know a lot about books and have quickly fit right in with us. I work afternoons, but Mom won't let me lift anything heavy. Which to her, means anything over five pounds. I'm allowed to work the register, help people over the phone, maybe walk them to a bookshelf, but anything more and she does it herself or gets someone else to do it.

Talissa has figured it out. Or Mom flat out told her and won't admit it. She's been careful not to talk about it in front of the other employees. I want to tell Jesse before the whole world knows. Lucky for me, it's not showing at all yet. And I've been so sick that so far I haven't really gained any weight.

Jesse will be here less than two weeks. His plane arrives at BWI airport in Maryland at noon on the 27th. Which, with the traffic, means he should be here down here by midnight.

Hunter has cut his hours back. Our computer system seems to be working the way it should. I've even been able to solve a couple problems myself without having to resort to texting or calling him. It's a big relief. The atmosphere of the store is different when he's not here. It's hard to describe how. The air is lighter. I don't feel like I have to check over my shoulder every five minutes. I'll be glad when his contract is up.

I've done some research on freeing trapped spirits. Unfortunately, it's all kind of vague. Talk about white candles, sage smudging, stuff like that. That's great for a house, but what about a spirit trapped in an open space? I can't sage the entire woods. I've felt too tired and sick to venture back down there since we went before the 4th of July. But Maggie hasn't left the back of my mind.

We had a full moon on the 1st of this month. That means we have another on the 31st, the so called 'blue moon'. I read that it is easier for spirits to make contact during a blue moon, just like Mom said. So I guess the blue moon makes it more intense, somehow? I know it was supposed to be a full moon when Maggie died. All the stories about her say it was. Who's to say it wasn't the extra power of a blue moon that trapped her? What if she died on a particularly cosmically auspicious night, and it hasn't let go?

I researched all the blue moons in the latter 19th century. There were several around the appropriate time: July 1872, March 1877, May 1880, August 1883. Any one of these could be the day it happened.

I'm going back down August 31st and try to contact her again. Take the spirit box with me. Try to see if I can talk to her. If I miss this chance, I won't have another until May of 2026. Three years from now. So I'm hunting the stacks in the metaphysical section for any advice, since I really don't know what I am doing.

'Claire?" I hear Mom call, "Are you in here? You ok, sweetie?" I'm sitting on the floor, behind the standing bookshelf, out of her view. I swear, she's such a mother hen.

"Yes, Mother! I am trying to straighten the shelves," I come out and show her I am still alive, "When I get around to running a marathon or lifting the store off the foundation I'll be sure to let you know."

She rolls her eyes, "I need you. Can you help?" I follow her to the small upstairs office, "I'm confused about the computer. I hit some button that I'd never seen before, and now I've got this weird screen asking me for a password."

"What in the world were you trying to do?"

"There was a little icon on the desktop. I sat down to do payroll and I decided to change the background photo first. I was wasting time really. Payroll gives me a headache. The new picture came up and I noticed it down in the corner. It was visible once I'd changed the picture. So I clicked it. This is what popped up. Now I can't get off the screen. What is it?"

"Looks like password protected files of some sort. I've never noticed it before either. Do you think it's Hunter's?"

"He wouldn't have any private stuff on our work computer. Maybe it has something to do with security. I can ask him when he's in on Thursday." I manage exit out to the desktop screen and pull the POS system backup.

"Go ahead and do the payroll, Mom. I'll see what I can figure out it later." That's weird. It looks kind of suspish to me. But I am not the computer expert that Hunter is. Not by a long shot.

Thursday is two days away. Plenty of time for me to fool around with it.

* * *

When I let myself into the house later, Mom is not home yet, even though we left at the same time. She must have stopped at the store. Her obsession with feeding me grows bigger by the day. Tim's office door is closed. He came home a couple weeks ago, to Mom's great relief. I don't shout a welcome, I don't want to disturb him.

"What are you doing!?"

"Hello?"

"HELLO!"

"I wanna come OUT!

"Num nums!"

"MA? MA!"

"SLUT!"

Jesus, this is not the house to try and sneak into. I hear Tim start to laugh.

"Sorry for the racket!" I yell, "It's just me!"

"I'm used to it!" he yells back, "Come see me!"

I let myself into his office. He is surrounded by four different computer monitors, stacks of books, each one bookmarked with a dozen slips of paper. I see probably twenty empty, dried out coffee cups. This is a fantastic room. I get inspired just standing in it. I want one just like it someday.

"So how is the world of the Native American in the old West?"

"Heartbreaking. How is the fast-paced world of retail book sales?"

"Riveting…" I sit on the arm of the soft wide chair near the desk. The only empty spot in the room. "Tim, what made you decide to write American history novels?"

"Ahh, my mom was a history teacher, and my dad was a civics teacher. I grew up in a house where discussions about the Civil War were common at the dinner table. I guess I just was always fascinated by it. I majored in History in college, always figuring I would be a teacher like my parents. But I got into writing about halfway through. Figured I'd give it a shot. It's worked out so far." He laughed.

"I think I want to give it a real try. But fiction. I deal better with stuff I make up than trying to make sense of the past. That seems so intimidating."

"Just remember, the past is all out there. It already happened. I just have to find all the information, try and understand it, and present it in a way that people haven't considered and want to read about. In fiction, it's all on you. The whole world.

"But hey, write something. I'll read it. If it's good I can send it to my agent. The next great writer is always out there." He winked at me.

"That would be amazing! Thank you!" The idea terrifies me. Putting a story out there. Being judged by strangers. My family has always enjoyed the stories I write but that's a totally different thing.

I'm still going to do it though.

"MA!"

'Good baby!"

"I love you."

"I'm a good boy!"

"MA!"

"Your mother must be home," he laughed, "I can always tell. They are quite the warning signal."

"Humans?" we hear her shout, "People I love? Where are you guys? I'm making spaghetti carbonara. You have 45 minutes!"

"I swear, I think that woman is trying to keep me here forever with food."

"She is nervous that you will move to the other side of the country with her grandbaby. So, you may be right."

August 15th, 2023

I arrive at the store early this afternoon. I want some time before I'm on the clock to try and solve the computer mystery.

"Good afternoon, Talissa," I smile at her standing at the front counter running a customer's credit card. The customer, sunburned, and in just a bathing suit with a long shirt and flip flops, turns to eye me up and down.

"Well look who's here. To what do I owe the pleasure of seeing your face two hours early?"

"Just some computer stuff I want to do without any other responsibilities to distract me," I smile as I head up the stairs, stepping to the side to allow two middle aged women with their arms full of books, to move down past me.

I sit my travel mug of woefully decaffeinated coffee on the desk, drop my bag on the floor and shut the door behind me. The smallest room in the house, it was a former sitting room, just off the largest bedroom. This office is really just a storage room with a computer. Mom uses it for paperwork, payroll, ordering, etc. The screen for all the security cameras is behind the front desk on a dedicated monitor. So the person working the counter can keep an eye on the whole store at once. The desk chair is an old one of Tim's. Broken in, but still comfortable.

I turn on the monitor and the screen comes to life. I see the regular icons displayed as usual. But Mom is right, down in the right corner is a tiny icon, practically a dot, really. I'd have never notice it before. It blended seamlessly into the old background photo of the macaws sitting on their giant bird stand staring out the front windows at the Nanticoke River. This new photo of the front of the store made the small transparent square just visible.

I click it, and it brings up the same screen Mom found yesterday. If I were Hunter, what password would I use?

* * *

This is pissing me off. Talk about frustrated. I have tried his whole name, his first name, his last name, parts of his last name, his birthdate. The name of the store, book titles he told me he loved, and any number of other things. Nothing. His phone number, even his social security number off his payroll information. It must be one of those really secure letter/number combinations you're always told to use but I never do because it's too damn hard to remember. And I am in no way a hacker.

Oh forget this. I give up in frustration and head downstairs to start my shift. The store is pretty quiet today, only three or four people milling about in the rooms, clearly browsing for fun and soaking up the charm of the place. The advertising worked great, but I think that word of mouth is working even better.

Talissa is retrieving the books left randomly on shelves where they don't belong. I believe deep down; people have no idea how to be neat. They will drop anything, anywhere.

225

"Solve your problems?"

"Not yet, but there is always hope."

I take the spot behind the front counter, in the padded chair Mom brought in just for me. Evidently, even my butt needs to be comfortable while I am pregnant. I start processing an order for an early edition. We've started getting a lot of these. Older folks who want to replace their well-worn paperback favorites with a beautiful original hardback.

"The Collector," by John Fowles. Printed in 1963. That shouldn't be too hard, it's not that old. I've never heard of it. I check the used book sites and find quite a few for almost two grand. Yikes. The customer's budget is $500 and no higher. For that I can find a first edition fifth printing. Not in perfect shape but very good, for $325. With our fee added they are still well under budget. I buy it.

I wonder, do we have a new copy here in the store? It's an old book but Mom has a habit of buying popular books regardless of age.

"Talissa," she is in the next room, "Can you come here? Are you busy?"

She appears, "Are you ok? What is it? Are you sick?"

I groan. Do people think pregnant women are about to explode or something? I pride myself on being fairly self-sufficient. This being treated as some fragile flower about to collapse any moment is getting old.

"I'm fine. I'm just wondering if you've ever heard of a book called The Collector?"

"John Fowles? Oh yes. It's excellent. Double POV. This soft spoken, outcast loner guy wins some money in the lottery and buys a house in a remote area to kidnap this young woman. He keeps her in the basement and expects her to fall in love with him. We have it, I'll go grab it."

She's back momentarily, handing the book to me. "They made an excellent movie adaptation. I'd bet money your mom has it."

"You'd probably win. She has everything."

I'm caught up with the work so I can sit here and start reading. It grabs me right from the start. This guy, you almost feel *sympathetic* towards him. Like...why wouldn't she want to come live in his basement? She should be grateful at all the trouble he went to. Look at all the nice stuff he bought her! It's natural that she would get to know and love him. Obviously. How dare she try to escape? He's just in love with her. Doesn't she get that?

These thoughts make me feel skeevy. He also reminds me of Hunter in a way. I can too easily picture Hunter bringing food down to a tiny dark room he's set up with everything I like.

But, what if he *is* a little obsessed with me? An idea, a terrible idea, comes into my head. I stand and slowly climb the stairs back to the office.

I sit, flick the monitor back on and click the tiny icon, bringing back the password box.

I slowly type out...C...l...a...i...r...e and hit Enter. The screen immediately changes.

I'm in.

Thumbnails appear. Dozens of thumbnails. I scroll down. They just keep going and going. What looks to be over a hundred video thumbnails. I click one.

The screen fills with an image of Mom and me, standing in the Children's Book room, talking about who knows what.

I'm baffled. What are these? The regular security videos? I didn't know we recorded anything. I though our system is just visual, so we can watch for shoplifters. This video shows the store not even open to the public yet. There are boxes stacked everywhere. This must be from back in mid-May. Maybe it's a test of some kind.

I click another, and there's me on top of a ladder, the camera right in my face. It's me adjusting the placement for Hunter. My lips are moving, I'm saying something. A soft mumbling noise comes out of the computer. I reach and turn the volume up. It's my voice. These have *sound* too??

I click through more.

Me, manning the front counter, chewing on the end of a pencil.

Me, in the Vintage room surrounded by stacks of old books.

Me, in the Horror room organizing shelves.

Me, in the Children's room reading a picture book to a little girl.

Me, having a conversation with Talissa by the front windows.

Me asleep. Oh my God.

My eyes widen in horror looking at myself. There's my face resting on a pillow, sitting at the table in the break room.

Video after video. The only thing consistent in them is me.

My shoulders rise up somewhere around my ears as my body curls in on itself. My knees press tight together. I honestly feel violated. He's recording me and saving all the videos. He has my voice, my face, saved forever. Who's to say he didn't set this up somehow so that he can watch these anytime he wants…from his house…from his phone? Oh god, when he's in bed at night? What if he's watching me right now? We really have no idea where he may have set up cameras. This is repulsive. Mom *trusted* him. He could literally have done anything. Can he see the video feed live from his house or does it just record here? I jump up and search the room. I check every shelf, every box, every corner. There is no obvious camera in here. What if it's hidden? A tiny little camera tucked inside something innocuous? If he is doing this, what *else* is he doing? Does he have Mom's passwords? Access to the store bank account? The credit cards?

This wonderful place, that I have grown to love so much, feels like a trap. I suppress the urge to run out the door.

Vomit rises up in the back of my throat with an audible burp and I run for the bathroom, dropping to my knees in front of the toilet, painfully losing everything I've managed to eat today.

I sit on the cold tile of the bathroom floor, waiting for my stomach to settle and try to think. Is that illegal? It must be. I know video is not illegal. People are on video everywhere they go. But what about audio? Isn't it the law that at least one of the parties has to know it's happening? Right now that feels like not enough. At the very least it's an invasion of privacy. I have to tell Mom. I check my phone; she's due in any minute.

I wipe my face and stand up carefully. Rinsing my mouth out in the sink, I feel my legs are still shaking. I head downstairs, stopping to close the office door on my way out.

* * *

"I'm calling the police," Mom is apoplectic, "This is ridiculous. That crazy stalker *asshat* is not setting foot back in this store." She wraps her arms around me. "How did I not realize? I should have seen it. Honey, I'm so sorry."

Talissa looks stunned. She has hardly spoken since I told them what I found. She knew of course that he liked me. But this...this is so much more. I'm sure she feels guilty, she's the one who found him in the first place.

I had showed them the videos the moment Mom arrived. Her confusion quickly turning to anger.

"Hello?" she says into the phone, "Who should I talk to if I want to report staking behavior from an employee?"

That makes it seem even more real. My knees feel weak, and I drop into one of the soft chairs by the window.

"They are sending an officer over right now to confiscate the videos. Claire, he's going to want to talk to you. Are you up for it?"

"If it means we don't have to see Hunter in this store again, then yes. Let's get it over with."

Officer Little is very kind. He sits across from me and listens to the whole sordid tale. I tell him everything: all the text messages he sent, his invading my personal space, the dinner with his inappropriate remarks. I watch Mom's face lose the bright color that had suffused her cheeks. When I get to the part about him touching my leg and me smacking him with my phone, she turns white.

"Oh my God. Oh, honey. Why didn't you tell me?"

"He was helping us. I didn't want to rock the boat."

"Claire, you are more important than the damn store, you should have told me!"

"Well, I can't say for sure the legality or illegality of what you have here. If you want to press charges over the physical assault that's up to you. You'll need to go over the terms of your contract in regard to the videos."

"He's fired. Absolutely fired for putting his hands on you. He won't be setting foot in here again," Mom is shaking, "I'll be calling a lawyer."

Chapter 30

I have never known fury like this. It fills me completely. Throughout every part of my being. I was a good person. I cared for my family. I went to church every Sunday. I prayed for forgiveness for my mistakes. I was kind to everyone. I did everything that was asked of me. There is no reason I should be punished this way. I have been here for an endless amount of time. It is limitless. When the people come, I no longer try to reach them for help. I hate them. I want them to suffer as badly as I am suffering. To make them feel as frightened as I have been for an eternity.

I want to hurt them.

When I hear them, I scream. When I see their ephemeral shapes, the fury wells up inside me. I am not able to touch them. I reach out to them but cannot feel them. It brings me peace when they run in horror. They could help me if they wanted to. But they don't.

Their fear makes me laugh. I can feel the energy from it crackle through the air. If they are not going to save me I will make them leave me alone.

May 31st, 1880

Afternoon

From the outside I appear calm and proper. On the inside I am screaming...HE IS NOT HERE! Where is he? How is he going to know I cannot meet him tonight? His parents are here. They smile politely and nod as we file past them. I take my seat, my mind racing. Now what do I do? Perhaps he is also making preparations for us to leave. Taking this time when he can be alone in his house to secret things away so that he may retrieve them quickly tonight. His tools? Supplies to care for Roger and the buggy? Confident that he can take this time because our plans are firmly in place. He doesn't know how desperately I need to see him.

All through the next hour as our preacher drones on and on about the importance of honesty, my thoughts are in a whirl. I turn the problem over and over in my mind. I have to know where he is.

I sip the note into the hymnal anyway. If I do not show up tonight he may think to check it.

When the service ends and we stand to file out, I time my steps carefully, so that Arba Hastings and his wife are waiting at the end of their row as I approach. I demurely signal that they should precede me. They smile, and walk ahead, meaning our families are next to each other as we come out into the bright sunshine.

Elias's mother turns to speak to me. "Good afternoon, young Maggie. How are you on this beautiful Sunday?"

"I am doing quite well, thank you ma'am. How are you and um...your family?"

"Doing just fine. Although I am short a son on this Lord's Day."

"Is he well?" I try to keep the worry out of my voice and merely sound curious.

"He is fine. Working the sabbath. I don't approve, but he is determined to finish the job for the Morgan family before the sun sets. Just as stubborn as his father about working."

"Well, good luck to him. I hope he accomplishes his goal. It's commendable that he is so dedicated."

"Thank you dear." She gives me a rare smile.

My thoughts are a jumble the whole ride home. He is completing the job so that he can be paid. So that we can have a bit more money to make our start with. Perhaps he also does not wish to leave the job unfinished. He will be expecting me tonight. What will he do if I do not come? Will he be angry? Will he give me the chance to explain?

"I will be heading out in a couple of hours. I want to have a rest before I leave. Maggie, will you take care of Roger when we arrive? Unhitch him and feed him. Let him rest a bit. We will wait to have our meal till I awaken. So we may eat together. Is that alright?"

"Of course Robert, the stew will keep."

"Please pack my overnight bag while I am sleeping."

"Yes, Robert."

In the barn I unhitch Roger, rub him down and feed him. Kissing him softly on his velvety nose. I wander back and see the pile of hay that covers my secret belongings. I will need to move these back into the house. They may be discovered if we must wait another week. The idea brings tears to my eyes. I do not want to wait. I want to run. To get away with the man that I love and my precious baby. I reach down and rub the hard, gently rounded belly hidden under the voluminous skirts. He is safe. He must remain safe. He must remain with his parents who love him.

Should I run away now? Just hitch Roger back up, put my things in the buggy and go. Adrenaline rushes through me. Just as I am about to start moving I realize; Elias is not home. How would I explain my sudden arrival at the Hastings home in the middle of the afternoon? I am not thinking clearly.

I could run away at night on foot! Just take what I can carry and head off down the road. We can ride double on Elias's horse. No, that will not work either. We need the buggy. We cannot take any of what we need simply on horseback. Nor can we move fast.

"Maggie! Come inside dear," my mother calls to me.

I cast a last, desperate glance around me, praying for a solution to appear out of thin air, but it does not. I walk dispiritedly into the house.

"I'm heading upstairs to see to your father's belongings. Will you check the stew please? It may need more spices."

"Of course."

It is simmering in a large pot over the fire. I lift the lid and stir it gently. Large chunks of venison and vegetables give off a wonderful rich smell. I lift a spoonful to my lips. Hot, delicious. Not quite as peppery as we usually have. I sit down the spoon and open the cabinet holding all our spices and medicinal tinctures. I add several dashes of pepper, stir, and try it again. Much better.

Returning the pepper to the shelf, my eyes fall on our small collection of palliatives. The thin glass bottle of One Night Cough Syrup is nestled among the jars. I have had it before. Just a bit. Two years ago I had been taken with a wicked fever. My mother had dosed me with it, and I had slept the entire day away. I know for a fact she often uses a single drop to treat the pain of her monthlies. Hers are particularly bad. Often confining her to bed for several days. Even that much of the medicine will make her sleep for hours. To my recollection, I have never seen my father take it. A horrifying idea begins to form in my mind.

Could I dose him somehow? Make him too sleepy to travel? Do I dare? By the time he awoke in the morning, I would be long gone.

How? I certainly cannot convince him to take it. I have to dose him some other way. I light up inside with excitement and daring. It could work, I could do it! I take the slim bottle and slip it into the pocket in my dress.

MAGGIE I HAVE YOUR BABY

Mother and I spend the next two hours reading our bibles in the quiet living room. Talking very little. Mother engrossed in the scriptures and I too nervous to concentrate. Surely God will forgive this slight sin I want to commit in the light of protecting my unborn child.

My father rises shortly before the hour of three, dresses and comes out of their bedroom. Smiling, my mother stands to get supper on the table. "Robert, I hope you are rested for your trip."

"I shall be fine. I should reach the hotel in just a few hours. Plenty of time to settle in before dark."

"Can I prepare coffee for you, Father?

"I'd enjoy that Maggie, thank you."

I grab the boiling kettle hanging over the fire. Dropping in several scoops of ground coffee. I stir it and leave it to steep and let the grounds settle while I help mother set the table. Pulling down my father's cup I glance over my shoulder. Mother has her back to me dishing stew into bowls at the table. Carefully I slip the glass bottle out of my skirts. Uncorking it, I quickly tip it over and place a large dollop in the cup. Hopefully, that will be enough. Father is much larger than either my mother or myself. I plunge the cork back in the top and slide it into my pocket just as my mother appears behind me.

"Maggie, are you ready?"

"Yes Mother. I am going to pour the coffee, then I will sit down."

237

I pour the steaming liquid in, watching the medicine swirl and disappear. I add a heaping teaspoon of sugar and stir as I carry it to his place. I hope he cannot detect the taste. It has a bitter flavor.

We always hold hands during the blessing. I sit to the right of my father. Taking his hand in mine, I cast my eyes down as I bow my head.

Our hands are clasped directly over the cup of coffee. I can feel the gentle steam against my wrist. Am I really sure I want to do this? It is absolutely wrong. If I do not wish to sink to this level, I need to stop him now.

"Please bless this food to the nourishment of our bodies, and thus to thy service. In Jesus's name, Amen."

"Amen"

I do nothing. My desire for what I want overshadows any guilt I feel. He finishes the prayer and immediately picks up the cup and takes a hearty swallow. Then another. And then a third. Sitting the cup back down I see only a small bit left. A grimace crosses his face, and he glances at the cup.

He knows I did it! He can taste it! He will figure out everything! However, just picks up his spoon and begins to eat.

I glance often at my father as I eat my stew; forcing it down as I will need my strength. I watch him closely, waiting for the drug to take effect. How long does it take? It will not do for him to fall asleep after he is already on the road.

"There were some clouds in the sky this afternoon. It may be wishful thinking but perhaps we will get some rain tonight."

"I hope so Robert. The garden will not be able to go on much longer without. Although I do wish for you to reach Georgetown before it begins. No sense in you getting wet."

He continues to talk to my mother as if nothing were amiss. As if his own daughter had not drugged him and is now waiting for him to fall asleep.

I rise and get second helpings for everyone. "Father, may I refill your cup?"

"Yes, thank you dear."

They linger over the table. I busy myself clearing up, putting the bowls and silverware in the dishpan to soak, wiping the counters.

Father checks the clock. "I should be getting on the road. Maggie dear, can you go hitch up Roger for me? I best be starting if I want to reach Georgetown by nightfall.

"Of course, Father," I head out the door, trying to hide my disappointment. I must have not used enough. There is no way to give him more. I have missed my opportunity.

Inside the barn, Roger is waiting; nickering as soon as I go inside. He is always happy to see me. Despite my distress, my heart warms at his playful whinny. I enter his stall, reaching my hand out for his bridle.

"MAGGIE!" I hear Mother scream, *"OH MAGGIE, COME QUICKLY! HELP ME!"*

I spin on my feet and run back to the house. Inside, my mother is holding my father by the waist. He is leaning all his

239

weight on her. He looks confused and unsteady. I rush to his other side and pull his arm around my shoulder, bracing myself under it to help support him.

"I am...alright Joan. I feel...a bit dizzy. If I could just lie down for a bit. I am sure I will be well in a minute or two."

"Maggie, let us lay him on the bed. Can you make it?"

I am sure my face is flushed with shame. This is a terrible thing to witness. I have done this to my father. This is my fault. "I can make it," I reply. When he leans his weight against me I feel a sharp twinge and a pull low down, across my belly. I must stay mindful of the baby.

We get my father over to the bed. As he turns to lay down his legs give out from under him, and he falls forward, collapsing onto the quilt. My mother lifts his head and slides his pillow underneath it. I busy myself removing his shoes, hiding my face from my mother. I do not want her to see the guilt there.

"Maggie, what are we going to do? What is happening to him? Shall we go for a doctor?" Her face is lined with worry.

Just at that moment, my father begins to snore. Settled on his pillow, a calm and peaceful expression on his face.

"I think he is fine. Perhaps he was more tired than he thought he was. We should let him sleep. If he feels poorly tomorrow morning I will ride for the doctor."

"If you think that is best. I will sit here with him and read. I want to stay by his side."

"Of course, Mother. I will straighten up the kitchen for you. May I bring you some tea?"

"Thank you dear. You are a good girl."

She smiles weakly, taking her place in the chair at the window.

I walk back to the kitchen, my body filling with satisfaction. Wrong or not, I have *done* it. I am one step closer to freedom.

Off in the distance comes the soft rumble of thunder.

Chapter 31

Claire

August 26th, 2023

Jesse will be here tomorrow! He will actually be standing right in this living room in less than twenty-four hours. The thought won't stop spinning wildly around in my head. Most of me is so excited I can hardly breathe. I can't sit still. I feel like I haven't seen him in a lifetime. A small part of me is absolutely terrified. I'm still not showing, not really. You can't tell when I am dressed. Undressed, it's getting sort of obvious. I really need to tell him before he can get me *'alone'* alone. Mom and Tim are sworn to secrecy. It's my news to give. If Mom had her way she'd probably blurt it out the minute he comes in the door.

She's given me off work till after he leaves. Things are running smoothly now that Hunter is gone. He was fired that next morning when he arrived at the store. Mom made me stay home so I wouldn't have to see it. She didn't want me upset. It was a good thing too. Evidentially he made quite a scene screaming at her that she called the cops to get him out of the store. Screaming about how it was his job, and she is overreacting. She won't tell me anything more.

It's Sunday, and Mom and I have been in the kitchen all morning baking. Right now she's trying to teach to make meringue.

"Now, you have to respect Caroline. And she will treat you right."

"Caroline?"

"The Kitchen Aid stand mixer. I named her after my Aunt Caroline. She taught me everything I know. My Aunt did, not the mixer." She laughs as she practically caresses the beautiful dark teal appliance.

"I'm thinking that maybe Tim and I will head down to the beach tomorrow night. Leave you two alone for the evening. Give you some privacy. It's been awhile since you've seen him," she winks hugely at me.

"Mom."

"What? You think I don't know how you got knocked up? I'm not an idiot, honey." She laughs, "Besides, maybe you'd like to tell him your news without an audience. It's a special moment. He might want a special moment too."

She's as subtle as a bulldozer.

We spend the morning cleaning the house. I'm trying in vain to stay relaxed as she bounces around like a madwoman. "Is this how you were right before I got here?"

"Worse. Poor Tim. No wonder he hid in his office."

243

She's exhausting. Thankfully, she heads to the store in the afternoon so I can take a nap. Pregnancy has cured my nightmares. I sleep so hard I rarely dream at all. My bodies way of banking rest for when the baby comes, I guess.

When I wake up, the sun is setting. A beam of light coming through the far window lights up the corner of the room. It is still stacked with books and covered with clothes. It's sort of cleaned up. Mom would disagree but it's as good as it's going to get. I did get some books on the shelves. Even that took a while. At least it made it so I have a few clean surfaces in here. It's cleaner than Tim's office, at least. Besides, Jesse is used to my normal state of quasi neatness, so I've not been inspired to organize too much.

Underneath the books is the box of things Toby brought down from the attic. Elias's things. I haven't decided what to do with the toys we found. Mom agrees with me that what was found in the house should stay in the house. So it's all still sitting there. The two pictures we found and the writing in the Shakespeare book are the only hints of anything relating to his family or himself.

I hope I can convince Jesse to go down to the bridge with me on the 31st. Can you imagine that conversation? Hi honey! Welcome. Haven't seen you in months. Wanna come release a trapped spirit with me? Oh, by the way, I've got a bat in the cave.

August 27th

I wake up fairly late. Dragging my eyes open. The blackout curtains really cut the light. It's still dim in here. I yawn and stretch out wide in the bed, feeling a slight twinge down low in my belly. Ouch, sorry kid.

Oh God, it's today. Just a few more hours to go. The faint sound of The Bee Gees, 'Stayin Alive' drifts up from the room below me. The birds favorite song. Mom must be playing them music to keep them from making too much noise.

I get up, head to the bathroom, and splash cold water on my face. I catch my eyes in the mirror. Geez, I look so nervous. I don't have much experience with makeup, but I might need Mom's help later covering up these circles under my eyes. I couldn't settle down last night. My brain wouldn't stop racing. I have to tell him *today*. As soon as I get the chance. I've spent the last two months worrying about his reaction, and now I'm only a few hours away from it.

Heading down the stairs into the kitchen I find Mom at the coffee machine, filling a giant mug. God, how I miss coffee. I walk over and suck in the smell as hard as I can, trying to inhale caffeine through my nose.

"Good morning my Clarity. How are you feeling? Nervous? Excited? Need to barf a little?" Smiling, she hands me a small cup, "Use this."

"Yes, yes, and it's very possible, so thank you."

"How about I make you some breakfast? Scrambled eggs perhaps? Kippers? Raw oysters? Glass of clam juice??"

"Oh gross, Mom. Do you actually *want* me to throw up?"

"I'm kidding! How about some wheat toast with peanut butter?"

"Ok. That I can handle."

She toasts the bread and spreads it with thick chunky peanut butter, while I sit at the table with my head in my hands. "I'm freaking out! What is he going to say? I have this beautiful idea in my head of how I want it to go, but what if this totally turns him off to me? What if he's not ready for this? What if he doesn't want me?"

Mom sits down across from me, pulls my hands from my face and takes them in hers. "Honey, please don't do this to yourself. From what I know of Jesse he loves you more than anything in the world. Whatever happens, he's going to stick by you."

"Mom, you don't *know* that. Anything could happen."

"I have a feeling this day will turn out better than you could have ever dreamed. Try not to worry. It's not good for my precious grandbaby. Try and be happy. You've been waiting for weeks. How long has it been since you have seen him?"

"In person? One hundred and seven days."

She laughs. "Just try and enjoy the time that he is here. Is there anything else you need before I head in?"

"Nothing, unless you know a way to make the day go by faster."

* * *

By three in the afternoon I am, bathed, perfumed, and groomed within an inch of my life. I spent an hour in the bathroom buffing, shaving, and moisturizing myself. Then almost as long trying to get my hair to behave. In humidity like this all I can do is try to tame the waves in the right direction. My dark circles somewhat disappeared. A light layer of power and some lipstick and I look pretty good. I have hunted and hunted through every bit of clothing in the drawers and cannot find any of my good sexy underwear. They must be in the attic with the winter clothes, damn it. All I can find in the drawer are my plain boring cotton panties. But I don't suppose Jesse will really care; it's been months. I choose a relaxed pair of cutoff jeans and a sort of floaty blue top with wide sleeves. You can't see a bit of the bump in this outfit, but the jeans are starting to get snug.

My phone buzzes.

Jesse: I landed!

Claire: OMG. I can't wait to see you!

Jesse: As soon as I pick up my bag, and grab the rental, I will be on my way.

Claire: Be safe driving. Let me know when you get close.

I pick up a book and try to settle on a couch to read. I've got to distract myself, so the anxiety doesn't totally make me sick. I read the same paragraph five times before I give up and get to my feet. That's not working. I pace the room from window to window, knowing full well it's far too soon for him to get here. I don't want to take a walk outside because that will just get me all sweaty and gross. Not how I want to greet Jesse. Tim is hard at work in his office, I don't want to disturb him.

A movie! I drop back on the sofa, grab the remote, and pull up Netflix. I scroll, and scroll, and scroll. Nothing looks even remotely interesting. I finally settle on Invasion of The Body Snatchers, the original. I snuggle into the couch, my cell phone by my hip.

* * *

A featherlight touch on my face. Across my forehead. The gentle brush of a finger down my cheek. I sense the light touch fan across my eyebrow and around my ear, stopping and gently cupping my chin.

"Tiny?"

My lids crack open just a bit and I see beautiful green eyes. A smiling face with a thick five o'clock shadow staring back at me. His hair is a mess, he looks sweaty and tired, but it is Jesse. He is here. My eyes grow wide, I'm trying to clear my head and understand. "Wha...what...how? How did you get here?"

"A big airplane and a small car." He leans over and gently touches his lips to mine.

The desire that I've been trying to ignore all summer explodes through me. My arms reach out and pull him close. He is kneeling on the floor in front of the sofa, so he easily molds the top of himself down over me. His lips find mine again and I wonder if I am actually dreaming, the feel and taste of him so exquisite that it doesn't feel real. A minute later he slowly pulls himself back from me and helps me sit up.

"You didn't answer my texts or my phone calls, so I called your mom. You didn't answer her either, so she called Tim and he let me in when I got here. Did you not hear your phone?"

"My phone? It's right here..." I hunt around me and see nothing. I shift in my seat, and there it is. It must have slipped under me while I was asleep, and my butt muffled the sounds. Brilliant. Five missed texts and three missed phone calls. So much for welcoming him here with open arms.

"I'm so sorry baby, this is not how I wanted to greet you."

"Are you kidding? You looked like an angel laying here sleeping. It reminds me of those nights I'd come home late from class and find you trying to wait up for me, passed out over a bowl of popcorn, with the TV playing in the background. Waiting up just to see me. God, I've missed you."

"I love you Yeti. I missed you so much."

We sit here, just holding each other, for a long time. It feels unreal to have him in my arms again. I lean into his neck and breathe in his smell. A little dusty, a little dirty, but all Jesse. I even missed this. "So Tim just let you in and snuck away?

He squeezed me tighter, "Yep. He tiptoed across the room so he wouldn't wake you up. I told him I wanted to be the one to do it."

I lift my head from his shoulder, "Want to see the house?" I get up and wobble a bit. Jesse reaches out his hands to steady me and stands up. Holy crap, he is tall. I forget just how tall until he is standing right next to me. I look up at him, "You are lucky the house is renovated. They pulled out the drop ceiling. Otherwise your head would smack right into it."

He swats me playfully on the butt, "I even missed your bad jokes."

"Bad? Are you telling me you don't appreciate my world class humor? You need to expand your horizons, baby." I take his hand and start leading him back to the kitchen. I give him the grand tour. Mom will be glad to know that every room but mine and Tim's looks like it's ready for the President to show up. Upstairs, I open the door to my room. He laughs as he looks around. My signature style is evident; clean, but cluttered.

"I see you haven't changed any."

"Would you want me to?"

"Not at all. You are perfect just the way you are." He reached down and scoops me up in his arms. Running his lips over my neck, he walks over and gently places me in the middle of my bed. Kicking off his shoes he drops down next to me and takes my face in his hands.

"I've thought about you so much. I have missed you every day that I've been gone," he leans down and trails kisses down my neck, "I can't believe I am finally alone with you again,"

There is nothing I want more that to stay right here on this bed with Jesse, but I don't want him finding out about our baby like *this*. I want to tell him over dinner. Set the mood a little bit. Make it a moment he can remember.

I push him gently away and sit up, "Yeti, Tim is right downstairs. Mom is going to be here any minute. They promised they are going out tonight and leaving us the house.

We will get a chance to be alone together really soon, I promise."

"You're right." he sighs, his hand resting high up on my thigh, dangerously close to my stomach, "Let's get downstairs and get my mind on other stuff. You are far too beautiful right now."

* * *

"So you travel every day?" Mom is grilling Jesse about the internship as the four of us sit on the couches with the setting sun blazing through the side windows.

"Most days I do. Dr. Schwartz's practice does a great deal of mobile work. We travel from farm to farm for calls. You can't exactly load a young bull in a truck to come get castrated. They aren't the most mellow of animals. And pregnancy checks are usually done a few dozen at a time."

"So a pregnant cow feels different inside? How soon can you tell?"

"Actually, right away. You can tell when they are 'open' or not pregnant and you can tell how far along they are when they are pregnant. It's really fascinating. I'm learning it on horses too. Dr. Schwartz is great about letting me get in there and get all the experience I can handle. I even got to try an LDA. That's when a cow gets a twisted abomasum, and we flip them over to let it float back into place. Then we stich it to the body wall. It's wild. I love it."

"I'm so happy for you. You are out there doing just what you said you would do," I said. So proud of him I can hardly deal with it. Seeing him so confident and proud of himself is so sexy. I want to wrap my arms around him and climb him like a tree right here. It's unreal. He's sitting right here after being away from me for so long. I'm so glad to see him that I can hardly look at him. Like if I look too long it's going to burn my eyes, or something.

"Ok, babe. Let's get ourselves together and get out of here. I'm getting hungry," Mom stands and heads for the stairs.

"Is the bathroom free? I was hoping to take a quick shower and get the travel funk off me."

"Absolutely Doc, I'll show you were the towels are."

They all head upstairs and leave me alone. I need to get our food ready for dinner. Mom picked up crab cakes for us on her way home, thank God. So things will be less stressful for me. I am making her famous macaroni and cheese to go with it. Fancy, right? She taught me this summer. The trick is *five* different kinds of cheese and a little cayenne pepper. I layer it all together and slip it in the oven.

I'm standing at the kitchen at the sink, rinsing dishes when Mom comes up behind me, wraps her arms around me, and whispers in my ear, "Good luck tonight honey. It's going to go great, I promise. I love you. Send me a text if you need me, ok?"

"Thanks." I exhale a huge breath and follow her out of the kitchen. Tim and Jesse are waiting at the front door. Mom reaches up and hugs Jesse around the neck, whispers something in his ear, and kisses his cheek.

"You guys enjoy yourselves; I will keep your mother away until at least midnight." Tim is smiling at me, "Maybe even later if I can convince her to walk with me on the beach after dinner."

"You can absolutely convince me. Let's go. Romance me!" We laugh as they head out.

Jesse and I eye each other when they drive away. His expression slowly darkening with desire. He takes a step toward me...

"I...uh...need to go check the mac and cheese and set the table," I scurry away from him. I *really* have to tell him. This is getting awkward. I leave him standing alone by the doorway.

The table looks perfect. I light candles between us and shut off the overhead lamp. With the only light coming from the candles, the room is bathed in a flickering glow. We take our places across from each other at the end of the table. The crab cakes smell amazing. Jesse moans as he takes a bite. "Tiny, these are incredible."

"I can't take credit for those. Mom brought them home. The mac and cheese, however, is all me." He lifts a forkful into his mouth, the cheeses dripping and hanging down from his chin in long strings. His eyes close.

"I thought you loved me. I did. I thought I meant something to you. Why have you *never* made this for me before?

"Because I only just learned how to make it this summer, that's why."

"This is definitely worth flying down for," he smirks at my indignant expression, "You too of course."

253

"Eat. Before your mouth gets you into trouble."

We talk all though dinner. I hear about the people he works with in the vet practice. Jesse describes them so vividly I feel like I know them myself. I tell him about the store, and how it's going. Leaving out anything about Hunter. I don't want to spoil the mood. It's magical to be able to just sit and talk with him. We each clean our plates, then lean back and sigh. I really need to get to the point here, I've put it off long enough.

"Want to sit in the living room?" I ask, "I need to talk to you about something."

"Actually, come for a walk with me. Please?" He holds out his hand. His face is suddenly serious.

"Ok." A twinge of real fear goes through me. Omg. He's found someone else. He came down here to break the news in person. I take his hand and can feel the trembling in his fingers. My stomach drops. Damn, I hope I'm just paranoid. Don't cry. Don't cry. I'm sure everything is fine. He leads me out the door and we walk to the corner of the yard.

"Is that your mom's dock there?" pointing across the road.

"Yes, I haven't been over there yet. As you know, I don't fish."

He laughs, "Let's go see it. I bet the view is amazing"

We walk hand in hand across the road and head out onto the boards. The river is calm, and I can see the light from the almost full moon sparkling like a diamond on the water. Oh wow. I should have come down here before. Mom and Tim walk down here sometimes at night and now I understand why. This is crazy romantic. My unspoken news is on the tip of my tongue. I have to tell him. I'm going to do it right now. Do it. Just do it. Deep breath, girl.

I turn to face him, "Jess-"

The words die in my throat. He is down on one knee in the moonlight, holding up tiny box. My jaw drops.

"Claire, I knew I would fall in love with you from the first moment I saw you at that party. Your sense of humor, your dedication. How brave you are. How committed you are to the people you love. You are the most amazing woman I have ever known. Your hopes and dreams. The way you support mine. I want to grow with you. Discover the world together. I never want to be without you. Please, please marry me."

I can't speak. I am gob smacked. Absolutely floored. Happiness suffuses my body and crowds out the nerves. I start to shake. Tears fill my eyes as I drop to my knees in front of him.

"YES! Oh my God, Jesse. Of course I will. I love you so much." I kiss him. Hauling him against me hard, rocking us off balance.

"Careful babe. There's water underneath us, and I'm clumsy. Let's put this on you first. I don't want to drop it. It took me forever to pick it out." He takes the ring out of the box and slides it on my finger. A beautiful square cut sapphire set flush in gleaming white gold band. Just my taste. It fits perfectly.

"It fits!" I can't believe it, "How did you do that? My ring size is a 4 3/4, I have to have everything sized special."

He smiles at me sheepishly, "There is a *small* chance your mother was involved."

That explains a lot. Poor Mom! She's been keeping *two* secrets. I can't imagine how hard that was. "I'll bet she loved that. Nothing makes her happier than a juicy secret."

"She didn't tell you did she?"

"Not a word."

"Are you surprised? I had planned to wait until after the internship was over but being without you this summer, I realized I didn't want to wait anymore. Could we get married when I get back next May? It will give us some time to get ready. Then when I get a job somewhere the two of us can move together as man and wife."

"Speaking of the two of us..." I swallow hard. Here we go. Now or never. "I have a bit of news, myself."

"As exciting as mine?" he laughs.

"Depends. You know how you are trained to be able to spot pregnancy in animals?"

"Yeah..."

I stand and lift the hem of my shirt, slowly turning from side to side, my belly level with his face. Showing the tight roundness stretching the waist of my shorts to the limit.

His look of confusion changes to one of wonder. He gently places one hand on my hip and touches my lower belly with the other, carefully feeling the hard, rounded skin. "I...wha...are... Oh Tiny. This is unbelievable! Are you serious?"

"Absolutely. You can feel it right there. I didn't want to tell you in a phone call. I really wanted to be able to see you face to face for something this important. I hope I did the right thing. I've been kind of terrified. You do want kids, don't you?"

"I've wanted a family my whole life! I figured I wouldn't get to it for a while because my education is taking such a long time. This is the greatest news you could possibly have given me. Besides saying yes to marrying me, of course."

"Seems we each had a surprise tonight," I smirk.

"Your secret is the best. You're having our baby. All I brought was a piece of jewelry I had made."

"You *did* help me make mine, though."

He gets to his feet and wraps me in his arms. I'm so relaxed now. And happier than I have ever been before.

"When are you due? Have you been to the doctor? Is everything ok? Have you been sick? I'm so sorry I haven't been able to be here for you."

"I'm perfect. I'm due February 1st. I have a great doctor and a mother who watches me like I'm a fragile vase in an earthquake, but I am healthy as I can get."

He exhales in relief. "But honey?" I ask, "Can we finish this conversation inside? The mosquitoes are going to drain us dry."

He laughs and scoops me up in his arms, shouting into the air, "Claire is going to marry me! We are having a baby!" I

257

tighten my arms around his neck and kiss him as carries me back across the road.

We lay in my bed later, replete, happy, our limbs intertwined, my damp hair spread across his bare chest. Watching him slowly undress me and kiss the small naked bump of my stomach caused a storm of feeling inside me. I am grateful we were alone in the house.

Chapter 32

Maggie

May 31st,1880

Evening

Father has been sleeping for hours. Night is falling. A gentle rain has begun, thunder rumbling ominously off to the west. I am waiting for mother to give up her vigil and join him in bed. She has been sitting and fretting for hours. Wiping his brow, laying her head on his chest to hear his slow steady breathing. I have to give her constant assurance that he will be alright. She is so distraught that I cannot bear to simply run away and leave her sitting here alone next to his prone body. At least in the morning Father should be awake to comfort her when I am nowhere to be found.

"Mother, do you need anything? I am going out to do the chores before it is too dark."

"I'm alright child. Hurry back. I do not want to be alone."

"Yes, Mother."

Out in the barn I make quick work of feeding the stock. I give Roger an extra helping of grain and hay. He needs his strength for the night to come. It will be difficult if the rain does not let up. Roger is sometimes a stubborn horse. He does not enjoy being out in a storm.

The stock fed, I turn my attention to the pile of things I have hidden. It takes just a few minutes to pack everything behind the buggy seat. I should leave some room for the things Elias wishes to bring. I grab the blanket upon which our baby was made and use it to cover my things from the rain. I'm happy for a reason to bring it along.

I look around, everything is place. All that is left is for me to hitch up Roger and leave. I want so much to do it right now. If I can just convince Mother to go to bed! Elias is already waiting for me. I can feel it. What if she waits up all night? I have come this far, I have to see it through, no matter how much guilt I feel.

Coming out of the barn to head back into the house, I see my mother's face in their bedroom window. Anxiously waiting for my return. She appears wide awake. As I look at her worried face, my resolve hardens. The cough syrup is still in my pocket. In for a penny, in for a pound.

I brew her another cup of tea and add a good drop of the cough syrup. More than I have ever seen her take. Stirring it as I walk in; I hand it to her and sit myself on the bench at the foot of their bed. She slowly sips the hot tea until it is gone. We sit; she watches, I wait. Soon enough, my patience is depleted.

"Mother, hadn't you better get some rest?" I try, "When Father awakes in the morning you need to be at your best to help him. Let us go to sleep, it is almost 9:30."

"In a while, my dear. It distresses me so to see him like this. He is such a strong man. I do not know what I would do without him. Or you. I rely on you both so much. I am not a strong woman. I admit it. I have never been able to get by on my will alone. The day you get married and leave us will be a big adjustment for me." She gives me a sad smile.

"It will be alright Mother; you worry too much."

I can no longer sit still, I rise to my feet and take the empty cup from my mother's lap, "Come Mother, let us go to bed now. You need sleep."

"All right; you are probably right. Thank you for sitting with me. I am sorry to have kept you up so late. I shall be fine; you head on up to bed."

I sit the cup down on the side table and put my arms around her; holding her close, "You are more than welcome. I love you Mother."

She holds me tight; probably surprised at my embrace. We are not an affectionate home. "I love you too dear. Goodnight."

I look at her, remembering all the things she has taught me. This may be the last time I see her face. At best, this is the last time before she knows my secret. My eyes try to fill with tears, but I force them back. I cannot show weakness to her when I am so close to success. I turn and walk away, leaving

261

her standing in the bedroom next to the still and sleeping body of my father. I do not stop to kiss him goodbye.

I wait upstairs. I do not change my dress or remove my shoes. Mother does not climb up to my loft bedroom on many occasions. I must hope that she does not tonight. Time is growing short. Elias is surely waiting at his window. Watching the darkness to see me appear. I have taken my mother's cloak from the hook on my way up. It has the large hood that I will need to cover my head from the storm. It is not weakening. It only grows stronger as the hours go by. Travel will be slower in the rain.

I hear Mother downstairs preparing to get into bed. I listen close to make sure she makes it safely; I do not want her collapsing on the floor. I could not bear to witness that. Or to have to try and lift her into the sheets by myself.

Finally, I hear the bed squeak as she climbs in. It is almost imperceptible through the sound of the rain and thunder. The best aspect of the storm is it may mask the sounds of my leaving the house and driving Roger out of the yard.

I wait, poised to move, at the end of my bed. There is finally quiet in the house. The only sounds are the storm, and the faint sound that I know to be my father's gentle snore. I count to three hundred for good measure and can wait no more. Slowly I ease myself down the stairs, being careful not to step in any spot that might make a noise. I check the clock. It is close to midnight. Only twenty minutes away. I ease the back door open and slip out into the pouring rain.

By the time I reach the barn I am already drenched to the skin. The cloak is sopping with water. It feels as if the sky is crying.

Roger is pleased to see me. Nuzzling into my hand, hoping I have brought him a treat. I kiss him swiftly on his velvety nose and lead him out of his stall. He balks when he realizes what I am trying to do, pulling back against me. It is difficult to keep hold of his head. He pulls and fights me, refusing to move. He can hear the thunder pounding louder with each passing minute. But we have to go right now. There is no choice.

I coax him and soothe him as best I can. Gently stroking his neck and whispering, "Roger, sweetheart, come on. Be a good boy for Maggie. Everything is going to be just fine. I just need your help right now. Can you help me, honey? Let me get you hitched up. Please?"

He finally allows me to hitch him to the buggy. I am awash with fresh new blame. He is such a loyal animal, only doing what I ask. Wanting to please me. I walk to the barn door and open it wide. There, standing in the pouring rain, is my father.

"Maggie, what be you doing, child?"

"I have to…I have to go out, Father. I cannot say why."

"You will not."

"I will Father, you will not stop me."

He begins to stagger towards me, still groggy from the medication. What do I do? It feels as if time slows to a crawl as I try to think. He will reach me and take hold of me and I will be trapped here forever. I cannot allow it. I search around me and my eyes fall upon the pitchfork leaning against the barn wall by the door. I grab it in my hands just as he reaches me. I do not think but swing it towards his head with all my might. It cracks against his head with the sound of an ax splitting wood. He falls, and slumps to the ground in a heap directly in front of the barn doors.

There is not time to reflect on what I have just done. I take hold of his arm and brace my feet on the ground, pulling him out of the way of the buggy. Pain shoots across my belly. The muscles protecting the baby stretched too far. A scream of pain comes out of me like a feral animal caught in a trap. Which I am. I leave my father unconscious in the rain and head back into the barn.

Climbing into the buggy seat I drive Roger out into the dark.

BOOM!

The giant clap of thunder cracks through the sky with a bright flash of lightning. Roger rears up and whinnies loudly. Trying to pull away as I grab for his bridle. That was so loud! Did my mother hear it? Did it wake her? I have to get out of here.

Roger feels my hands on the lines and takes off racing down the dirt packed path from the barn towards the road in front of the house. I fight to keep control of his head.

I manage to slow Roger just enough to round the curve that adjoins the barn path to the road. The wheels on the inside lifting off the ground before dropping back with a thud as we shift straight. Roger is frightened. We head off at great speed down the road.

I have made it!

We race off into the storm. I am almost free.

Chapter 33

Claire

August 28th, 2023

Waking up with Jesse's arms around me is the greatest feeling. And just think, soon I will get to do this every morning for forever. I stretch luxuriously.

"Hey there fiancé. Sleep ok? I didn't crowd you did I?" he rolls to the side and his smile appears above my face.

"You did actually, and I loved every bit of it," I pull him down to kiss me. He flops back down next to me, reaching his hand down and resting it gently on the baby, "Good morning, little one."

"Stop being adorable. You're killing me. If it weren't for the smell of your feet, I'd think you were an angel."

"You know you love it," he laughs, "And every masterpiece has to have a flaw, it helps you appreciate it's beauty.

"So what it's been like living here? This house is awesome. How old is it again?"

"It was built in 1860. It's been great actually. For a while it freaked me out that it is so close to…you know…the bridge," I take a deep breath, "But I've learned some stuff I didn't know before. About Maggie."

I feel him stiffen slightly. His breath speeding up. "Maggie? What did you learn?"

"Well I'm not exactly *positive* but I think the man she was running away to meet when she died lived in this house. They, uh, found some of his things in the walls when they redid the place."

"You're joking."

"Nope."

"Show me everything."

I climb out of bed, throw my robe on, and slide the box over from the corner. I pull out the Shakespeare book and flip to the right page. The two photos are stuck there like a bookmark.

"Here is the name Maggie. Right by this very romantic sonnet." He runs his fingers over the name on the page.

I hand him the portraits, "We also found these pictures in the stuff. They are labeled with the names of the family that lived here. Elias here would have been just the right age at the right time."

He marvels at it for a while, "What else did you find?"

I hand him the folklore book, "This is her. I found this at the store."

His eyes grow wide at the sight of her. I see him grip the book tightly.

"The other books they found in the wall have no markings of any kind. Although they are old enough to fit the right period. There are these toys, and that weird piece of wood," I point into the box.

"Weird piece of wood?"

I fish it out and hand it to him, "It doesn't open. It's just a carved square. Pretty though. Elias could have made it. Who knows?"

"Claire honey, this is a puzzle box."

"A what?"

"A puzzle box. People have them to hide valuable things. They have to be solved to get them open. My dad has one from Japan."

"So you can open it?"

"Maybe, I can try, but I have to be careful. This is so old, if I try the wrong move I could break it. And it's incredible. Let me get some breakfast in me and I'll give it a shot."

Bird voices carry up to us from downstairs.

"Slut potato!"

"Hi! Hi! Hi!"

"Wanna come out?"

"Imma good girl!

"Jeepers!"

Jesse busts out laughing, "OMG. Which one of them is that?"

"That's Finn. Mom will be quick to point out that she did not teach her bad words. That they came from her previous home. I have my doubts. But in Mom's defense, I've never heard her call anyone a slut potato."

"We should probably get down there. I'm sure she's dying to get her hands on us and find out how everything went."

* * *

I'm not wrong. The moment we start down the stairs Mom breaks into tears at the sight of my grinning face. Jesse walks over and picks her right up off the floor, "Hey Grandma!"

"Oh god. We have to think of a better name than that. It makes me sound so *old*! I'm guessing everything went according to plan?"

"Your daughter and grandbaby signed up for a lifetime of me. If you consider that a good thing."

"I very much do," she walks over to me with her hand out, "Let's see it. I've only been hearing about it for weeks. You know, it's not easy to keep two huge secrets from two different people. I'm not an undercover spy. I think half my hair has turned grey this last month." She pulls my hand up to her face and closely examines my ring. Turning it back and forth in the morning light.

"That's gorgeous baby, congratulations," she hugs me, "Now everyone in the kitchen, Tim will be out of the shower in a minute. I made a celebratory breakfast of chocolate chip pancakes."

Everyone happily talks while we eat. Mom is fairly bursting with the excitement of being able to plan a small wedding. Where is the woman who was complaining to me last week about how busy she is? I look around at each of their faces, shining with excitement for us. I am so lucky. I have a loving mother to support me. I have an amazing partner, who wants to stand by my side forever. This is just how I dreamed it. It could have turned out so differently. If Mom had not approved and pushed me away. If Jesse didn't want the baby and left me to raise it alone.

Again, unbidden, thoughts of Maggie pop into my head. This was not the experience she had. She had to run away from home. In the dark, alone. Hoping for a happy ending that she never got.

"Earth to Claire? Are you with us?" Mom is looking at me, "You zoned out there for a minute."

"Sorry, what did I miss?"

"I asked if you guys want to have a Horror Fest tonight? We can order pizza with everything and watch disgusting movies till it's really late."

"Sounds excellent. Count us in."

"I'll clean up," Tim offers, "You guys just enjoy the day." He leans over conspiratorially to Jesse, "I think Claire here has missed you. If the mopey expression on her face and love songs coming out of her room at night mean anything"

"Tim…please don't embarrass me. I'll be forced to tell him about the sappy songs you sing to Mom when you drink wine," I say with a slight shake of my head.

He laughs and throws up his hands, "I know when I'm beat. Not another word about it."

We head back upstairs. Jesse sits on the edge of the bed, "Let's hang out here for a while, then we can take a ride and you can show me the bookstore. Maybe have lunch in Georgetown?"

"Absolutely. But don't forget, you promised to try and open the puzzle box."

"You got it doll. Hand it over. I'll try right now."

First, he grabs a damp paper towel from the bathroom, and takes the time to wipe the dust off every inch of the surface. Then he spends several minutes holding it close to his face and staring intently, turning it in all directions.

"What exactly are you doing? Trying to will it open with your mind?" I tease, "Using the Force, maybe?"

"Somewhere there is a seam and I need to find it. These boxes are a series of small moves, that have to be done in just the right order. That's what makes them so difficult to get into. If you don't do it just right, forget it. I don't want to damage this thing."

"I see. Well I'm glad you're on the case." I kiss him on the head and go crawl back in bed. The giant breakfast made me sleepy. I lay and stare at him, just happy that he is here. Watching him flip the box over and over in the beam of light coming in through the front windows. My eyes slowly close.

I slip seamlessly into a dream. Jesse is proposing. We are at the end of the pier in the dark, a million stars all around. I say yes, feeling the joy all over again. He reaches to hug me, and his eyes drop to my stomach, horrified at the sight of my giant, straining, pregnant belly. He grabs me by the shoulders and shoves me back. I fall slowly, endlessly, backwards into the river. I see disgust on his face as water closes over my head. I sink to the bottom. As I struggle to reach air again, hands reach up from the muck of the riverbed and clutch at my ankles. I open my mouth to scream, and it fills with river water. The hands hold me down and I cannot get free. I am trapped down in the dark with no escape.

"Claire? Honey? Wake up."

I struggle my eyes open. The dream is still with me. I feel held down by hands I can't break free from. I pull Jesse close to me. "Damn. I had a terrible dream." I draw in a shaky breath. He squeezes me tight.

"You did? Looked like you were sleeping just fine. I'm sorry Tiny. I only woke you because I almost have it open. I didn't want you to miss it."

I struggle to sit up, rubbing my eyes, "Really?"

"It took a few minutes, but I think I figured it out."

He has the box sitting on the bed next to us. He lifts it gently, holding it up in front of me. He takes the box in his left hand and with his right he places two fingers cattycorner on the end. Just the top right and bottom left edges.

"Watch this," and he gently squeezes them together. A tiny sliver of wood slides out. He slides his finger against the top

271

and bottom right in the center and the two thin panels shift. Suddenly the patten of the carving takes on a more uniform shape. A rose. He wiggles it a tiny bit, trying to get an idea of what to move next. He tries shifting the panels a few different ways, and nothing happens. Then he stops, takes two fingers and presses gently down on either end of the inlaid mother of pearl. I hear a faint click, and the side pops off.

"Yeti! You got it!"

"Damn Claire, whoever made this was very skilled. Really incredibly talented at woodworking. The seams are tight and even. It is totally smooth to open. This has almost as many moves as my father's does. His is a valuable antique. It was years before he'd even let me touch it."

"Is it empty?"

We look inside. At first it appears that way. I hold the end up to the light. There are many small slips of paper stacked together and wedged as far back in the narrow space as possible. I reach in the opening and gently pull them out. Old paper, thin and fragile. I unfold the stack and see words written in beautiful, elegant script. I look up at Jesse and gently open the first page on the top of the pile.

Elias,

November 1879

You should not stare at me in church so. Your Mother gives me looks like I am about to steal her only son away.

Little does she know that she is right. I have warm and tender feelings for you that I do not understand.

Please be patient with me.

I am only 16 and do not much understand the ways of the world yet.

Maggie

"Jesse! It's her. I know it is. Oh my god." I flip gently through the pages, "These are from her to Elias. I am right! I knew it!"

"How do you know that this Maggie is *the* Maggie?"

"I'm hoping to find out for sure. But these letters will need to prove me wrong. I know deep down that this is her."

I read through more letters. None are from him. All her. His responses to her are lost forever.

After working my way through some of the notes, I don't find anything significant. All they are taking about is silly unimportant things. Things people getting to know each other would talk about. Sort of like notes my mother would have passed in high school before we had cell phones and text messages.

Love notes. These are love notes.

I read one out loud.

My dearest Elias,

December 1879

If you will allow me a moment to share a passage from Middlemarch.

It is my favorite. I'd love to be able to share with you my copy so that you too could enjoy it.

'If we had keen vision and feeling of all ordinary human life, it would be like hearing the grass grow and the squirrels heartbeat, and we should die of that roar which lies on the other side of silence.

All my love,

Maggie

Well, she obviously loved him. And if her letters are any indication, he loved her too. Near the bottom of the stack I find one that has a bit more information…

Elias,

February 1880

Be so very careful.

I am very excited that you will be building the cabinets,

but I worry that you will give away our secret.

We must be very careful in front of my parents.

We must not show the least sign of our feelings.

Know now, that every smile that I give you will be just like the first one you asked for.

My love forever,

Maggie

After that there are only two more notes. The handwriting is much less clear in them. It looks like it was written in a shaking, nervous hand.

Elias,

May 1880

I must speak to you immediately.

Come to my house tonight at midnight.

Meet me in the back stall of the barn. Be very quiet.

It is imperative that I see you.

Maggie

The last one is dateless. The ink is smeared and hard to read.

Elias,

Father is going out. We must change the plan.

Give me 3 days? Wait for me.

Maggie

I look up at Jesse, "Something major happened between these two notes and the ones before," I hold them out, "February to May."

Jesse looks at me, "Time enough to get pregnant and find out about it? Maybe she asked him there to tell him about the pregnancy. The last one sounds like the plan to leave, but there's no way to know."

"So you believe me now?

"It's hard not to. It all makes sense."

"There's more I haven't told you yet. Toby and I have been down there at night twice this summer. He bought me a spirit box that records EVPs. We caught a voice," I get up and pull the small black box out of the closet, "You sure you want to hear these?"

"I might as well know it all. It's important to you. But Claire, what do you hope to accomplish with this?"

"Just listen and then we will talk about it. Listen close in the silences. In the static."

I fidget on the bed as he works his way through the two recordings. His eyes confused then growing wider and wider as he reaches the end. He starts it over and listens to them a second time. He pulls the earbuds out of his ears, "Claire…"

"Can you hear her?"

"I…do…hear a voice."

"Ah! So now you believe she is real?"

He rolls the desk chair he is sitting in over to me at the end of the bed and takes both my hands in his. His expression is grave.

"Claire, I need to confess something to you. Please don't be upset, but I have *always* believed she was real. I spent years trying to convince myself that what I saw that night was just my imagination. But…when you saw first saw the lights on the bridge that night, before the screaming started, I saw something at the edge of the woods. A shape. A female shape…without a head. The moonlight made the shape clearly visible. It scared me so bad. I couldn't move. I couldn't breathe. It wasn't till you called me that I could get my feet to work. After the screaming started I was so worried about making sure you were ok and getting you out of there safely, I didn't think about what I had actually seen.

"You seemed so scared in the car; I couldn't bring myself to tell you the truth. I tried the best I could to help you rationalize the lights and sounds. I didn't want to scare you more.

"I'm so sorry now that I didn't tell you. But you may want to leave this alone. It's not something you want to see. Especially now that you are pregnant. She was hideous. I've had nightmares about her for years."

He's surprised when I smile and start to giggle. I stand, lean over, and wrap my arms around his neck, "Yeti. We are both a mess. I kept my own secret about that night. I looked back that night after we got in the car. I saw her too. Here I am thinking I was protecting you all this time. Ha!"

His eyes grow wide. A smile seeps onto his face. He slowly chuckles. I bust out laughing and he joins me, loudly cracking up. Tears squeeze out of my tightly closed eyes. I am so relieved.

Once we get control of ourselves I lift my head and stand up, "Babe, I've been pregnant both times I went down there this summer and I've been just fine. I have a plan. Thursday night is the blue moon. Our best shot at reaching her, spiritually. According to my research. For the next few years, anyway. I'm hoping to somehow release her spirit from that place. So if you'll help me, I say we go down there and…"

Chapter 34

Maggie

May 31st, 1880

Midnight

We race hell bent through the storm. My arms are aching from trying to control Roger. He is petrified. It takes all my strength just to hang on to the reins. I cannot control him. I cannot even slow him down. He is not used to travelling in the dark. Father has never brought him out on a night like this in his life. In my hurry, I did not think to put his blinders on. The poor animal can see the lightning flashes in the sky and the darkness of the woods as we pass through it. The sky screams…

CLACK!

The blame for his terror is mine and mine alone, but there is nothing that can be done about it.

CRACK! BOOM!

He is running so hard his sides heave with the effort. Bits of mud from his hooves fly up into my face and hair. My hood has blown back, and the rain is hitting me full in the face. It is so cold. The downpour is obscuring my vision. I dare not let go of the reins to wipe my eyes. I blink hard to try and clear them, but it does no good. I feel as if I am travelling blind. My only goal is to reach Elias. If I can just reach him all will be well. From there he can take over. Roger will feel better with a more confident driver.

What circumstances conspired to make this bid for happiness so difficult?

Why did my father have to choose today to travel?

Why did Elias have to choose this day to run away?

Why must the drought break tonight in such a mighty fashion?

Why could we not simply go to my parents and have them accept what happened with love and understanding?

Why must we lie?

Why must we run?

The road is pitted with muddy holes. I cannot avoid them as Roger is running so fast my arms are not strong enough to steer him around them. It jostles the buggy so hard my teeth clack together and my bones rattle. My belongings behind the seat lift and drop with each bump.

It is nearly impossible to see the road ahead. The good news is the road is an easy one that Roger has been over many times. There is nowhere for him to go but forward. And ahead of us, at the end of the road, is my love, waiting for me. The sky lights up with a brilliant flash of light.

BOOM!

Roger rears his front legs into the air. Making a sound ripped from hell itself. I see his back rising up in front of me. Growing larger and larger as it comes nearer to my face. Dear God, he is going to flip back on top of the buggy! He hangs in the air for an endless moment till his front legs crash back down again. Showering me in a wash of muddy water. The jolt shifts the buggy hard and I hear and feel my belongings lift right out of the back to fall to the road. Roger takes off again as fast as he can go. Shivers rippling down his body as he runs.

There is a change in the space around me. The woods have shifted further back. The bridge is coming! In trying to fight the storm and control Roger I have forgotten about it. I am halfway to my love.

I grip the right rein even more tightly in my hand. I will need to pull it hard to turn Roger as we prepare to cross over.

There is little time to think. We are there in an instant. I brace my feet hard against the buggy as we approach, and I pull hard to the right.

The sky lights up with a flash of lightning so bright the entire woods is visible. The bolt strikes a large tree on the far side of the water, exploding the wood and showering sparks everywhere. The clap of thunder splits the night with horrifying noise.

BOOM! CRASH!

Roger rears again, screaming in fright. At that exact moment, the wheels of the buggy catch the outer edge of the wooden planks at the base of the bridge where the pounding water wore away the packed dirt of the road. The wheels lift into the air and the whole buggy starts to twist. Roger turns his head back, and I see his crazed and panicked eyes staring up at me as it rises over his back. The buggy is going to land on him, and I cannot stop it. His hooves skid on the wet wood. The buggy and I coming down as we slide towards the edge of the bridge. The ground rushing up to meet m-

Chapter 35

Claire

August 31st, 2023

J esse is cooing in a baby voice, "Who's a pretty girl? Who's my best baby? I wuvs you so much. I'm gonna sneak you into my suitcase when I go. Yes I am."

"You know Jesse, Rufus and I are…right…here. Is it necessary to flaunt your new love right in front of us? We have feelings, you know!"

Finn has taken a liking to Jesse this week. I'd say the feelings are mutual. The macaws generally adore my mother and are at best, standoffish with everyone else, including me. Finn wanting to sit on Jesse and preen the hair by his ear, is tantamount to adultery in Rufus's eyes. We have to leave him in the cage when Jesse plays with her. Rufus would very much like to murder him. The 2nd clutch of babies went to the hand feeder last week, so they are making the switch back to being just pets.

"I have spent every minute with you for the last four days. I know you have it in your heart to share me for just a few minutes to love on this sweetie-weetie-boo-precious darling." He nuzzles her beak with his nose, and she purrs like a cat. "You smell like maple syrup and gingerbread. You're just my wittle snacky cake, yes you are."

"I love you."

"You a good boy."

"Jeepers bird."

"Omg. I can't handle this. I hope you two are very happy together," laughing, I head upstairs. Wait. I stop still at the top of the stairs. Did Finn say jeepers? We never say that. In fact, the only person I know that ever uses that word is *Hunter*. How could she learn that? He was never here. Never.

The things we are taking to the bridge tonight are laid out on the desk. The spirit box. A smudge stick made with sage. The large cast iron pan I will be using to hold a small fire. A box of matches. Some balled up paper, sticks and dried moss to burn. A bottle of water to put out the fire with. A small baggie of tobacco that's really just a cigarette I bummed from Mom's neighbor across the street, cut open and shaken out. The notepaper with the words I want to say. The picture of Elias. The picture of Maggie photocopied out of the old folklore book. Maggie's love notes to him. I'm really glad I found something that belonged to her to bring. It should help attract her to us and help focus the energy. I pack everything but the pan into my corduroy bookbag and sit it and the pan next to the bedroom door. The forecast for tonight is clear and warm, without much wind. Ideal for what we are doing. I better remember to put on bug spray before we go. I don't want to need a blood transfusion tomorrow.

* * *

Tim and Jesse are fishing. I find it hard to believe but all I have to do is look out the window and I can see them. Their bright, sun-lit shapes over at the end of the pier. I don't know if they are catching anything this afternoon, but they look like they are laughing and having a great time. I guess actually catching the fish is not all that important.

I look around my room for something to read and my eyes fall on my open laptop. I was rechecking Google last night to make sure I had everything I needed to take later. Maybe I'll sit down and try to write for a while. I've been toying with the idea of a non-fiction account of Maggie's story. Tim said all the information is out there. I only have to find it. Take the old legend and try and flesh it out a bit. Talk to some locals, do some more research. I have new information of my own from the walls of this house, plus my own experiences at the bridge this Summer. After tonight I may have even more. I open up a new document and stare at the blank page.

2 hours later the sound of Jesse bounding up the stairs breaks my concentration. He bursts into the bedroom, his face exuberant and pink from the sun.

"Tiny! I caught three fish! I threw them back, of course, but you should have seen 'em." He stretches his arms out as wide as they will reach, "They were *this* big!"

"Riiiiight."

He laughs, "Ok, maybe not quite that big. But I did catch three. Which is three more than I've ever caught before."

"I'm all for male bonding, but maybe you want to shower? I can smell you from here and it ain't Chanel."

"Yes, dear." He blows me a kiss as he heads to the bathroom.

I check to make sure the document is saved and shut the computer down. I've gotten almost six pages in. I'm surprised at how easily the words are coming to me when I am writing about something I care about. Maybe Tim is right. I think I might tell Maggie's story. As much as it can be told.

* * *

Mom and Tim went upstairs after dinner and are watching old Mystery Science Theater episodes on YouTube in their bedroom. It's after nine and we have the living room to ourselves.

"Tiny, if we are going to do this tonight will you please go upstairs and try to sleep for a while? I promise I will wake you up in plenty of time to get ready. We are going to be up late tonight. Please?"

"Ok, but what will you do?"

"Sit at your desk and play around online. I'll set an alarm on my phone. If I get sleepy I'll lay down next to you. I promise."

I yawn, convinced.

* * *

I wake later to the sound of raised voices. Prying my eyes open in the dim room I see Jesse at my open door looking out into the hallway flooded with light.

"I'm coming with you if you are going," Tim voice sounds high and tight.

"Honey, the officer said there is no danger, but he wants me to come and inspect the damage. See what's missing. I'll be perfectly safe. But come if you need to. You can drive. You see better in the dark than I do."

I get up and walk to the doorway. Jesse moves close behind me and puts his hands on my shoulders.

Mom sees me, "Claire honey, it's fine. Don't get upset, but someone broke into the store. It set off the alarms. Whoever did it knocked around some stuff at the front counter and tried to remove the safe. When that didn't work, it seems they took off. I have to go over there and talk to the officers on scene," she cups my chin in her hand, "Everything is fine. I'm taking Tim with me. I will be perfectly safe, don't worry. We'll be back in a few hours."

"Ok Mom, just be careful, both of you."

They hustle quickly down the stairs and out the side door. I hear Tim's SUV start up and drive away.

"Well! I was about to wake you when I heard your mom's phone ring. Then she was shouting. The next thing I know they're both out in the hall. I'm sure it's nothing to worry about. Probably just someone looking for a quick buck."

"Damn. I hope they didn't wreck stuff. We worked so hard on the place."

"Try not to worry about it. We've got a plan to get ready for. Why don't you get dressed? It's after eleven."

Ten minutes later we're at the doorway, dressed in long sleeves and long pants. Faces and hands covered with bug spray, bag in hand.

Outside, the moon is bright overhead as we climb into Jesse's rental and pull out onto the street. A car is passing just as he backs out. We follow its taillights into the woods.

The brief drive is long enough for me to be hit by a warm wave of nostalgia. Maybe it's pregnancy hormones, maybe it's the fact that he asked me to marry him but heading back down this road next to Jesse makes me feel all gooey and love struck. I lean into his arm, "I love you. Thank you for doing this with me."

"Anything for you babe. I'll gladly face a ghost if that is what thou doth desire," he laughs, "Next week, dragon slaying. In the meantime please keep your eyes open for cars. We don't want to get run over in the middle of the road. It may be almost midnight, but people do live down here."

"Pull over where we did before. Up and on the right."

I sound confident, but the moment the car stops, doubt creeps in. Is this nuts? Am I crazy? What in the world am I doing out here in the middle of the night getting ready to light a fire in a pan and wave sage around? We climb out and stand together on the edge of the road. I've never felt more ridiculous. I look to my right and there is Jesse, right next to me. Either he really loves me or he's just as crazy as I am.

The moon is high overhead. I can smell the river. The air is thick with humidity and totally silent. No crickets, no frogs, not even the buzzing of mosquitoes.

"We need to face each other in the center of the bridge. Let's get set up. I'll sprinkle the tobacco in the four directions. To me that means each corner like where we stood before when we called her. That is supposed to consecrate the ground."

"You want me to set up the stuff in the pan?"

"Please."

I walk to each corner and take a pinch between my fingers. I blow each pinch out across my palm into the light breeze. When I finish the four corners, I turn and see Jesse sitting in the middle of the road, facing the way we had come, with the pan ready to go. He's filled it with the kindling; the water and matches set next to it on the road. The sage stick and spirit box are on the opposite side. He has the notes in one hand and the photos in the other. His eyes shine at me in the dim light. I love him so much right now. He is all in. Crazy idea or not.

I walk over and sit cross-legged facing him, the cast iron between us. He leans toward me in the dark, and I meet him in the middle. We share a slow, soft kiss. "Thank you Yeti. You are the greatest. I know I'm a weirdo."

"If you are a weirdo, so am I. This whole thing makes me nervous but hey, maybe we can actually do something. And if nothing happens, we will still have a great story to tell our kid someday."

I pick up the box of matches, and turn on the EVP recorder, "Ok, let's start." I strike a match and touch it to the paper at the bottom of the small pyre. The fire catches and light flares up on our faces. It quickly spreads to the moss and small twigs he arranged in a pyramid shape.

I light the sage stick on the edge of the burning paper and let it burn for a moment before blowing it out. The fragrant smoke starts to rise and fill the air around us. I place the smoking stick in front of my crossed legs and use my hands to wave the smoke over my face and back across my head. I repeat the movement several times till I feel and smell the scent clinging to my clothes and hair. Passing the stick to Jesse I watch as he repeats the movements I just made. When he finishes he rubs the embers out on the surface of the road and looks into my eyes.

"Now what?"

"We call her. I tell her why we are here. If nothing happens I will start asking her questions. Ready?"

He nods.

"Maggie, we have your baby!"

"Maggie, we have your baby!"

"Maggie, we have your baby!"

I pause for a few seconds before I speak out loudly…

"Maggie? My name is Claire Ludlow. This is Jesse Mumford. We are here to try and help you."

Silence.

"I live in Elias Hastings's house just down this road. Maggie, he died a long time ago. You died too. You have been here for years and years."

Silence.

"I found your letters. Your messages to Elias? He kept them his whole life. He boarded them up in the walls of his house so they could never be lost. He loved you."

Silence.

"I want to help you get out of this place. I know you loved him. I know you loved your baby."

Silence.

"Your baby is not here. It will never be here. Your baby moved on when you died. I am so sorry that happened. You should not have had to run away."

Silence.

"I got pregnant by accident too. My family accepts me. Yours should have too. I'm so sorry that they didn't. It was so unfair. Jesse is my baby's father. He is here to help you too."

Silence.

"You need to move on. Look at our light. Focus on the light. Elias is in the light. Your baby is in the light. Let go of this place and go to them."

We sit in silence for almost a minute. Looking at each other over the bright flames coming from the pan between us. This fire is messing with my night vision. It's so bright that when I try and scan the woods the afterimage of flames on my retinas makes everything fuzzy and dark. If Maggie is out here it's not going to be easy to see her.

There is a soft sound. A rapid thumping. Coming from ahead of me, behind Jesse. "Do you hear that?" I whisper. I squint, trying see the road. If it just wasn't so damn dark! I see faint movement move up close behind him. Maggie? My heart leaps and when I open my mouth to tell Jesse an arm comes out of the dark and closes tight around his neck, dragging him backwards along the road. I scream.

I can hear the sounds of struggling but I can't *see*! Jesse's legs and feet make scrambling sounds on the pavement as he struggles to pull away the arm choking him. Still screaming, I push myself back from the fire and try to get to my feet. My legs have fallen asleep. As I get them under me a loud cracking thud rings through the air.

There is deafening silence. I freeze. There are footsteps. A smiling face appears in the firelight.

"Hello, Claire."

"Hunter."

"In the flesh. Long time no see, huh? Missed me?"

"What have you done to Jesse?"

"He's not a part of this conversation. I must admit, when I made this little plan to get you alone, I never thought I'd get you way out here in the dark. What in the hell were you two doing out here? Some kinky sex ritual shit? If you wanted kinky all you had to do was ask. I think it's about time you had a real man."

I have to stay calm. I have to. I feel my fingernails digging into my palms, "Hunter, we can talk, no problem. But I need to call 911. Jesse may be hurt." At the very least. I won't even consider the alternative.

"911? I don't think so. I had quite enough of the god damn *police* thanks to you, little Claire. Ophelia's precious girl that can do no wrong. I swear, some days I was blinded by the sun that shines out of your flat ass."

I slowly back up in little steps as he talks. Don't panic. Don't panic. I want to put as much distance as I can between us without him noticing.

All my muscles are locked tight. My heart is thumping so hard it's making spots in my vision. If I can get enough of a lead I'll try running into the woods. Maybe I can make my way back to the house away from the road. The housekeys are in my pocket.

My cellphone! Damn it all to hell, it's in the car. Jesse has the keys in his pocket. I know the car is locked. He always locks the doors, a habit from living in NYC.

"So, little girl, you think you can destroy my life and just go on like nothing happened? There are consequences for screwing with me," he laughs, "And you haven't even screwed me…yet.

"So I kept videos of you? So what? So I sent you text messages. Is that a crime? I touched your leg when I was drunk. SO WHAT!? I'm a handsome, successful guy. You should be flattered I even wanted a mousy little thing like you. You *ruined* my god damn life, you stupid bitch!"

"I…I'm sorry Hunter, you're right," trying to placate him somehow. Buy myself some time.

"You bet your skinny ass I'm right. It was easy to get your mom away so you and I could have a little *talk*. Anything wrong with her precious store and she comes running. I was planning to come back in the house so I was confused when I saw you two leaving right after she did. But instead of having to cut you off down the road, you guys were nice enough to stop right here in the damn middle of the woods. Thanks for that. You made it really easy."

"They will come looking for me when they get back. It's not going to take them long."

He rushes me and grabs me by the arms. Digging his fingers into my flesh, hauling me up close to his face.

"Little Claire, even if they do come back and you aren't there, they'll think you're out with your piece of crap, jackass boyfriend. They won't worry about you for *hours*. Hell, they'll go back to bed! Plenty of time for me to have a good time before I shut your stupid mouth up forever and head out of this god forsaken state." He releases one arm and slaps me hard. My face reels back, stars exploding in my head. He wraps his arms around me and squeezes me so tight I cannot take a breath. Our faces are inches apart and I smell his fetid breath.

"*That* one is for hitting me with your stupid phone, you bitch. And that's just the start. I'm going to make you pay for every damn problem you have caused me. Hell, I'll even make up a few new ones.

"I can picture your air-head mothers face when they find your used up body in the woods tomorrow with nothing but your cheap old ripped blue underwear lying next to you. That will be so sweet. Sorry I won't get to see it."

Oh Christ. *HE* has my missing underwear. He was in the house. Our house. *MY* house. That's why Finn learned that damn word. When the hell did he get in there? What else did he do? I was an idiot in so many ways. I underestimated Hunter and how psycho is really is. I thought he was a disgusting sexist pig, not an actual physical danger. I'm so stupid. It can't end like this. I won't let it end like this.

I drive my knee up into his groin, then rear my head back and slam my forehead into his nose as hard as I can. Wrenching myself free from his grip, I fall backward and hit the ground hard. Landing half on my backside. Pain shoots like a lightning bolt up my back. Hunter screams and bends over at the waist, clutching at his crotch and his face.

"Agghh…You CUNT. Ah, god dammit. Are you ever going to get it now."

I try to ignore the pain and get myself up off the ground. This is my chance to get out of here. But it's too much pain. My head is spinning, and it feels like fire is shooting down my leg where I hit the ground. I can't move yet. I am trapped here till the pain subsides.

Oh god, the baby! Its poor vulnerable little life, dragged along into this mess. There were three of us on this bridge the whole time. Now there are four. My poor defenseless baby is along for the ride.

295

Four

FOUR!

Lifting my face to the sky I take a huge breath and scream, "MAGGIE! I HAVE YOUR BABY! HELP ME!"

Hunters expression turns puzzled through his pain.

"MAGGIE PLEASE! I NEED YOU RIGHT NOW!"

He lifts up his head to look at me, "Bitch, what baby? What the hell are you talki.."

An unearthly scream pierces the night. Making my eardrums ring. Hunter ducks as if trying to escape the sound. He throws his hands over his ears, moaning loudly.

The sound dies off and he straightens up. Looking back in my direction. On his face I see a slowly dawning horror. Stretching his features into a near grimace.

Maggie is between us. Looking as she did 6 years ago. Her wet, mud-covered dress glistening in the light from the dying fire. So much more visible in the glow. Dark red blood runs in rivers from the jagged stump of her neck. Her contorted face swinging near the ground from her outstretched arm. She is a ghastly sight.

I do not move. I will not run from her. I will not be afraid of her. She is standing between me and real danger.

Hunter screams in abject terror. He tries to back away, and I watch Maggie raise her arm, and swing her hanging head directly at his face.

THOCK!

The sound of the contact fills my head. It was so hard his feet lift off the ground. He falls backwards onto the hard asphalt. Landing on his back, he screams up at the vision of Maggie.

(clairenow)

A voice in my head. Clear as if it were spoken directly in my ear.

(stophimsavebaby)

A power swells up in me. A strength. I will do anything to protect this child. Protect myself. Protect Jesse.

I push myself to my feet, ignoring the pain that shoots across my lower back, and run to the pan of burning embers. Pulling my arm into the sleeve of my shirt, I grip the handle tightly with my covered hand. The heat quickly sears though the fabric and I feel burning pain in my flesh. I turn and dump the guttering fire out onto the blacktop.

Hunter continues screaming at the sight of Maggie standing over him. Too afraid to move, or take his eyes off her. He does not see me coming up behind him. Swinging with all my might, I bring the hot cast iron down across the side of his face. The thud is enormous. It rings in my ears. The vibrations travel up my arm and pass through my whole body. He falls silent and limp. I am shaking. Shock overwhelms me, and I sink to my knees.

(claire)

I look up, she is in front of me. Looking as young and beautiful as she is in the photo I found in the book. The way she was before all this happened to her. She is looking down at the road. At her feet are the two photos. They had fallen out of Jesse's hand and are laying side by side. Maggie and Elias. Young and hopeful. Her notes have scattered across the bridge. She looks back up at me, her face is wet with tears. Her voice fills my head again.

(baby?)

I whisper to her, "No Maggie, your baby is not here. Look for the light Maggie. They are there. They are waiting for you. Thank you so much."

She raises her arm and points to my stomach.

(baby)

She smiles. I see her raise her eyes to the sky shining with points of light and the full moon above our heads.

(iseestars)

She slowly dissolves away in front of me, and I am alone.

Chapter 36

Claire

September 1st, 2023

Officer Little smiles at me, "You're doing great Claire. We are almost done. If you could just tell me one more time what happened after you hit him with the pan."

This hospital bed is high and uncomfortable. They admitted me for a few days observation because of the baby. My bandaged hand is held carefully against my stomach. The mild painkillers aren't quite numbing the pain in my skull from slamming my forehead into Hunter's nose or the 2nd degree burns on my palm. The other hand is trailing an IV line. My ass cheek is sporting a hell of a bruise from hitting the ground so hard. I'm practically helpless.

"He fell down and went still. I got myself up and went over to Jesse. He was just starting to come around a bit. I fished the keys out of his pocket and made my way over to the car.

Once I got inside I got my cell phone and called 911. I waited there with Jesse till the ambulance and police arrived.

"Were you aware that Hunter was dead?"

"Not then, not until the paramedics told me."

"You were very courageous, facing him alone. You did an excellent job of defending yourself. It's a good thing you did. Look, I don't want to upset you, but we found rope and duct tape in his car. Along with a switchblade. You saved yourself, your fiancé, and your baby last night."

I blanch. Good God.

"We have your EVP recorder. It has the entire incident recorded. It will be returned to you eventually but for now it's evidence. May I ask what you and Jesse were trying to do out there?"

"It's..um..silly. We were trying to contact a ghost. It was a full moon last night," I stare down into my lap.

"Let me guess…Maggie Bloxom?"

"Familiar with the story?"

"Who isn't? I've gone out there a few times, myself."

"I think everybody has."

"Of course, I was younger then. See anything?"

"Um…maybe, I'm not sure. Hunter was on us so fast, and I was too involved with him. It's still a bit fuzzy."

"Sorry to disappoint you but we didn't hear anything on the recording except a nice big confession from Hunter. You're lucky it was running. It's going to save you a lot of trouble."

"I've had enough trouble for a while."

"I'll just bet you have. You feel better. I'll be in contact if we need anything else. Get some rest."

"Thank you, officer," I lay back on the flat, antiseptic smelling pillow. Closing my eyes, I try to relax to the sounds of never-ending intercom pages, people walking past my open door, and the banging of the food delivery cart down the hall. I wish I were in my own bed with Jesse lying next to me.

He has a concussion and seven stitches in his head from the laceration where it hit the road. His room is just down the hall. He'll be here for a few days at least. I got wheeled down to see him earlier. He's groggy and in pain but he knows who I am. I can tell from his expression that he's confused about what went down last night. We're going to have quite a lot to talk about when we are finally alone again.

I turn ever so slowly and carefully onto my unbruised side. Trying not to pull on the IV or put any kind of pressure on my bandaged hand. I hope I have some time to rest before Mom gets back with food and who knows how many more flowers. I've been here less than a day and this room already looks like a meadow in the spring. I think she went over to the flower shop and bought everything they had. She went home an hour ago to make me chicken soup. Lucky for me, her way takes four solid hours. No cheap stuff for her Claire. Soup for me means homemade stock and fresh noodles. I know what happened last night scared her really badly. Tim told me this morning she was hysterical and had to be sedated when they got to the hospital. If making amazing soup from scratch helps her calm down, who am I to say no? I'm starving. I may be hurt but I am still eating for two.

The baby made it through last night just fine. Or so they tell me. I still have to be watched for a couple of days. Till my head clears and I'm not considered a fall risk.

I roll onto my back, unable to get comfortable. It smells gross in here, like bland meatloaf, latex gloves, and bleach. Yuck. Reaching down with my unburned hand I gently rub my hard belly, "Well kid, we made it through. I promise you; I'm always going to protect you. You are going to be the most loved baby in the world."

There's movement under my hand. What feels like the soft flutter of butterfly wings tickle me from the inside. The baby! It's the most incredible sensation I've ever felt. I press my hands to the spot. There it is again! Just the faintest movement. But it's definitely there.

"I guess you are alright in there, little one," I giggle in relief.

One question is looming huge inside my head. Did Maggie leave? Did she find peace? It looked to me as if she did. Someday I will get to hear the EVP recording. I might be able to detect her voice even if the police couldn't hear it.

But do I even want to? I know what happened. I trust my eyes and my heart. I don't need to hear her voice as proof. I also don't ever want to hear Hunter's voice, to experience that horrible exchange again. His words are already going to live forever in my head.

I realize now that many things could have turned out differently if I had just been honest with everyone from the beginning. Jesse and I kept the secret of Maggie from each other for years. That was wrong. I should have told Mom from the beginning that Hunter was bothering me. If I had, she would have fired him long ago, and he may not have gotten as fixated on me as he was. I have to understand that I need to stand up for myself in any situation. Now I have another life to be responsible for.

I'm going to focus on the future. Jesse and me together. Our baby who is safe and healthy inside me because of Maggie's help. I decided this morning when the sun rose on a day that could have started without me; I'm going to tell her story. Be honest about everything that happened. She deserves to be more than folklore. More than a fun game that teenagers play on a lonely road in the dark. More than a cautionary tale.

She was real. She was a person with a life.

She deserves to be remembered that way.

Epilogue

Jesse smiles widely at me as we pull into Mom's driveway. "Look at all the stuff she has out. Holy crap."

The lawn is covered with a long picnic table and chairs. The grill is open, and Tim is in front of it flipping burgers. There are American flags circling the entire property. A baby pool is set up by the side door with a giant stuffed bear next to it. The bear is wearing a flag t-shirt for god's sake. A badminton net is strung up near the front of the lawn. Along the corner facing the river are fireworks lined up ready to go for tonight.

"Her granddaughter only has one first 4th of July. You can't expect her to behave *normally*."

He laughed and I went on, "Actually, I take that back, this is normal for her. Be happy she didn't hire a marching band."

He raises an eyebrow at me, "Day ain't over yet."

"I shudder to think what Halloween is going to be like."

"She won't be able to trick or treat this year. Relax."

"HA! I was only a few months old my first Halloween, and she dressed up like Dorothy from The Wizard of Oz."

"Oh…oh no…she didn't do with I think she did."

"If you are thinking she put me in a dress and a wig and carried me around as a Munchkin, you'd be right."

As we open our doors Talissa's head rises from the lawn chair she is stretched out in. She waves, "You're here!"

Just at that moment Mom head pokes out of the kitchen window. "Where is my baby? Bring her in here. I want to bite her. Just a little bit."

"Watch it crazy lady. I'm on to you. I'm going to lay her down for a while longer. She needs her nap to be ready for everything you have planned here."

"I'll start bringing in the stuff, you grab the kid," Jesse walks to the back of the SUV and raises the gate. Even for a day trip, packing for everything a baby needs takes a large vehicle and military level coordination.

I open the back door and look down at the face of my daughter, sleepy safely in her car seat.

Maggie June Mumford made her entrance to the world on February 7th. A full week after her due date. Mom says she came in her own sweet time. She's five months old and just learning to push herself up on her hands and knees. Rocking back and forth with her diaper clad butt in the air. Not crawling yet but she's getting really close.

Mom held Maggie in her arms the day her parents got married. May 11th at sunset. Just Jesse and I with the officiant, standing at the end of the dock. Simple and sweet. Our friends standing behind us, watching us promise to love each other. It was wonderful.

I lift Maggie out of the seat and take her in the house. She doesn't stir. She's out like a light. Mom has set up a brand-new crib in the guest room. I lay my sleeping daughter down and sit on the bed, looking out at the river and thinking of all that's happened since last August.

Jesse fully recovered and returned to Vermont to finish his internship. It took a couple weeks longer than he intended. But the concussion didn't do any permanent damage. He was able to get back here in time to spend the last couple weeks of my pregnancy with me and was right there, holding my hand, when I brought Maggie into the world.

He found a job with a practice in Milton, just a few miles up the road from Georgetown, so we have moved into the recently renovated top floor of the bookstore. Temporarily, till Jesse gets settled in the job and we can find a house we like. I'm staying on at the store for now. It feels like my place, too.

Mom is thrilled we decided to stay local. At least for a while. It's nice having built in babysitters for Maggie.

My book should be coming out in a few months. Being pregnant and too uncomfortable to walk around is very conducive to writing a lot. I told the truth about Maggie, as I see it. I just hope the world wants to hear it.

Soft sounds come from the crib. I quietly walk over and look down at my baby. She is wide awake. Her arms waving in the air, reaching. Her tiny fingers grasping at nothing. She is smiling at the air above her. Not at me, I am behind, out of her line of sight. She giggles. Stretching up as far as she can reach. Holding her arms out for something only she can see.

The End

Acknowledgements

There are a few people who encouraged this book into being.

My wonderful son Kaiden, who shows me every day how to live your truth.

My sweetheart, Jason Ryder, who supports all my crazy ideas. I love you.

My internet best friend, James Nafz, who talked me down from my tree many a day and was the first person to actually get through this thing.

And of course, my macaws Rufus and Finn, who are as real as they can be and provided background vocals for the entire writing process.

Thanks also to my good friends Nicki Shumway and Bob Schwartz, who helped make me who I am today.

It's your fault.

About The Author

Kelly Lidji lives in Lewes, Delaware with Jason and her two macaws, Rufus and Finn.

She grew up in the 80's trying to raise the ghost of Maggie Bloxom with her friends out at Maggie's Bridge in Woodland, DE.

Inquiries please contact the author at:

littlegreenbirdsofficial@gmail.com.